# STARDANCER

# STARDANCER

## A NOVEL

## STEVEN KENT

WordCrafts Press

Hardback ISBN: 978-1-967649-01-3
Paperback ISBN: 978-1-967649-02-0

**Stardancer**


Cover art by ArtSpree, Adobe Stock Images
Cover design by Mike Parker



Published by WordCrafts Press
Cody, Wyoming 82414
www.wordcrafts.net

For Prof. Lewis

a small show of thanks,
if I may

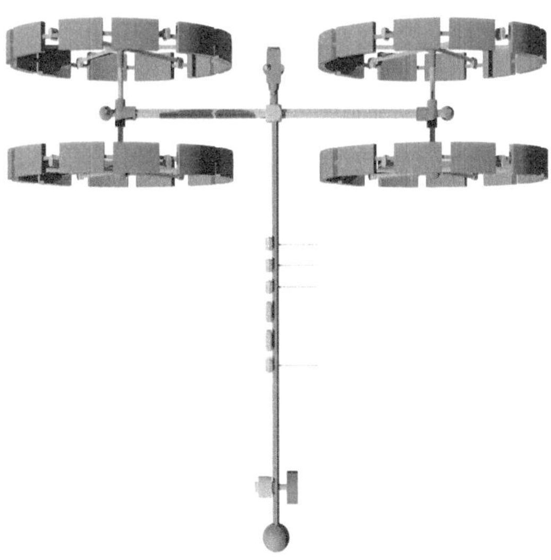

# CHAPTER ONE

*B*elow my catwalk, at the far end of the vast chamber, robots shaped like giant safari ants bury the floor in soil. Grownups install irrigation sprinklers while high schoolers rivet floor plates into place. These are critical, foundational tasks to build a garden chamber for growing crops aboard a space station. But *my* job is to paint the walls. All one hundred and twenty thousand boring square meters of it. A job that could easily be handled by a bot. Instead, Chief Engineer Kapurthala assigned it to me, to isolate me, because he knows I supervise the construction crew better than he does.

"Little girls shouldn't handle rivet guns," he said.

A tiny drip oozes down the wall behind me. Only by smoothing it out with a brush can I suppress the feeling that it's slithering down my spine.

Sunlight filters through crystal panels overhead and shines off my perfect paint job. If I didn't have to spend two weeks with a spray gun, I would probably think this was a pretty color. Other crewmembers call it *sky blue*, but that must be an Earth term. Our sky outside *Prelude* station is always black with stars.

Raised voices below make me lean over the rail to see who Mr. K is snapping at this time. He makes exaggerated gestures at a pile of dirt and a tree-well, while a high school girl cringes before him, on the verge of tears. She dropped her pine tree into the well before filling it most of the way with dirt, so that the top of the sapling barely rises above the floor. But yelling at her won't fix anything.

I rush down the stairs and plant myself between the girl and Mr. K. His orange flight suit practically glows in contrast to his cocoa-colored, dusty face and hands.

"Nabhitha, you should be painting," he says in his precise Indian accent.

I grit my teeth as he messes up my name. "And you should be doing something more important, instead of driving rivets and terrorizing your workers. Besides, my name is pronounced *nah-Mee-da.*"

He wearily holsters his rivet gun. "Of course it is, *Namida.* My apologies, but you remind me of my little sister. And, as I often say to her, it is not your place to correct me."

"Somebody has to." I shine my omni-dev's laser pointer to highlight his row of rivets. "Look. They waver three centimeters off line! Redo those."

Omni-devs are handy devices, like a super computer with gadgets in your pocket.

Sounds of work stop echoing as high school apprentices pause to watch. The girl who doesn't know how to plant trees keeps her lovely, almond-shaped eyes to the floor. The grownups pretend not to notice.

Mr. K growls low enough so no one else hears. "For the last time, stop pestering me and my crew. Finish. Your. Assignment."

"But your rivets are wobbly."

He pinches the bridge of his nose in irritation. "Do you know the word 'fastidious?'"

Strange. He suddenly changed subjects. But I look up the word on my omni-dev anyway.

"It means, 'to pay obsessive attention to detail.'"

"Precisely!" he shouts. "And you can obey orders, or be fastidious somewhere else."

Hmm. Tough choice. But how is attention to detail a bad thing?

"Get little details perfect at the beginning, or it'll mess up big things later on."

Mr. K suddenly plucks the construction insignia pin off my collar. "You are done."

Blast! Fired again. Now I'm down to only three active team pins. One for robotics. Another for medical. And the last for education. I've been a gardener, a beekeeper, a data cable monkey, a hydroponics tech, an aquarium feeder, and a bunch of others. Some lasted a few days, some a couple of years, but I make a point to save each pin.

Someday I hope to get kicked off the cold fusion team, if I ever get to join.

I hold out my hand for the pin, but Mr. K stubbornly folds his arms. Fine. Best not to argue. I spin on one heel and march toward the airlock exit. The high school kids send me off with a smattering of mock applause. Bunch of jerks. Except maybe for that inept tree girl. She mumbles, "Tài xièxie nǐ," as I leave. That was either Chinese for, "thank you," or "mind your own business." Too many languages aboard *Prelude* to learn them all.

I hate the thought of joining high school in two years, but my teacher assures me I'll still be in a league of my own, since the material I'm studying in middle school is college level. High school for me would mainly be for social interaction.

Oh, joy. My teacher must think mental scars are a vital part of growing up.

Mr. K shuts down their applause with a scowl. Everyone returns to work.

Before I reach the exit, my omni-dev rings. I tap it to answer.

"Namida?" Mom says. "A new crewman named Colton has gone missing."

"A shuttle passenger? Roger that. I'm on it."

It's her subtle way of reminding me I should have been in the hangar an hour ago to help process new arrivals.

I climb the stairs to the airlock, and the operator processes me through. From the antechamber on the other side, it's forty-two steps to the spoke junction. I count them in case the lights ever fail. Prepare for the worst, and you might live.

*Prelude* station has four enormous wheels, where people live and work. They rotate to simulate gravity. Their spokes also serve as elevator shafts for large freight. For crewmembers, it's easier to use the smaller people-lifts. One lift goes up one side of the spoke; the other runs down the opposite side.

I step into the people lift, a simple wire cage, hook both feet into stirrups on the floor, then twist the handle. Magnetic rails pull the cage up toward the hub. As I rise toward the hub, fake gravity gets weaker, because things don't spin near the hub as fast as they do at the rim. All my internal organs float to my chest. My hair bounces in slow motion, so I tame it with a scrunchie.

When the lift stops, I'm completely weightless. I float out the top of the cage, and wave to the crew behind the broad hub control window. With a twist of my wrist, my jetpack throttle flips into my palm, and I soar into the axle that connects two of our wheels. The smooth, peach-colored axle interior is comforting and warm.

As I redirect my flightpath up the industrialized main corridor, a text comes through my omni-dev. *Jingle, jingle, tinkle ring.* It's from Dad.

    O jsyr nihd.

This again. I picture a keyboard in my head to work it out, and notice that if all the characters were one letter off to the left, it would say, "I hate bugs." I'm sure he means programming bugs, not real ones.

I type,

    r u OK?

He's slow to reply.

    A;ll is wwel. Dissr3gARD.

A bit weird, but I'll accept that. It's possible his fingers tremble from too much caffeine. But a little sleep loss or a few missed meals are a small price to pay for humanity's future. At least I know he gets the vitamins I slip into his coffee. I make a mental note to tell Mom about his shakes. Being *Prelude's* chief surgeon, she'll want to know.

I keep my eyes peeled for the missing crewman. Now, if I were a pinheaded noob, where would I get into the most trouble? I open my jets to full, then air-brake when I reach the corridor's halfway point. To my left, a big red sign that reads, *Authorized Personnel Only*, is plastered on the giant, shipyard airlock. It's sealed, so the lost crewman couldn't go there. To my right is the hatch to the shuttle hangar. Above that is a side passage that leads to Flight Control.

I zip over and, sure enough, there's an older kid bumping around, confused, wearing nothing but a unitard. He's lean and wiry, and probably taller than I am. Maybe a year older. Crud! Should have known Colton was a boy's name. Would've been nice if the shuttle had delivered a girl this time; I'd have a second friend. Maybe I'll get lucky, and Colton won't be a jerk, but I don't have much hope that he's very smart. He's yanking on an airlock, even though warning lights indicate it will open to empty space.

I float up close to him. "If you don't want to die, pay attention. That hatch's doorframe is lit up red, which means, don't open it. See these five gauges? Conditions are not safe on the other side." He nods, but my guess is, this guy won't live long. "We have proper ways to do everything. They're called *protocols*. If you get sloppy, people could be blown into space. They'll either freeze to death, burn up in direct sunlight, or run out of oxygen. Always remember, death waits behind every door."

That's the kind of stress I live with every day. By now I'm sort of used to it, like having a comforting little rope knotted in the pit of my stomach.

His response is slurred. "Must escape! Diodes taste yellow… before penguins sing."

"I'll remember that," I say, and take his hand.

We float down the side corridor that leads to the hangar.

Inside, eight parents and other techs crowd the hangar's ante-room, all bustling to get five newly-arrived second-graders out of their space suits and into less bulky flight suits. Under normal circumstances, it would be a headache to get five children to listen and change, but in zero gravity it's a special challenge. Only the adults make use of the stirrups on the wall to stay "grounded." Gloves and boots keep drifting away, and the kids won't stop giggling. One girl, a red-haired cutie somewhat older than the rest, buckles her flight suit with dress shoes still on. So many protocols are being ignored that I want to scream.

From the anteroom's observation window, we see the delivery shuttle, the *Jules Verne*, clamped in its bay like an arrowhead in a display case. The outer hangar doors begin to close to shield the bay from the deadly emptiness of space. Crewmembers in red space suits crawl over the shuttle's surface, examining every centimeter of its heat shield for damage, so the *Jules Verne* won't become a fireball on re-entry to Earth's atmosphere.

I salute the *Prelude's* captain, and he touches the brim of his sailor's cap with a smile. It only ever rains in garden chambers, so he doesn't need it. But I once told Captain Binnacle his cap made him look dashing, and he's worn it everywhere ever since.

"Found him," I announce.

Mom helps two female engineers into flight suits, conversing in Cantonese. She relaxes when she sees me holding onto Colton. I detect the aromatic perfume of antiseptic from her med uniform. When she's on rounds, she plaits her hair into braids that join behind her neck, and clips the ends to her belt.

"He wandered away while we were distracted with the kids," she explains.

Captain drifts over. "Thank you, Namida. My son's been listing to port the whole trip, so they kept him sedated."

His son? Unlike the captain, Colton has curly blond hair, and wears it long and pulled into a tight low-knot in back. His bright blue eyes sparkle through half-closed eyelids. I'd kill for long lashes like that. Metaphorically, anyway.

Mom floats over to give Colton an injection with a hyospray.

To the captain, she says, "This will give him enough slow-release adrenaline to walk to your apartment."

I retrieve a fresh flight suit from lockers next to the bio-facilities, where newcomers can shower and stuff.

When I return, Mom is shining a penlight in Colton's eyes. "Are you awake?"

Colton nods and mumbles.

Captain Binnacle introduces me. "This is Namida. She'll get you squared away."

Colton starts to wake up. He glances down at the soft white unitard he wears as though he's lost something, then his ears turn red when he sees all the people in the room.

"Here." I shove the flight suit into his arms.

He manages to get one leg into a sleeve and one arm into a pant leg. He'll never get it buckled with it all twisted, flapping around like that. *Oh, for star's sake!*

"Stop!" I beg. "Please. Just stop." I untangle the suit, then hold it open. "Grab the belt and shove both legs in first." Once he's in, I snap his unitard sensors onto the belt while Mom seals his boots. "Now hold your arms back so I can get the sleeves on."

Finally, I'm able to start a standard check. "Bio readouts are green. Emergency oxygen hood tucked into the collar. Liquid $CO_2$ jets pressurized." I make sure that when he twists his wrists, the jetpack control-grips on his sleeves flip into his palms.

"Of course, the most important thing is your locator tag." I slap it to the nape of his neck hard enough to make him wince. "Help can always find you if you wear your tag." For each item, I recite what I'm doing so Colton will learn. "Do it right," I lecture. "Check it. Then check it again. Your life depends on it."

When I look up, Colton asks, "You expect me to remember all that?"

Captain Binnacle chuckles. "Don't worry. Namida won't let you forget. That's why we let her train newcomers. We ought to have a whole team of kids like her to keep this station from falling apart."

A flush of gratitude warms my heart, and I set an omni-dev reminder to request more kids on the next supply run. "Good idea, but the Coalition might have trouble matching my skills profile."

Captain and Mom exchange an amused glance. People don't think I notice when they do that, and I've learned it's best to ignore it.

I offer Colton a pistol that shoots a powerful magnet, tethered by wires. Mag-pistols can come in handy in zero-gravity. "Do you know how to use this?"

Colton yanks it from my hands. "Of course! In Texas, you never go anywhere unless you're packing."

"Don't tease her, son," says the captain.

I'm not sure how *packing* and *mag-pistols* are related, but Colton straps it on correctly.

Mom fits dizzy-phones behind Colton's ears. "Motion orientation headsets override signals from your inner ear to counteract the nausea and dizziness you'll feel in simulated gravity. In zero gravity, it helps if you think of *down* as always being toward your feet."

Newcomers always wear dizzy-phones. A lot of the more experienced crew *still* need them, but I've never worn any.

"Honey," says Mom, "take Colton to the captain's quarters."

"Roger that, Dr. Mom. Follow me, Colton."

I kick off from a nearby locker, and as I sail across the room, I look down. Colton is using handgrips on the wall to pull himself weightlessly along, as if he expects to fall. I wait at the hatch and try not to laugh.

It occurs to me that I've forgotten to mention Dad's shakes. Mom looks pretty busy, though, so I suppose it can wait.

# CHAPTER 2

$W$e glide through a narrow passage to our main corridor, the Yoke. Colton's mouth drops open as it comes into full view.

"Whoa! You could drive several trains through here. And it's got to be at least two miles long."

"*Miles*? What *century* are you from? But as long as we're using ancient measurements, we could also say it's twenty-three Olympic stadia. And who knows how many cubits!"

"All right. No reason to get snotty."

He's right. Not supposed to mock the noobs.

"Other than size, this place doesn't look like much," he says.

"Excuse me? You're insulting my home." I take a second to tamp down my irritation. "Maybe if you saw the whole station at once it'd be more impressive."

We backtrack and turn up the side corridor, where I first found him. Without thinking to warn him first, I check the gauges and swing the hatch open to the observation room. It's a large dome of shatter-proof glass, with nothing obstructing our view of infinity.

"Holy hand grenades!" Colton clings to the doorframe, so I float in and tap on the glass to assure him it's safe.

And there it is. Big and bright and beautiful: Earth. Covered in sparkling oceans and swirling clouds, its dazzle fills the room with bluish-white radiance that makes me shiver, even in my insulated suit. I can't help but reach for it and imagine the planet is cool and wet to the touch, like holding a peeled orange. Mountains scratch my fingertips. Desert sands warm my palms. Forests tickle like moss. Off to the right, the moon's pearly white disk tries to out-shine its glory, but it's not nearly as pretty.

"Can you see your home?" Mom says if I get nervous people talking, they'll calm down.

"No. That's India showing." His voice trembles. "Texas is on the other side." He works up enough bravery to let go of the doorframe. "Do you see *your* home?"

I have to laugh. "All the time."

"No, I mean where you're from originally."

"I'm from *Prelude* originally." I smile with pride. "Never been to Earth."

And…there it is. That slack-jawed disbelief every time I tell people.

"*Seriously?*" he says. "Well, shuttles come once a month, don't they? You could visit any time."

"Crewmembers have told me about it. My friend Ash reads post-apocalyptic stories about it, too. They gush about Earth absolutely *teeming* with life. Slimy fish in your drinking water, trees filled with screaming birds, and tons of bugs everywhere. Makes my skin crawl."

"Well, that's a screwy way to look at it," he says. "What about good stuff, like horseback riding, or sunshine for a change?"

"Around here, if we don't filter sunlight through ozone windows, it'd smoke us worse than Mom's Thanksgiving biscuits. No thanks. Earth is disgusting, full of filth and chaos. Sorry, but that's what you get when your planet forms through a long chain of random accidents."

"*Accidents?*" He sounds surprised.

"Earth *is* beautiful, I admit, but best admired from a distance. Preferably from about three hundred eighty-five thousand kilometers, which is how far it stays from us."

"But don't you get bored up here?"

"Bored? There's too much to do! Besides, I happen to like my home." I quote my lines from the Space Coalition's video we made last year. "Look at it! *Prelude* is almost eight kilometers wide and over seven kilometers long. It's a technological wonder of super-strong composite materials! Elegant and clean. Nestled in a Lagrange gravity pocket. Designed by thoughtful engineers, and built by robots to precise specifications. A heaven set in the heavens!"

Colton scoffs. "You sound like a dopey Coalition commercial."

"Well, it's true," I pout. He remembers the commercial, but not my face in it. "Anyway, I brought you here to get you oriented. Look outside. *Prelude* is shaped like a cross. Shuttle hangar and Flight Control are at the head. The crossbar is called the Yoke. It's the main corridor that ties it all together. And, from where we are, you can see down the Trunk to our main fusion reactor."

He admires the view, then frowns. "I thought the doctor said something about artificial gravity. When do they turn that on?"

"*Turn it on*? It's not that silly movie stuff. We simulate gravity by spinning the wheels," He looks confused, as though he hadn't noticed. I drift close to him, the way I do to make little kids feel safer. "Two wheels on starboard," I say gently and point. Colton sites down my arm as I trace the wide arc of the wheels with my finger. My ponytail brushes his nose. "Those are Eagle and Lion. Think of them as enormous Ferris wheels."

Captain suggested I describe our habitats as a carnival ride. He was right; newcomers always get it. But from pictures I've seen, there's only a superficial resemblance.

"Those flat buildings on the wheel rims are gondolas, where people live and work." I spin to face the other way, but Colton doesn't turn with me. Instead, he hangs in midair, his face an awkward elbow's length away. "On the Yoke's port branch, are Adam and Ox. Go on. Look."

He's startled, but still doesn't turn around, and his ears turn red again. I don't think he knows how to pivot in weightlessness.

"You're staying in Adam's rim," I say, then lead him out and seal the hatch behind us.

We return to the intersection, and I check for traffic. A group of builders approaches from Eagle with a bright red construction- bot. It tows an equipment crate and resembles a gigantic ant struggling with an equally giant sugar cube. The *Authorized Personnel Only* sign on the Trunk's airlock splits in two, as the immense hatch swings open.

Colton breezes by me as he rounds the corner. When he sees the construction-bot, he screams a phrase so bad that he'll have to pay extra to the swear jar. Whatever made him panic also makes him miss the corner handhold. He tumbles into the middle of traffic, flapping arms and legs, headed for a slow-motion collision.

"Mag-pistol!" I shout.

Colton draws and fires. The magnet flies out on two wires and sticks to the robot's broad head, but he fails to hold the trigger, so the magnet deactivates. Colton continues to sail past and smacks against the far wall. The builders laugh and continue on.

Once the robot has helped steer the equipment into the Trunk, I join Colton on the corridor wall, avoiding his mag-pistol wires floating loose. The impact knocked his dizzy-phones down around his neck.

"For every action," I recite, "there is an equal and opposite… blah, blah, physics. Same effort you use to get going, you have to use to stop."

"I *know*," he grumbles.

"Then *act* like you know it." I check him for damage. "Why'd you panic?"

"Didn't you see that monster space bug?"

"That's not a *bug*. Construction-bots are designed after safari ants."

"Then why'd you tell me to shoot if you didn't want me to kill it?"

"*Kill* it? You big dope! If you can't air-brake, use your mag-pistol so you don't fly into somebody. Look. The trigger activates the magnet." I aim my own mag-pistol, shoot, and its magnet sticks to the wall. "Press this thumb button to reel it back in. Release the trigger, and the magnet turns off." I reach around him to press the thumb button on his pistol, and his magnet reels in. My ponytail brushes his face, but he doesn't complain.

"Oh." His anger fades, and he looks sheepish.

"We have enough problems with micro-meteors; we don't need people shooting extra holes in our hull. Why'd you think you'd need a real gun anyway?"

He gives me the cutest lop-sided grin. "Space pirates?"

Colton tries to hold it in, but we both get giggle fits. It's adorable the way his nose crinkles when he laughs. After a minute, we manage to calm down.

"Oh wow," I gasp for air. "You're going to be fun, if you don't kill yourself first."

"I guess I'm not the sharpest egg in the attic."

With that, my mind pauses, trying to make sense of his words. Maybe the impact scrambled his brain. Maybe it's best to ignore that and resume our trip.

The Yoke has always reminded me of a colossal, industrial elevator shaft turned on its side, but full of storage compartments and tunnels in the walls. Some crew complain it gives them nightmares about falling. Harsh lights run up the four corners but never brighten things enough. In contrast, the peachy light from the axles at both ends is warm and inviting.

High schoolers painted murals on the axle that joins Adam and Ox wheels. At the end closest to Ox, they painted animals. At the Adam end, they painted people. I would prefer they had left it blank, like the second axle at the other end of the Yoke.

Colton doesn't seem to notice the artwork as we turn up the axle, but he's fascinated how Adam's disk-shaped hub slowly rotates while we float motionless in the middle. On the flat wall ahead is a broad window that reveals the wheel's control center where technicians, and computers with twinkling lights, keep Adam in balance.

I tow Colton over to one of the six spokes and point to a people-lift cage.

"Shove one boot into that stirrup on the cage floor and face the blue stripe."

There is just enough room for two people in the wire cage. I anchor myself in the second stirrup and twist the handgrip, which starts the cage gliding on the spoke's magnetic rails. We head out toward the rim, feet first. Halfway along the spoke, I feel Adam Wheel's spin push me backward, forcing me to rest my head on Colton's collar bone.

"What are you doing?" He sounds nervous, but happy.

"The spin presses us backward. The direction of the blue stripe is spinward. Red stripe means anti-spinward."

Entering simulated gravity messes with a person's senses. My eyes say I'm standing upright, but my balance says the cage is tilting. The closer we get to the rim, the heavier my limbs get and the more it feels like I'm lying on a table, rolling downhill. Plus, the hill gets steeper as fake gravity increases. That's when my brain warns that I'm about to be dumped into a bottomless hole. People-lifts are a blast!

Almost to the bottom, Colton's knees buckle as Adam Wheel's centrifugal force pushes us down. I try to brace him up. "Put your dizzy-phones back on!"

"I didn't expect this," he says. His stomach heaves as if he's about to be sick. "My arms and legs feel like sacks of wet clay, like I've been swimming all day."

Colton fumbles the dizzy-phones behind his ears before our cage stops, then staggers off and drops to his hands and knees. Here at the rim, we now feel a sense of *up* and *down*, but not in a way Colton enjoys. He's looking somewhat pale in the bright corridor. I hope his nausea passes soon—maintenance bots recently polished this floor. I fetch an airsick bag from the nearby bio-facility and hold it under his chin.

He waves it away.

"Give me a minute. Or, are minutes an ancient measurement?"

"No. We use minutes."

Colton is a helpless puppy. There must be something I can do to make him feel better. A sympathetic hug would probably make him hurl. Explaining the system I invented to divide days into ten hours, and one hundred minutes each hour, wouldn't help either.

I fetch a cup of water from the bio-facility and kneel next to him. He manages a few sips, then I coach him to inhale in slow breaths, the way I do for my panic attacks. Other people that pass by offer help, but I wave them on. After Colton recovers, I help him stand. He's wobbly, so I steady him through the rim's tube-shaped passageway. Its gentle curve terminates in gondola anterooms at both ends. The biggest difficulty is to keep Colton from face-planting onto the floor.

"Most noobs—um, I mean, newcomers have this reaction. You've traveled three days in zero gravity. Now you're spinning at one hundred and twenty-seven meters a second." I do a quick mental calculation. "That's about two hundred and eighty-four Texas miles per hour. So don't be embarrassed."

"If it doesn't look like I'm going to survive," he moans, "please make sure my death is quick and painless."

Protocol says that potential suicides must be reported to my mom, the chief surgeon. For now, I should probably humor him.

"Sure. I'll put you out of your misery with a mag-pistol."

He snorts a laugh, which means he was kidding. That's a relief. Still running on Mom's adrenaline shot, Colton manages the short walk to Adam's third gondola.

"Your heart rate is fast," I say, checking his readouts. "Breathing irregular. Temperature up a bit. Here, maybe this'll help." I unzip his jacket down to his navel to cool him off, but his pulse goes all wonky, and his ears turn red again. *Ooops.* That had the opposite effect.

"I'm fine!" He brushes me away. "Stop touching me."

"Sorry!" I know he doesn't feel well, but that's no excuse to be rude.

The captain's quarters are on the gondola's third deck, below the garden chamber. We ride a regular elevator down to the cozy apartment level, where the floors are carpeted and the walls covered in simulated wood paneling. Distance between gondola decks is relatively small, so the fake gravity only makes you slightly heavier on the lowest deck. Unlike the extreme difference felt while riding along the fifteen-hundred-meter spokes.

I herd Colton into Captain's apartment without touching him, and watch him weave through the furniture with eyes half closed, still groggy from sedatives.

Captain has become used to the way I keep his apartment organized, but now I get to show off to someone new! Every detail according to the living quarters procedure manual, with a few improvements. Kitchenette towels hang perfectly straight, and flatware is arranged in their proper bins so they can be found in an emergency. Every bottle, drawer, and can is labeled with the same font so that people with food allergies don't get confused.

I've even dusted what I've come to think of as Captain's shrine. It's a silver-framed portrait of a woman holding a six-year-old girl. On a table beneath it, Captain keeps a wooden hairbrush and a doll made of taffeta scraps and yarn.

Colton sways and nods, breathing heavily. He doesn't seem to care about any of this.

"I just want to lie down," he moans.

"Oh. Okay, fine."

He staggers to the bedroom as if the floor is lurching, then flops face down onto fresh sheets without taking off his flight suit. I roll him over so he can breathe. Maybe his illness is more than just the return to gravity. Does he have a fever? My hands are too cold to tell from touching his neck, so I press my lips to his forehead, and he mumbles something. He is a little warm. A good sleep should make him feel better.

But how can anybody sleep in boots and a lumpy flight suit? He's pretty much unconscious, so I'll have to do it for him. I sigh as I yank the first boot off.

"What are you *doing*?" He kicks at me and sits up. "You're still *here*?"

Now that one hurt. "Those widgets on your flight suit will snag the sheets."

"Get out!" he barks.

My mind goes blank, searching for words and reasons. *Why is he so mean?*

"Get. OUT!" He throws a pillow at my head. The dip-switch misses by a Texas mile, but his words sting and leave me speechless. When I realize I'm standing there spluttering like a muppet, I run blindly out, slamming the apartment door behind me.

In the peaceful hallway, I collapse against a wall and try to figure out what I did wrong. I don't get it. One minute he's nice, and the next he's incredibly rude. I can't decide if I'm angry or want to cry. Vitals on my readout crawl up the scale from green to yellow. I've been making huffing noises and twisting my ponytail without realizing it.

I use my breathing exercises to force myself to settle down. Slow inhale through the nose. Count to three. Force exhale through pursed lips. Repeat until heart rate returns to normal. Once I'm calm again, I still feel lousy.

Sometimes I *hate* learning new people.

# CHAPTER 3

After giving my orientation class the next day, I head over to Dad's lab, which is way over in Eagle Wheel. An eight-kilometer journey, door to door. Traffic is sparse, and I have the entire Yoke to myself. Since Dad isn't expecting me for another thirty minutes, I have a perfect opportunity.

I pause over the opening of a maintenance tunnel in the Yoke's wall to make sure no one is watching, then duck inside. I plug wireless ear-buttons in and call up a playlist on my omni-dev. People make fun of my electronic dance music since it's so old. But I like it. Normally, if I'm on a leisurely, weightless glide, I'll choose artists who play the Ambient Nova Sizzle genre because it's relaxing. Today, I'm more in the mood for Base Runner. Better for air-dancing.

I undo my ponytail and shake my hair free as the melody immerses me and the bass rumbles through my bones. I kick off from one wall at an angle, sail across the passage, and cartwheel off the opposite corner. Using the momentum, I spin in mid-air and kick, then spread my arms and gently land.

While I air-dance, I become one with the station. My palms hold *Prelude's* four wheels. Atomic fire from the reactor at my feet makes my nerves sing with electricity. My heart pumps life-giving water, and the air recycling system scrubs the air fresh as I exhale. I am the conductor of a grand symphony! I am *Prelude* station.

Right before the song ends, a yellow tennis ball streaks by. It rebounds off a wall and tags my face. "Perfect shot!" crows Ash. "Did you see that, Namida?"

"How could I *not* see it? You almost hit my eye!"

Ash hangs onto the tunnel's rim, grinning like it's Christmas—or in his case, Diwali. He's slender as a willow sapling and has the face of an angel. The fact that he's heart-stoppingly cute isn't going to save that little scrub, though. I'll make him pay.

Snatching the ball from mid-air, I dart straight toward him. Ash yelps when he sees murder in my eyes and launches himself up the Yoke. I leap from the tunnel and give a short blast from my jets. As I pass over him, I sling the ball and bean him on the back of the head, which only makes him laugh.

"Ash, stop picking on me!"

He rolls over as he sails along. "Just trying to get your attention."

I jet up close and lower my voice the way Captain does. "I don't have time for this. I'm delivering materials vital to robotic research," I say, as I bind my hair back into a ponytail.

My cheek still stings from where he tagged me. I should be mad enough to spit in his face, but it's hard to stay mad at the only friend I have my own age. We stare each other down, his eyes defiant and playful. Gorgeous, soulful brown eyes. A Teddy bear, even when he's being a royal pain.

"Yeah, right," he says. "And the fate of humanity rests on *you*."

A sarcastic pain-in-the-neck Teddy bear.

"It just might." I jet ahead before he notices the grin twitching at my lips.

Ash catches up, then drags his hand against the wall to slow down and match my speed.

I frown at him. "Why do you always turn up everywhere I go?"

He shrugs. "Don't you want me around?"

"Usually. It's like having a pet that can talk."

"Gee, thanks. That's not insulting at all."

"Well, it wasn't meant to be. A talking pet would be cool."

Four years ago, Ash's father brought him up from Punjab, and we've been friends ever since. I found Punjab on a map once, but it resembled every other place on Earth. Lots of squiggly colored lines and dots. Before Ash, I only had scientists, engineers, and programmers to talk to. And adults don't like to play.

He notices the backpack strapped between my jets. "Mind if I inspect the materials?"

I lightly slap his hand away. "Not for you."

He backs off and pouts. When I don't give in, he changes the topic. "You've not been in class this week."

"Mom's calibrating lab equipment," I lie. "She uses my brain scans as a baseline."

Ash looks away. "Oh, I see."

"No, no, really. I'm not sick or anything." I grip him by the shoulders. "Why? Do I look sick?"

"You look fine!" A blush rises in his coffee-colored face. "In fact, you look super fine. You're a sleek tigress with the luxurious black mane of a mustang filly."

Comparing me to a cross between a meat-eater and a plant-eater is Ash's way of implying that I'm a freak. I never take his subtle insults seriously, but now isn't a good time for Ash to tag along. I puff my jets to speed up and give him a hint, but he catches up again.

"You are *not* following me," I insist. "Dad doesn't need any more assistants."

We reach the end of the Yoke and turn up the peach-colored axle to Eagle Wheel's hub.

Impishness glints in Ash's eyes as he zips on ahead. "Then maybe you should go home. I code INTERCAL better than you do."

"Not hardly," I snort. "Besides, I know how to keep quiet while Dad works."

"I can keep quiet."

"Since when?" There is no changing his mind, and if I argue I'll make it worse. "Fine! I give up." Maybe today will be one of Dad's good days, anyway. When he spends so much time in his lab, Mom relies on me to make sure he takes care of himself.

Before we reach the axle, Ash and I hear a *pop!* It's followed by a high-pitched hiss, and we know that a micro-meteor has pierced the hull. I follow the sound and find a hole not quite large enough to stick my finger through. Ash floats up behind me, and we watch as carbon fiber mesh closes over the hole, and epoxy leaks out from the inner layers to seal the breach. The hissing stops. Our hull is self-healing.

"The universe took another shot at us," Ash jokes. "Good thing it has bad aim."

*Prelude*'s magnetic field stops iron meteors, but not silicon rocks. "We should find it, before it jams equipment."

"Don't worry," Ash tugs at my collar. "Air scrubbers will filter it out."

Once in Eagle's hub, we head for the people-lift in Spoke Four. Ash drifts into the wire cage head first. He likes to free-float upside-down until centrifugal force drags him to the floor.

"Flip around," I tell him. "You're not doing it right."

"Namida, for the billionth time, I am not one of your students. Get in."

I shake my head. "Not if you're doing stunts."

Because he knows he's gorgeous, he thinks he can get away with murder. Sometimes, I can't help but sneak up behind him and ruffle my fingers through all that curly black hair. I have to admit, it does make his mischief hard to resist. But safety comes first.

Ash doesn't know it yet, but we're going to be married someday.

I wrote that in my diary in fourth grade, so I'm committed now. To undo it, I'd have to purge it from thousands of my omni-dev's backup copies. Probably easier just to get married.

"By the way, little Miss Protocol, you left a tennis ball bouncing around the Yoke." He twists the handle, and the wire cage whisks him away.

Or maybe it'd be easier to box him up and ship him back to Earth.

# CHAPTER 4

Ash thinks it's funny! What if that tennis ball jams equipment? What if someone runs into it and…well, I don't know. But what if there are Unforeseen Consequences and people die in horrifying ways? I head toward the axle, then stop. It'll take an hour to backtrack and find it. I'll be late. I jet back to the spoke and chew the end of my ponytail.

"*Carpe diem!*" I swear. Ash knew this would drive me nuts.

"Is there a problem, Miss Wiles?" someone says over the intercom.

"I left debris in the intersection, near the Trunk."

I see a stranger through the huge Hub Control window. With over two thousand crewmembers arriving and leaving in two-year shifts, I can't recognize everybody.

"We have a maintenance bot free to collect it," he says.

"Thank you!" That anxiety knot in my stomach eases up a bit.

Being married to Ash will be *agony*. Either I'll have to fix him, or we'll have to live in separate wheels. There's plenty of time to worry about that. After all, I only just turned thirteen a couple of months ago. Or, more accurately, I'm one-hundred fifty-eight months since birth. On the bright side, maybe those sections of our personnel manual about married couples will make sense afterward.

I board the next cage after it clicks into place. It glides along the spoke, and when it reaches gravity at the bottom, I join Ash on the benches to recover from being weightless. Crewmembers and robots pass by. After that, it's a short walk to Gondola E-6 where we take an elevator down to the bare metal hallway outside Dad's workshop.

The door's security system detects my omni-dev, and I start to punch in my keycode as I always do. Instead, I pause. Something isn't right. It's similar to when I air-dance and the health of the whole station pulses through my body. But this feels more like we're a balloon that's about to burst.

"Did you forget your code?"

Ash's question snaps me back to reality, and I realize that I'm fiddling with the snaps on the oxygen hood rolled up in my collar. I key in my access code and enter. Dad isn't at his console. The only light comes from several large screens on the wall. Random electronics and robot parts litter the desktop. The adjoining workshop is open with a squad of deactivated test bots staring at us from out of the dark. Everything seems normal.

Ash plops down in a swivel chair as I shed my backpack of vital materials and straighten up until the office looks like the diagram on page 512 of our operations manual. Ash again tries to sneak a hand into my backpack.

"Stay out of that!"

He recoils and acts innocent. Then one screen flickers and changes views. It shows live video from the garden chamber above, where Dad sets up tests for his robots. We see him kneeling in the bare dirt where crops would normally grow. His back is to us, and he faces a TNK robot with its chest panel open.

This bot's frame is covered in tough green plastic, and it stands tall enough on four legs to look Dad in the eye. Two arms, joined at the shoulders, can switch out multi-purpose claws for various tools and are strong enough to bend metal bars. A stubby abdomen stretches out behind it like a fat tail. The overall design is like a stubby praying mantis.

Dad is installing one of our R.E.D. safety devices into its open chest. It's a silver cube, about the size of an apple. Beyond him is the wide, empty field with the transparent quartz ceiling above. White shutters outside have angled themselves to reflect sunlight into the chamber.

"What's that on his head?" Ash asks.

The helmet he wears has two bulky headphones and a thick band around the head. It's similar to the one Mom uses to graph my brain.

"That's the interface helmet Dad designed, so he doesn't have to text instructions to our robots."

I turn around and see Ash holding a small box that has a fractal antenna and a big red button on it. He flips open the safety cover, and I snatch it out of his hand.

"Don't mess with that!"

"Why? What is it?"

"It's the Annihilation Button. Press it and the whole station explodes."

"*Really?*" For once, he's impressed.

"No, you dope. But this is exactly why I didn't want you to tag along."

Dad must have the console's mic activated because he turns to the camera and says, "Is that you, Kitty Doodle?"

Ash snickers at my nickname. I don't know why he calls me that. Must be a Dad thing.

"Yes. Ash is here, too, and he's *touching* stuff."

"Snitch," says Ash, and grins to let me know he doesn't care.

"Okay," Dad says. "I'm on my way down."

While I'm dividing up a lunch meant for two into three equal shares, Dad walks in, slips off his helmet, and leans exhausted against the wall. His brick-red hair is a mess, and polyuria grease stains his rumpled flight suit, but I don't care. It's been days since I've seen him. I rush over and give him a big squeeze. He smells of ozone.

"Mom sent a package."

He strokes my ponytail and kisses my forehead. "Smells

wonderful. Lamb and potatoes?" He lays his helmet on top of a tool chest and settles into his chair.

I wipe off Dad's kiss with an antiseptic cloth from the case in my pocket. Can't be too careful about germs. Then I hand him a plate and flatware. His fingers tremble as he tries to get a bite of stew, and most of it falls back on the plate.

"Maybe I'll save that for later," he says, and lays lunch aside.

"We've got coffee." I unscrew one thermos to pour him a steaming cup. I had already taken a sip earlier to make sure he couldn't taste the sedatives. "Of course, it's a crime to have coffee without these." I open the box of vital research materials and pull out a torus.

Dad's face lights up. "You are an angel of mercy!"

Ash stops fidgeting and sits up straight. This is the real reason he followed me here.

*Prelude* grows most of our food in Ox Wheel—with a few exceptions. For instance, nobody knew how to make a decent doughnut. Naturally, our engineers ordered some to be delivered, since doughnuts are an essential part of their diet. But Captain Binnacle proclaimed it "frivolous" and scratched them off the supply shuttle's manifest. Soon, he had a near mutiny on his hands. Engineers and programmers refused to meet deadlines.

Captain displayed expert wisdom, as usual. He had a chemist write out the formula and technical description, yet labeled it as specifications for "disaccharide tori," which is a fancy term for sugar doughnuts. Someone at Ground Control must have developed a sense of humor because, in the end, we got our shipment. Afterward, the entire crew swore an oath to call a doughnut a "torus" for fear the supply might stop.

I take the oath seriously and report crewmembers when they slip up. Captain punishes them by making them eat asparagus.

Dad nibbles a torus and warms his hands on the cup. Computer screens reflect off the nervous ripples in his coffee. Ash doesn't notice because he's too busy stuffing his face.

Around a mouthful, Ash says, "My father's going to risk opening the wormhole to Starheim again." He gulps my milk straight from the second thermos. "Just wide enough to send another probe. He hopes to make contact with the terraform-bots again."

Dad nods. "Well, it won't do us a bit of good if I can't get my program to work."

"Have you figured out why the bots went berserk, Mr. Wiles?"

"Still no answer." He picks up the helmet and starts absently playing with the slider buttons on the side. "We must have fouled up their orders. Or else they misinterpreted something when we tried to send materials for the next phase."

Ash wrinkles his eyebrows. "But…robots do exactly what you tell them."

"Normally, yes." Dad lays the helmet aside. "Like any robot, though, the terraform-bots can't resolve *unexpected* problems. The difficulty is that a roboticist can't foresee every problem a bot may encounter in order to code for it. Although, we certainly tried.

"My colleague, Mr. Spencer, believed robotic intelligence could develop without guidance, the way human brains evolved in nature." Dad swipes at something invisible near his ear. "Therefore, we reproduced the entire terraforming operation, down to every rivet and wire, in a virtual reality simulation. After that, we inserted our AI programs into the simulation and mimicked countless system failures. The AI agents reasoned out how to handle every conceivable malfunction, but only through trial and error."

"Sounds like that'd take a while," says Ash.

"Hundreds of years," says Dad. "Except Mr. Spencer ran the simulations through high-speed computers. He condensed their training into a few weeks. We thought that when they faced problems in the real world, they would be prepared for every situation. Apparently, we were wrong."

"But Dad's got the problem solved."

"I hope so," he says. "My solution involves a human overseer who would live in a small space station at Starheim. That is, if I can get my program to work first." Dad sighs. "I'm so very close. But my problem might be that I'm not using a compatible decision matrix."

Ash looks to me for an interpretation, but I have only a vague idea what Dad means.

Dad tilts his head, then leaps to his feet and nearly knocks over the chair. He motions for us to keep still. Ash and I hold our breath while Dad creeps over and puts his ear to the wall. "Ash, come tell me if you hear a sizzle."

"Like an electrical short?" Ash hops out of his chair and presses an ear to the panel next to Dad. "I don't hear anything."

Dad backs away from the wall. "Maybe I ought to have Sidney check my ears."

There's nothing wrong with his hearing. "Ash, we should let Dad get back to work."

"No, it's okay," Dad says. "I need a break." He swats at his pant leg, then looks at his palm to see what he killed. Nothing there.

"Dad, why don't you unroll your sleeping bag and get some rest?"

"I'm fine." He waves off my suggestion and settles back at his desk to try some lamb stew. He pauses with the fork halfway to his mouth, then pounds a fist onto the keyboard so suddenly it makes us jump.

"Blasted pests are everywhere!" he hisses.

Ash stares wide-eyed at the sterile desk, then turns to me with an expression that asks, *What is going on*?

Dad snatches up the box of tori. "Namida! Are these from a farm?"

"No. They came straight from our fridge."

"Well, look at them!" He squeezes a handful of sugary deliciousness. "They're *crawling* with mantises! We'll have bugs in everything."

# CHAPTER 5

*D*ad grabs an electric screwdriver from a toolbox and removes the wall panel.

Ash scrambles out of his way and nervously turns to me. "Namida?"

"Call agriculture," Dad orders, laying the panel aside. "Tell them to get a cleanup crew down here with pesticides."

I whip out my omni-dev and call Mom instead. "Hello? Ag department?"

"Namida," she snaps, "I'm busy. Stop playing games."

I rush on. "We need emergency cleanup crew in Stirling Wiles' lab."

"Oh, no." Mom's tone fills with dread. "What's wrong?"

"Bug infestation."

"Oh, Judas Priest," Mom moans. "Okay. Get your father away from anything dangerous and keep him calm."

"Roger that." I sign off. "They're coming right away."

"Good girl!" Dad rips out a handful of network fiber.

Ash looks confused. "Mantises? But I don't see—"

"They told us to evacuate the lab and seal it," I improvise.

"Makes sense. Come on kids. Leave the food."

He herds us out and shuts the door. We find seats in the waiting area across from the elevators. Dad and I share a couch, and Ash lands in a chair facing us.

That's it. It's over. I've tried to keep Dad's episodes secret, but they've grown worse. I should have said something to Mom instead of sneaking him vitamins and sedatives. All that seemed to help, at first. Now they'll lock him in the infirmary. It'll drive him nuts not being able to peck at a keyboard.

Dad squeezes his fists as he rocks back and forth. I scoot closer and rest my head against his shoulder. He's trembling, but he isn't cold. After a few minutes, he stops rocking.

"Doesn't make sense, does it?" That's more of a statement than a question. "There *are* no bugs in the lab, are there?"

I slip an arm around him. "It's okay. You'll be fine."

Ash shifts uncomfortably in his chair and stares at the floor.

"No." Dad's voice is hoarse. "I've ruined everything. The Coalition was counting on me. Captain Binnacle was counting on me. Our hopes depend…" He trails off.

Grownups aren't supposed to act so lost. It makes the world cold and uncertain. I want to reach in and fix him. Flip a switch. Twist a dial. Except, people aren't robots. There's nothing I can do.

"If I can't invent a solution," he says, "then we'll abandon the whole project. People will be too afraid to reach for the stars."

"You'll figure it out," I assure him. "We *will* finish the new planet and do it right this time, leaving out the cruddy bits. No weeds. No diseases. Plus, if anybody starts a war or litters a forest, we'll kick them off the planet."

"Your mother isn't keen on leaving our solar system." One eye starts to twitch. "At first, she was thrilled about working in space, but after your grandfather died, she swore she would never travel through a wormhole."

"Well, that's Mom, all right. First female chief surgeon in space. Mother to the first human born and raised in space. Afraid to fly across the galaxy."

Dad frowns. "Don't fault her for that. She has a point."

We sit for a while, saying nothing. Ash finally breaks the silence. "Why'd you never tell me about your grandfather?"

"Because I don't like to talk about it." Most people either think I'm bragging, or they get overly sympathetic. Both reactions upset me. But Ash isn't most people, so I tell him, "My grandfather was Isaak Lachenderbar."

Ash sits up and his mouth drops open. "First guy to fly through a wormhole, from the Moon to Saturn?"

"Yeah. My family is full of firsts. When I was seventy-four months old, two years before you arrived, Grampa set another record for being the first to *die* in a wormhole, trying to reach Starheim. It was supposed to be a repair mission."

Ash softens his voice. "Sorry. I guess Coalition doesn't advertise that story."

Mom was devastated. We all were, but Mom took the shuttle to Earth and stayed away for twenty-six weeks, two days, and seven hours. In spite of how Grampa died, I always thought it would be cool to see a different sun. Mom didn't agree.

I try to lift Dad's spirits by changing the subject. "They say there's a nebula near Starheim that paints the sky in swirling blue and pink. Imagine seeing that every night!"

"It'll take a couple of centuries before Starheim is able to support humans," Dad reminds me. "Even if we solve the robot problem, whoever goes first will be doomed to live on a space station."

*Doomed?* Even my parents have never felt at home in space. They'd rather go crawl in the dirt on Earth, which is kind of redundant when you phrase it that way.

An elevator dings, and its door opens to reveal Captain Binnacle standing at ease. He doesn't step out until we hear footsteps from the hall that runs back to the lab. It's Ash's dad, Mr. K. He doesn't even glance at his son, but positions himself behind my end of the couch as Dad faces the captain with dread in his eyes.

Captain Binnacle approaches and folds his hands behind his back. He seems tense. His gray eyes glint beneath the brim of his navy sailing cap.

"How do you feel, Stirl?" asks the captain.

Dad runs a shaky hand over his face. "Not good, Winston. Overwork."

Captain purses his lips. "Yeah, maybe, but let's get you to the infirmary and let your Sydney have a look. What do you say?"

"*I'm fine*," Dad insists. "I don't need a doctor; I just need rest."

Mr. K wears a grim expression, and pulls a packing strap from his pocket. Ash flinches in reflex, and retreats to the elevators, but never takes his eyes off the strap.

"Not to worry," says Captain. "I'm sure Sydney will prescribe plenty of rest."

Dad squints suspiciously. "You believe it's more than lack of sleep, don't you?"

Captain hesitates. "Could be Jitters. Not likely, but the last thing I need is for my chief roboticist to toss somebody out an airlock because he's hallucinating."

Ash is puzzled. "Too much coffee makes you hallucinate?"

"Not now, son," growls Mr. K.

"No." I stand up between Mr. K and Dad. "You're wrong! Jitters only hits one in every thousand astronauts. And it shows up in the first few months. Except for occasional shore leave, Dad's been here for sixteen years!"

Captain nods. "I know, but we should let your mother make the diagnosis."

"I've almost got it solved," says Dad firmly. "Give me a few days to reset and run another test!"

Captain sighs. "It's a crying shame we're biological creatures. Gets in the way."

He's not listening. And he's not going to let Dad finish no matter what. I glare at Captain, balling my fists, and shout, "Dad doesn't have Jitters!"

"Settle down, Namida," says Mr. K. "Your protective instincts for your father are admirable but unnecessary."

I hate to admit it, but he's right. My brain should ignore my biology and think it through.

"Okay, but do you have to tie him up?"

Dad notices the packing strap and rises from the couch. "You don't need that, Kavi. Look at me." His eye twitches. "I'm fine."

"Then let us have Sydney confirm," says Mr. K.

"Fine. I'll come without a fuss." Dad turns to me as though he's going to cup my cheek, then recoils in horror. "Holy God!" he shouts, and strikes me hard across the face. The blow knocks me backward. The whole side of my face stings. His eyes are wild and unfocused.

Mr. K and Captain pounce on him and pin his arms. Captain holds him while Mr. K wraps him in the packing strap and cinches the buckle.

Dad struggles in their grip and shouts, "Quick! Get that bug off her face!"

"Nothing's there," says Captain, gripping the back of Dad's neck. He forces Dad to face me. "Look again."

Dad gapes at them as though they've lost their minds, then his face sags. "Oh my God," he moans. "I am so sorry, Kitty Doodle. I didn't—"

He doesn't finish. My cheek still stings, and I shrink away from him. I'm actually terrified of… *Who is this? That's not my Daddy!* Everything inside me quivers, but I hold back the tears. He has never hit me before. Sure, the slap hurt, but that's not the point. At this moment, he's a total stranger. His voice is full of agony, but his eyes are still lit by madness, darting back and forth. He's panicked, but there's no real reason for it.

"Time to go, Stirl." Captain ushers my father into the elevator.

"Namida?" Dad pleads with me. "I'm sorry! I thought…I thought—"

Mr. K leans close to Ash. "Take Namida straight home. Then go stay in your room."

Ash nods, staring at the madman that Captain hauls away.

"Talk to no one on the way," adds Mr. K.

"Right," says Ash.

"No chatting with friends on omni-dev, either. Understand?"

"For crying out loud, Father, I got it the first time."

Mr. K shakes a finger in Ash's face. "Do not take an attitude with me!" And Ash shuts down. He casts his eyes to the floor and presses his lips tight. "You get that smart mouth from your mother's DNA. Now, what do you say?"

Ash is scarcely audible. "Sorry, sir."

"Good. I am leaving. What *else* do you say?"

"I love you, Father." But Ash's voice rings hollow.

Mr. K turns away and boards the elevator with the captain and Dad. The doors close, and the elevator rises.

Ash and I stand in shocked silence.

My stomach curdles. My future is uncertain. The dream I imagined for years, of learning everything Dad knows and traveling to Starheim, has vanished. It can't be true. Dad can't have Jitters. But what will I do if he does? What will I become? Where will I live?

I motion for Ash to follow me to the lab, and he watches while I power off computer screens and plug in L-books to recharge. Wipe the dishes clean and fit them into my backpack. Mechanical pencils lined up where people can find them before they lose their train of thought.

Out of nowhere, Ash says, "He didn't mean it."

Every tool fits into a slot in a case. I sweep loose screws into a jar and sort the other electronic parts into bins until his comment starts to irritate me.

"Who didn't mean what?"

"Your dad. He didn't hurt you on purpose."

No. Maybe he didn't.

"It didn't hurt." My cheek has stopped smarting, but the moment replays itself in front of my eyes, complete with the stranger who wore Dad's face, and my chin starts to tremble. I love him. And he *slapped* me.

I squeeze my eyes shut, and the image fades.

"Oh, shizzle spit!" I slam the bin down. "I've put resistors in with capacitors. Now I have to sort them all again, or someone will get confused and a circuit board will short out, a robot will fail, then somebody will die."

I wipe at my eyes, trying to see clearly.

Ash touches my arm, and I face him. He rests his cheek on my shoulder and gives me a sympathy hug. I squeeze back. It's so comfortable in his arms, with the way I tuck my head against his neck. My friend who is always there for me. He steps back, and I notice he has powdered sugar on the tip of his nose. Not in the mood to laugh, I rub it off and turn back to work. Dad made a mess of the cables behind the access panel. I start wiping down surfaces for germs.

It's just that Dad has never hit me before. Ever. Not even when I deserved it.

The box of disaccharide tori, the ones that *don't* have bugs, fits into my pack but leaves crumbs all over. Good thing I keep a tiny whiskbroom handy in another pocket.

*Jitters made him do it.*

*Prelude* is out of balance now. A creeping dread tells me my world is crumbling, as if little bugs are picking it apart. And a grim idea, one without definite shape, curls up and hides in a dark corner of my mind, waiting like a hungry rat.

After a few minutes, I realize I'm standing motionless with a broom and dustpan, staring at nothing. Ash is nice enough for once not to crack a joke.

I hang Dad's interface helmet on the back of his chair. Ash turns the lights off and I lock the door on our way out.

# CHAPTER 6

*D*ad used to cook while I set the table. This morning Dad is missing, not because he's working, but because he's been strapped to a bed in Mom's infirmary for a day and a half. So Mom and I choose to make pancakes because they're easy. Crispy on the outside and runny on the inside, the way Mom likes them. At least, that's how she makes them.

All through breakfast I deliberately do not ask how Dad is doing. I'm afraid to know. He may already be drooling and screaming. Mom scrapes a plate and hands it to me. "Are your new students behaving?"

Water curves to anti-spinward as it spouts from the faucet while I wash the dish. I'm told on Earth, real gravity makes things fall straight down.

"They're decent kids. Bunch of button-pushers, though. Can't keep their grubby fingers off anything."

"You know they can't do any real damage."

I dry the plate and stack it away. "Colton still hasn't shown up. You think he's still mad at me for no good reason?"

"Namida, I've explained before. You have to respect other people's personal space. Some are more private than others."

"Why?"

Mom sighs and hands me a glass. "I think it's a product of their upbringing. You know the idea. Behavior comes down to either DNA or how a person is raised. Nature or nurture."

"Well, it's silly. This is a space station. We can't install changing booths everywhere because some people don't want to be seen in a unitard. Anyway, a unitard covers everything except hands, head, and feet, so what's to be embarrassed about?"

"I know how you see it, Namida, but you should be more sensitive—"

"If it's such a challenge to figure out where Colton's precious *personal space* begins and ends, then frankly I don't want to waste the time. He'll have to get over it."

"Honey, it's more than that." She takes the drying towel. "It's possible for boys or girls to send wrong signals, and it's possible he might mistake your intentions—"

And this is where I tune her out. *Blah, blah, blah.* I've heard this lecture, and all I get out of it is that Earth people make everything complicated, as if they need a secret code to make friends or go on dates.

When she finally stops talking, I say, "Glad *I* never send signals about anything."

Mom blinks, and her mouth drops open. No words come out. She does that when she can't organize her thoughts, but I don't have time to wait for her lights to click on.

"I'll be late." I stretch on tiptoes to give her a quick kiss on the cheek, and stop by the bathroom on my way out to rinse with mouthwash.

⸺⁂⸺

Parents drop my five new students off at the playroom, but I won't let them play on the jungle gym or crawl through the gerbil tubes until we straighten up the ball pit. I've never been able to keep it organized. Over forty-six thousand plastic balls of six different colors, all out of order. The best I can do is tell myself that their purpose is to *be* out of order. But I insist they at least stay in the pit. The problem is, none of the kids ever agree. So I send my students to hunt for wayward balls and toss them in, while I level it off as best as I can. They turn the hunt into a game and laugh and chase each other.

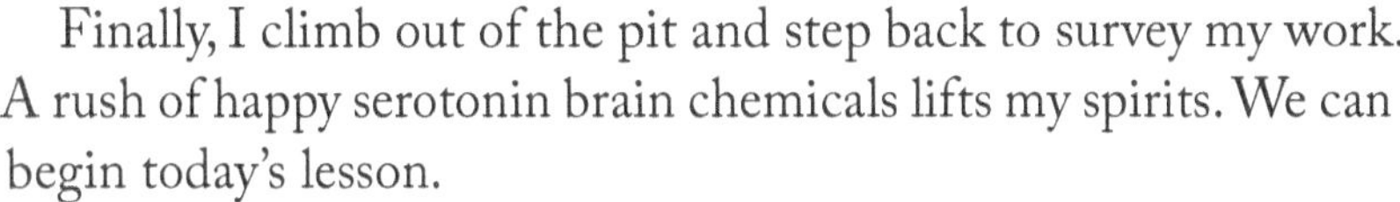

Finally, I climb out of the pit and step back to survey my work. A rush of happy serotonin brain chemicals lifts my spirits. We can begin today's lesson.

The kids seat themselves in a semicircle on the mat. I notice the red-haired girl still wears a type of leather shoes called Mary Janes.

"Wear your boots from now on," I scold.

While I fetch a jug of water, a bucket, and a rope, Colton wanders in and props himself against a batting cage with crossed arms.

"Join us, Colton?" I gesture to a spot on the floor.

He frowns. "I'm fine back here."

Okay, fine. I don't want him near me anyway.

"Has anybody tried getting water from a kitchen faucet?"

A bunch of them nod.

I uncap the jug and hold it a little to my right. When I upend it, the water curves and splashes into the bucket at my left foot with perfect aim. "Can anyone tell me why the water curves as it falls?"

"Magic!" shouts the class clown. There's always one.

"No," I say. "*Physics*. Right now, we're in a *gondola*, kind of like being in a big bucket."

As I talk, I uncoil the cotton rope tied to the bucket's handle. "What would happen if I turn this bucket upside down?" I start to swing the bucket back and forth. The kids smile in expectation as the bucket gets higher on each backswing. When I have enough momentum, I let it make a full circle, turning upside down over my head. Their mouths drop open in surprise.

"Centrifugal force keeps the water inside. The same force now pushes you to the floor, kind of like when you try to hang onto one of those mini merry-go-rounds, when someone spins it really fast."

I always love seeing that light of understanding flicker on. Except that this time, mischievousness twinkles behind my students' eyes. From behind me, somebody's hand stops my arm on the upswing. The bucket's arc is interrupted, and I am drenched.

The kids erupt in laughter.

Gasping from the shock of cold water, I let the bucket clatter to the floor. When I turn around, Ash grins in my face.

"That's an example of Newton's First Law," he says, then dashes away.

Colton breezes past me and tackles Ash before he can dive into a gerbil tube. Both boys get to their feet, but Colton grabs Ash's wrists and flings him into the ball pit. My students cheer, and they all jump in with him, scattering colored balls across the floor.

So much for organization.

Ash stands, waist-deep in the pit. "Namida, who is this dip-switch?"

"Everybody out!" I shout above the chaos, wiping my eyes. Water trickles down my back. My flight suit clings with uncomfortable wetness.

Three kids climb out and sheepishly put their hands behind their backs. The other two calm down only when I remind them, "Mrs. Kirkpatrick will be here soon."

Orientation is over until the real teacher arrives, and they want to squeeze out every minute of playtime. Everyone takes the hint and scatters to the jungle gym and rope swings. Some of the kids experiment with jumping straight up to see how long they can hover. They will drift sideways for a bit, before falling back to the floor amid giggles and classmates ready to catch them.

Ash turns big puppy dog eyes at me and holds up a hand for me to help him out. Instead, I squeeze water out of my ponytail onto his face. Sweet revenge!

Colton points to the kids. "So, you're their babysitter?"

What a horrible thought. "Wouldn't sitting on babies squish them?"

"I suppose it would," he laughs.

I look up "babysitter" on my omni-dev. It's not at all what it sounds like.

My clothes are drenched, but I can't leave the kids unattended to go change.

"You should go through full orientation," I tell him, "so you don't kill yourself or forget to zip a shower stall."

He pretends to be worried, "Oh no! That'd put us all in hot water, wouldn't it?" as though it's some kind of joke.

Mrs. Kirkpatrick enters the playroom. Her gray hair is twisted up in a bun, with a few curls escaping. She wears her forest green flight suit as regulations require, but she takes the liberty of modifying it. Today she has added a rough woolen scarf pinned by a silver brooch, shaped like a dragon chasing its tail. Somehow, she makes even a flight suit look stylish.

"I'm glad you already ken," she says, in heavy Scottish brogue, "how humidity causes electrical shorts and leads to fires, which is na laughing matter."

Colton looks puzzled, so I whisper a translation. "'Ken' means 'know,' and 'na' means 'no.'" For some reason, this doesn't clear it up for him.

Her accent was difficult to get used to. When we first met, I thought she kind of called me a rabbit's behind. After I told her she owed the swear jar, she made me apologize. Turns out she'd said, "bonnie lass," which means, "pretty girl."

Mrs. Kirkpatrick regards the boys. "Colton Binnacle, have you been fighting?"

"Swimming lessons," offers Colton, as he helps Ash out of the ball pit.

My teacher raises one eyebrow, and Colton withers. "Either you are dishonest, or you believe I'm a complete numpty. Which is it, Mister Binnacle?"

By his expression, I think Colton is trying to figure out if numpty is the same as idiot. "Can we call it a bad sense of comedic timing, ma'am?"

For a couple of heartbeats, Mrs. Kirkpatrick freezes Colton with a squint, and right when I think she's about to verbally shred him, she says, "Excellent. A third option presents itself. Aye, let us call it that."

Mrs. Kirkpatrick clucks her tongue at Ash in disapproval. "Tamonash Kapurthala, what did you do to deserve this?"

"Nothing," he says, then suddenly punches Colton on the shoulder.

Colton does not hit back. Instead, that lopsided grin gets bigger and turns the whole episode into a playful joke. It's the kind of smile Mom calls "infectious," like it's a disease.

"Okay, now we're even," Colton says, rubbing his shoulder. "But let that be a lesson to you. Back home in Corpus Christi, we don't stand for bullies picking on girls."

"Oh yeah? What about the *rest* of Texas?" quips Ash.

Colton has the right idea. Nobody had better tease any of my kids. Boys or girls. It takes me a few seconds to realize he's referring to *me*, and I am aware once more of how my drenched flight suit clings to my skin.

"Have you been swimming, Miss Wiles?"

"No, Mrs. Kirkpatrick. We…um…"

"We experienced localized aqueous spillage." Colton puffs out his chest, proud of his vocabulary.

My teacher nods knowingly, and I rush to assure her, "The leakage has been contained." She seems to accept that answer. "I thought I'd go home and change, then show Colton around."

"Wonderful. Try not to decompress the station."

As she gathers up the kids, we make our escape. Outside, I turn to Colton and block his way with arms crossed.

"What're you so mad about?" he says. "Didn't I just rush to your defense?"

"Last time we met you threw a pillow at my head."

His smile vanishes. "Really? I don't remember that. I must have still been groggy. But I do remember you about pushed me out a window."

"The observation room doesn't open to space," I say.

"Lucky me."

Ash tries to hide a grin. I wait, but Colton still doesn't apologize. I give up with a huff and lead the boys to the apartment deck. On the way, I show Colton how to use the *You Are Here* displays in case he ever gets lost.

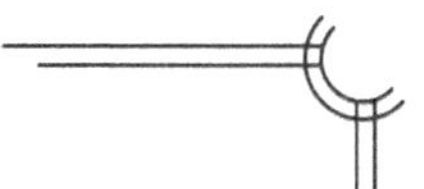

Colton turns to Ash. "By the way, is your name really *Ash*?"

"My full name is Tamonash Singh Kapurthala."

Colton grins again. "Well, ain't that a mouthful? Mind if I call you Tammy?"

"Sure. As long as I can call you Revoltin'."

"There ya go. Ash it is, then." He shoves his hands into his pockets. "So, what's first on the tour? Do I get to see where you hide your alien life forms?"

"Who told you that?" I ask. "We don't have aliens."

"Good job keeping a straight face," says Ash, then turns to Colton. "She's telling the truth. There are no aliens." He gives me an exaggerated wink, and Colton chuckles.

Okay, I'm not sure what that's all about.

My apartment is empty when we arrive. The boys wait by the door while I zip out of my flight suit and spread it on the common room's table. They watch with interest as I make a quick pass with a blow dryer over my damp unitard without taking it off; probably impressed by how unitards let moisture evaporate quickly. In my bedroom, I slip on a new flight suit and clip on fresh jet canisters from the $CO_2$ recharging station. Back in the common room, I finish my suit checks and make sure my pockets are stocked with handy items.

When I'm ready to go, the boys' expressions take me by surprise. Ash scowls with his arms folded, eyes cast to the floor, as he angrily grinds his teeth. Colton stares, eyes wide and standing perfectly still. His ears have turned bright red.

"Are you okay?" I ask, and glance at the readout on his sleeve.

He nods nervously.

Ash says, "Let's get this stupid tour over with." He throws the door open and stalks into the hall. I've given up long ago trying to figure out his moods.

"Let's show Colton the garden chamber," I suggest. "People always say it's the part of *Prelude* that's most like Earth."

We ride the elevator from the apartment deck up to the garden level and step out into the warm light of the chamber's anteroom. Through the huge open hatch to our left, the rim corridor curves up past the spoke junction. To our right is a matching hatch large enough to allow farm equipment through when it's unsealed. Across the anteroom, I can see an ag-tech in her monitoring booth. She recognizes me and waves us through a small open airlock next to the giant hatch.

Colton jerks a thumb back. "Don't we need to seal that behind us?"

"No. There's another one ahead."

Ash hangs back, sullen and silent. The cramped room beyond the airlock takes a minute to fill with ultraviolet light and antiseptic fog, then vents out again. Colton looks confused, but not alarmed, when hidden jets blow us clean of dust.

"It's so you don't infect the crops with your disease," Ash explains.

"When we leave," I say, "those blowers will keep bees from following us out."

This room opens onto the metal catwalk that overlooks the garden chamber. Ranks of cornstalks stand in perfect rows. Air vents send a light breeze through the pines that encircle the chamber, making their needles hiss softly. Behind them, the blue walls gently arch up to a transparent roof. Through quadruple layers of ozone and shatterproof crystal, we see the shutters outside automatically tilt to keep sunlight reflecting onto the crops, casting shadows that drift with the wheel's rotation.

"At night they fold the shutters away and darken the window. All the stars turn deep red. It's lovely, isn't it, Ash?"

"Yeah," he grumbles. "Just like the stars are burning out as the universe dies."

"Oh, don't be so morbid."

Colton asks, "Do you two watch it often?" It's an innocent question, but there's more in his tone than in his words. Ash turns away to sulk. "I see," says Colton.

I wish *I* did. It irritates me that I don't understand what's going on between them. For star's sake, I hope it's not a secret code thing.

Register zero patience for *that*. Ash perks up, and I recognize that cruel leer.

"You know, when you look up through the skylight, you're looking in toward the wheel's *center*. It seems like the whole station swings around our axle."

Colton grips the rail and leans over. His stomach heaves and his face goes pale.

Ash leans in close. "The station whizzes by about once a minute. When you realize there are two thousand people in that flimsy thing, it's awesome. A thin layer of aluminum is all that's between you and instant death."

Colton groans and makes a horrible noise at the back of his throat.

"Ash," I warn him, "you need to stop." I put a steadying arm around Colton and adjust his dizzy-phones. "Concentrate on how solid the rail is." Colton's grip tightens. "Good. Now think about how this platform *isn't* moving. Know that all of this—the trees, the soil, the walls—has been here for thirty years. *You are safe.*"

With effort, Colton straightens up. "Thanks. That helps."

Ash slumps, disappointed.

"Besides," I say, "Ash exaggerated about the walls being aluminum. They're made up of epoxy tubes, carbon fiber mesh, and honeycombed metallic—"

Colton puts a finger on my lips. "Please stop lecturing."

"Okay." I ease away from him and catch a death-glare from Ash. He's the one who's been teasing a noob, and he's mad at *me* again.

Colton breathes deeply the fresh scent of pines, soil, and mist as he admires the scenery. "Weird how the ground curves up all the way to the far end," he observes.

"It follows the curve of Adam's rim," I say. "If it didn't, you'd feel like you were walking downhill as you approached the far wall."

"Ever thought about building a baseball stadium in here?" asks Colton. "It would fit, bleachers and everything. And who would have thought you could grow trees in space?"

"Well, technically, they grow in dirt. Robots keep them trimmed so they don't get too tall. Robots also take care of the fields. See?" I point to several beetle-like ag-bots crawling between the rows, plucking up weeds, and checking the soil. "For a couple of years, I used to tend those beehives over there."

"I expected you to make your food in labs, like they do on Moon Base."

"We do that, too," I say. "We have two thousand forty-eight crew and guests aboard, but *Prelude* is designed to support over ten thousand. On decks below, aquariums supply fish, hydroponics grow an abundance of vegetables, and—"

Colton touches my lips again. "Ratchet down a notch, Namida."

Maybe I should be insulted, but his tender voice and gentle touch make me want to return the smile. He's different. Little kids hang all over me. Older kids are snobs. Adults either politely dismiss me or act as if I'm a trained monkey. Ash, being the one other kid close to my age, has been the only person I can play with or talk to. Until now.

I hold my breath and try to come up with something besides a lecture.

Nothing. I'm empty. Maybe I can get Colton to talk instead.

"Does this remind you of Corpus Christi?"

"Do you think everybody from Texas lives on a farm or cattle ranch?"

Wrong thing to ask, I suppose. With every word from my mouth, I shut him out. It surprises me to realize how badly I want him to like me.

Colton says, "We have stores, movie theaters, and laser tag arenas. Best of all, we have a beach right on the gulf. I spend a lot of time snorkeling."

"Ever been sailing?" asks Ash. He's always wanted to try it.

When Colton turns to answer, I discreetly look up *gulf* on my omni-dev. Another redundant word for "body of water," such as lake, ocean, or puddle.

"No," says Colton, "but I'd like to. My dad doesn't trust deep water."

Ash laughs. "But he's fine with deep space? Funny. What else do you do?"

"I make battle-bots for international tournaments."

"*That's* where I know your face! I've seen your bots." Admiration erases any irritation Ash showed before.

"What's a battle-bot?" I ask.

"It's a robot designed to destroy other robots in a contest," Colton explains.

"That's insane! Why would anyone want bots to rip each other apart?"

Colton spreads his hands as though it should be obvious. "It's fun?"

Ash says, "Mom often took me to tournaments before Father had me shipped here." He always mentions leaving Earth with a trace of bitterness.

Both of them seem so alien right now with their talk about destroying perfectly good machines. *Boys*! Normally I wouldn't care, but my friends are leaving me behind.

I interrupt to keep Colton's attention. "I know what you'd enjoy. It's not someplace most people see. Follow me."

We leave and take the elevators down to a lower level, then navigate through a maze of machinery. Tiny crab-shaped maintenance bots crawl over pipes.

When we reach the hatch, I rush through the sequence to unseal it, then pause for dramatic effect. Purple light spills into the corridor as I usher the boys onto the platform inside. Ripples on the water's surface reflect patterns of ultra-violet. Water reservoirs aren't as big as garden chambers, but they're the next largest space *Prelude* has to offer. I bite my lip as I eagerly watch Colton's reaction.

His eyes scan the reservoir with nothing more than polite interest.

"Ta da!" I say with a flourish, to encourage him.

Now he's puzzled and turns to Ash for help.

"Don't ask me," says Ash. "One of the greatest enigmas is how Namida's brain works. I usually just go with it."

How can they be so dense? "Gulf! Doesn't this remind you of your gulf back home?"

"You're kidding, right? Haven't you ever seen the ocean?"

Ash coughs. "Colton, she's never been to Earth. The most she's ever seen are pictures, because she won't go to movies, and omni-dev screens don't do it justice."

That isn't true about movies. Ash made me watch *Forbidden Planet*, even though I don't like science fiction. Sure, that movie is over a hundred and forty years old, but it does have a cool robot.

"Oh, right," Colton says. "You said that before, when I was still groggy, didn't you?"

Ash smirks. "Be glad you haven't seen her air-dance." He's trying to irritate me on purpose. "It's more like Kung Fu. She can be dangerous if you get too close."

Colton raises his eyebrows. "Really?"

My cheeks flush with embarrassment because I don't let anyone see me dance. Except, Ash has seen me because he sneaks around. Why would he pick on me like this in front of Colton? Is he trying to make me look goofy?

"Yeah," Ash continues, "and the music she listens to is this ancient electronic stuff."

"My EDM oldies are pure creative magic. Better than that painful Tech Screech of yours! I can produce better sound with feedback loops through broken speakers."

Instead of getting angry, Ash chuckles. I can't figure out why Colton is amused, but standing here while they both laugh at me makes me feel like such a muppet. Ash is deliberately trying to ruin a friendship before it even starts. *Blast him!*

*Jingle, jingle, tinkle ring*, my omni-dev chimes its nursery tune.

"Why do you always have to open your stupid mouth, Ash?"

"When did air-dancing become a secret?"

*Jingle, jingle, tinkle ring.*

I yell right in his face. "Since always!"

Colton nervously points at my pocket. "Aren't you going to answer that?"

*Jingle, jingle, tinkle ring.*

I rip my omni-dev out and stab the button. "What?!"

Both boys jump, and their grins disappear.

"Don't take that tone with me, young lady! I am *not* in the mood."

My first urge is to smash my omni-dev against the wall. Instead, I pull my ponytail and squeeze my eyes shut. In five seconds, I'm able to say in my sweetest tone, "Sorry, Mother *dearest*. What may I do for you?"

"Get your little…disposition to the infirmary. *Now.*"

# CHAPTER 7

 $M$ om finishes setting up after I locate her in an exam room off the neuro lab. A leather examination couch stands in the middle of the stark room, with wires and gizmos all around, waiting for me. The rest of the equipment is behind an observation window. By the way Mom taps at the keyboard and flits between workstations, I can tell she's agitated. I'm afraid it's because I've avoided the infirmary ever since Dad's incident.

"Look, I know I've missed several school days," I say, "but I've been busy."

She waves my excuse away to let me know she doesn't care about that, and points to the exam couch. I sit on the edge and lean over to slip off my boots and jet pack.

She hands me a scanning helmet. I buckle the strap under my chin and stretch out. The visor blocks out light, and the sensor studs press against my scalp. Mom hooks my flight suit to the computer to track my vitals, then fits the interfaced gloves on me.

"Since you brought it up," she says, "why haven't you visited your father?"

I picture the last time I saw Dad. *Smack!* A wild light in his eyes.

But I shrug and say, "I don't know."

"He misses you."

I hate that pleading tone she gets. My heart wilts. "Please don't."

Blind in the helmet, I listen to her bustle around the room.

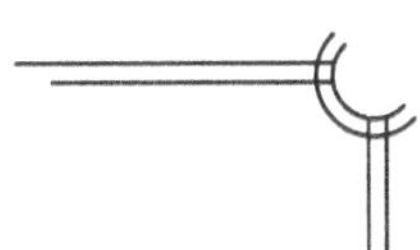

"We'll start with faces," she says.

"We did faces *months* ago."

"I know. We're starting over."

Oh, for the love of stars, I'll die of old age before I get out of here. First, there's emotional recognition. Then we'll record my reactions to a series of videos with sound. Then there's the visual dictionary, where I name off pictures of cats, types of trees, tools, and a million other items. It goes on forever. Motor functions. Memories. Language skills. Every little piece of my brain tested and mapped.

The single interesting part of the test is when we do simulations of a jammed airlock, or two people arguing. I'm supposed to solve whatever the problem is, like a role-playing video game. My decisions get recorded as a decision matrix.

All this so Mom can compare my brain patterns to recordings from when I was little, then compare them to scans of kids on Earth. She can map the bioelectricity that shines through every neural connection in my brain, but doesn't know what most of it means. Except she can see what's different from everyone else. Am I normal? That's the Big Question.

Well, I don't need a computer to figure that one out. Of course, I'm normal. It's everybody else that's messed up.

"Patient NW-CNH-0," she says into a mic. "Scan forty-two. May first, 2100."

People appear on my visor one at a time, and I call out what emotion they express: happy, sad, frightened, and so on. Today, every one of them looks idiotic.

"Annoyed," I answer, "because he has to make stupid faces for this test."

"Namida, be serious." There's a frazzled edge to her voice, and I know I should tread lightly, but why doesn't *she* ever tread lightly around *me*? Instead, she shoves me here, orders me there, without the least bit of scientific curiosity for how I feel.

"Bored. Depressed. Sly," I recite as more faces flash across my visor. "Asinine. Vapid. Dimwitted. Puerile. Obtuse."

"Namida! That's enough."

She unsnaps my chinstrap and yanks the helmet off. I expect to see rage in her eyes. Instead, I'm not sure what she's expressing. Grief? Maybe I do need more of these tests. The silence between us crackles with anger, then cools and gets awkward as she struggles to get the words out.

"Your father has Convulsive Neuropsychiatric Hallucinosis," she says. "Do you understand what that means?"

Part of me wants to rip off a stream of gibberish, then ask her if *she* understands. I mull that one over and decide it wouldn't be funny.

"In plain English, Mom, you mean he's got CNH. The Jitters. Yeah, I get it."

She holds my gaze with such intensity that I expect her to burst into tears. "Do you? It means this is serious, Namida. I need you to cooperate."

I cross my arms. "I've seen him, Mom. I know. Is he drooling yet? Has he tried to—" The words stick in my throat. "Has he tried to slap you?"

"Your father is sick. He was hallucinating."

"Right. He didn't mean to punch me. Not his fault. His brain made him do it. Except his brain is really him, isn't it? So, no, I *don't* get it."

Mom sighs and cups my cheeks in her hands. "Why your father struck you was the result of non-rational causes. It's like…" She gropes for an example. "It's like when your pancreas secretes insulin. It doesn't *mean* anything by that. It isn't trying to help you, that's just what a pancreas *does*, as a biological machine. If you get diabetes, it's because something has gone wrong with a long chain of chemical reactions, not because your pancreas hates you."

Why do her analogies always have to do with guts?

"You're telling me Dad's brain is broken, and when he saw praying mantises crawling out of his keyboard it didn't mean anything. Just a chemical glitch in his brain, like mixing baking soda with vinegar to make it fizz. And when he hit me, *that* didn't mean anything, either. Just another brain fizz."

Somewhat appeased, Mom backs away to her workstation to reset the test. She has something on her mind she's not telling me, and somehow another routine scan has turned into a battle. I fit the helmet back on and images flash across my visor. None of their expressions mean anything real or significant. They're all just brain fizzes.

"Serene. Sulking. Surprised." If I don't die of old age here, I'll die of boredom. "Afraid. Agonized. Affectionate." But I'd rather die as a girl, not as a lab rat. "Bubbly. *Effff*ervescent. Fizzing. Fizzled. Fizztacular. Fizzity-fizz-fizz-fizz."

The visor goes dark again. When I lift the helmet, Mom has her elbows propped on her desktop and pulls her hair. Frazzled. Also starts with an F. When she raises her head, her eyes look bruised. Defeated. I've hurt her without even trying.

Boredom flees along with impatience, and my throat gets tight. I *am* sorry. But that's not what comes out.

"Mom?" My eyes start to tear up. Then the thought slips out, the grim rat that's been hiding for days in the dark corner of my brain. Except that now I have words to shape it. "When Dad says he loves me, is that just another brain fizz?"

The lab falls silent, except for the equipment's electric humming.

"Oh, sweetie." Her expression melts and something warm comes through, even as her tears fall on her keyboard. "No. Your father loves you very much. That's precious and real."

"How do you *know*?"

She starts to speak, then her words evaporate before she can voice them. Her eyes dart around the room, as if searching desperately for an answer. Then she blurts out, "I know because I've lived with him for sixteen years, and for thirteen of those I've seen how he lights up when you're around. I've watched him sing to you, and read you bedtime stories."

Her words ought to be warm and assuring. These are facts, and I know them all and many more, but what do they *mean*? Dad does those things because that's the way his brain is wired. Ash tells his father he loves him, but he does it because his dad punishes him if he doesn't. None of it means anything.

"If a brain fizz can make him do a hurtful thing, then why can't it make him do a loving thing? What if it's all just brain fizzes?"

Mom's energy crumbles, and she turns a little gray.

"We're done for today." She powers off her monitor and leaves the room without glancing at me again.

Whatever battle Mom fought inside her head, it's been decided. Trouble is, I don't know if I won or lost.

# CHAPTER 8

After I buckle my boots, I go searching for Mom. I want to apologize. I'll take it all back, be a good little lab rat, and let the computer paint maps of my brain.

I check the lab next door, but none of the med-techs saw her come through. Turns out she's also not in the emergency room, or sick ward. Well, no sense chasing her around the wheel. I whip out my omni-dev and call up the locator app. A blinking red dot shows she's in her office. From here, it'll be quicker to use the service passage.

I sprint out a back door. The passages that run behind the scenes are narrow, full of power conduits, air ducts, and fiber chases for the network. Widely spaced LEDs provide minimal light. I cut through the deck's center, which makes it a short jog to Mom's back door.

Mom's office divides into two sections. The first is for consultations, with plush chairs and a couch, and the second is a space for her desk. The office is, in fact, a single room, but Mom had our craftsmen build a plastic dividing screen textured to look like a cascade of flowers.

My mind reels at the mess she's made. Her cabinets and drawers hang open. A dozen boxes litter the floor, half-filled with her stuff. Pictures, mementos, a few old-fashioned paper books, and her med projects.

Raised voices from the consultation section draw me to the screen. I'm able to watch them between the gaps in the flower pattern without being seen.

"I can't believe it, Sydney!" bellows Captain Binnacle.

"You're making progress, Winston. We finally found something you can't believe."

Mom plugs a thumb-drive into each picture on the wall, downloads the images, then powers off the frames.

Captain shakes a finger at her. "Clever shot, but now isn't the time for theological debates. No one has ever *resigned* from *Prelude*."

"You can't hold me prisoner." Mom drops the thumb-drive into a box.

"Don't think I haven't considered it." He takes the box out of Mom's hands and lays it on a coffee table. "Look. Let Stirl get some much-needed rack time while you finish out your tour."

A dangerous smirk curls Mom's lips as she braces her hands on her hips. I know that look, and I always make sure I'm not on the receiving end of it.

"Well, aren't *you* the magnanimous one!" She drips so much sarcasm we'll need a mop. "Where do I begin? First of all, a normal tour of duty is two years. Everyone else rotates out after one, maybe three tours, tops. I'm on my *eighth*!" Mom backs Captain against the wall. She's no taller than he is, but her attitude towers over him. "Would you care to guess why? I'll give you a clue. It isn't because I'm in love with space. It's because my daughter is the Coalition's shining example of how safe *Prelude* is. First child born in space! She's Public Relations' little darling. In the end, it doesn't matter if she loses one parent, so long as she has a spare. After all, we're all about redundant systems, aren't we?"

Wait. *Loses a parent*? My limbs go numb. Who said anything about losing a parent? Does she mean Dad's going to *die*?

"Sydney, that's not fair. You believe I'm heartless?"

"Oh, it's not your fault, Winston. The Coalition pulls your strings."

Captain straightens his spine. "I'm nobody's puppet!"

Mom takes a moment to breathe, then backs down. "Maybe that's true. I don't know anymore." She grips her hair with white knuckles. "All I know is that *Prelude* is no longer healthy for my husband, and I don't want to keep raising my daughter in a cage, no matter how big it is." She scans the room and tosses a vase into the box.

"Sydney, you're the best doctor I've ever shipped with. Not to mention I've become fond of you, Stirling, and Namida. Losing Stirl will take some of the wind out of our sails, but we'll work around it. Things'll be fine. You'll see."

Mom sags and has difficulty getting her next words out. "Stirling isn't going to bounce back. His career as an astronaut is over."

How can Dad live on *Prelude* and *not* be an astronaut? No. She *has* to be wrong.

Captain's brow furrows. "Wait. Why didn't CNH show up during admission screening?"

She shrugs. "It's not easy to detect, and we haven't pinpointed the cause, but specialists believe it has something to do with chemical vapor from the epoxy in our hull, combined with a conceptual-inanimate brain type that can't handle the wheel's constant spinning."

Captain spreads his hands, searching for words. "He doesn't need to work in a wheel."

"Working from the Trunk isn't the answer. Prolonged life in weightlessness has its own health problems. You know that. And if he continued his work from Earth, he would be too far out of the loop."

Mom sinks to the couch, exhausted, and Captain gingerly sits next to her. He runs his fingers through his hair, then puts his cap back on. "Give me a chance to work something out."

She pins him with her gaze. "CNH can be *hereditary*, Winston."

Captain's face turns ashen. "Have you tested her?"

"Every year since Papa died, yes. And recently I've stepped it up."

Grampa Isaak Lachenderbar was "Papa" to Mom. A giant of

a man, with a touch of gray at his temples, always laughing. I remember flying as he tossed me in the air. We would sail toy boats in water tanks and climb trees in garden chambers.

I was in Flight Control the day his ship got crushed. It was our sixteenth trip to Starheim. His ship passed through the reactor ring that creates the wormhole, one hundred kilometers from *Prelude*. Inside the ring, we had generated enough energy to squeeze thousands of light-years of space into itself. Four seconds in, the wormhole collapsed with a blinding flash of green light. Everyone gasped, but it took me several minutes to figure out that wasn't supposed to happen.

"What made you start testing her? Stirl only now started showing symptoms."

Mom squirms. "Maybe it's simple childhood fantasy, but Namida believes she senses the station as though it's part of her." She bites her lip and looks away.

Captain leans back. "Okay. That's a bit odd, I'll admit, but a belief in supernatural phenomena is no reason to panic."

"Let's not drag *your* religious delusions into this, Winston."

"Gee thanks, Sydney," he says flatly. "Because, logically, anyone who believes God exists must be mentally unstable. I suppose I should be grateful you don't have me declared unfit for duty."

Mom replies in her clinical tone. "If your personal beliefs interfered with your role as captain, I would, but let's not start that argument again."

He nods. "Sorry." After a pause, he asks, "Have your tests shown anything?"

"No. There's little difference between her scans and those of Earth children. Her corpus callosum is more active than normal, but other than that, she's the picture of health."

Of course, I'm normal, *because I don't have Jitters*! Mom can't handle anything that doesn't fit into her world of test tubes and med computers.

"Then nothing to worry about, right?"

"That's precisely it. *Stirl* passed the screening. Therefore, I can't be sure Namida doesn't have it, too." Mom rubs her face in her hands. "I'm not going to wait around for symptoms to manifest. I won't take that chance with my daughter."

I've heard what Jitters does to people. Hallucinations and convulsions. Dad's going to lose his mind. After that, will he even know me anymore? Will that scary light of madness I saw in his eyes be the only way he ever looks at me again? If that happens, the Dad I knew might as well be dead.

"I can't bear to see Stirl get sick," Captain sighs. "We'll do everything we can for him. To be safe, Namida can go ashore as well but, Sydney, that still doesn't mean *you* have to resign."

"No. I've already lost Papa to this project. I'm not trading my family to keep my career. Besides, it doesn't mean I'm giving up medicine."

Captain stands, accepting defeat. "I'll book your passage. Meanwhile, there's room enough for Stirling to leave on the next shuttle."

"Thank you, Winston."

Mom walks Captain Binnacle out the door and closes it before his words register with me. Leave on the next shuttle? Dad's *leaving*? I barge into the consultation area.

I shout, "No! That's not happening!" and scare Mom half to death. "Isn't there something *else* you can do for him?"

She spins around to face me. "How long have you been hiding in my office?"

Blood pulses through my ears. "Answer *my* question first!"

Oops. Wrong thing to say. Mom grips my shoulders. "I am your mother, and you will *not* speak to me that way. Do you hear?"

My chin starts to tremble. I open my mouth to apologize, but instead I squeak out, "Please don't send Daddy away."

Mom presses her lips tight, and her flash of anger fades. She releases me. "We *have to* send your father to Earth so he can get better."

"After he gets better, he can come back, right?"

"No. He can never live in space again."

"That's not fair! He's not sick."

"Trust me, Namida, he is."

"Then find a cure!" My hands start shaking, so I squeeze them under my armpits.

"Fresh air and living in normal Earth gravity *is* the cure."

She's talking in circles. There's no reasoning with her when she gets like this.

"It won't be forever, Namida. We'll join him, and we'll all be together."

How can she talk so sweetly about such horror? Even worse, she's still smiling! Blood freezes in my veins. She must be insane.

"Mom! We *can't* go to Earth." I fumble calling up the library app on my omni-dev. The buttons won't hold still. "Bugs, Mom. Trillions and trillions of bugs everywhere! And b-billions of people. How do they *fit*?" The very thought of crowds smothers me, and I start breathing deeper to make sure I still can.

"It's not as bad as it sounds," she soothes.

"No! Everybody says that, *but it is!*" I manage to find a picture of people dying on a battlefield. "They have wars, and p-pestilence, and starvation!" I hold the screen right up to her face, but she brushes it away.

"I know, but none of that happens in Duluth."

She's in denial. You can't argue with facts, but she refuses to see. My omni-dev clatters to the floor. "Direct sunlight! We'll fry like bacon! Skin…cancer. B-blindness." The words are hard to get out. When did the air get so thick? "Mom, p-please…don't send me to Earth! Everything's heavy, *all the time*. There's no weightlessness!"

No more flying through the Yoke. No more air-dancing. No more zero-gravity dodgeball. My home. Everything that I'm connected to, she's taking away. Might as well rip out my bones!

Blood pounds in my ears. I wind up on the floor, but I don't remember sitting. Mom sits behind me and draws me into a hug. It's already too warm in here, and her embrace makes it worse. I squirm to get free, but she holds me firmer.

"Sweetie, you need to calm down. Check your vitals."

Vitals. Right. I hold up my forearm to see the readouts. Yellow indicates warning, but I can't make sense of the numbers. What difference does it make? I'm going to die anyway.

"They named the whole planet after *dirt*, Mom. Dirt! Think of the germs!"

"You've been vaccinated. I've seen to that."

"Animals eat people there." How much more can I say to make her understand she'll kill us all? "Polar bears, and buffalo, and cats!"

"Calm down," she says slowly. "Inhale. Exhale. Concentrate on that."

She starts rocking me back and forth. I count out the seconds in my head for each breath. Inhale. Hold it. One, two, three. Let it out slowly. Then Mom starts to sing.

*"Hush-a-bye. Don't you cry.*
*Go to sleep my little angel."*

It's a kid's song Dad would sing at bedtime when I was little. The lyrics don't always rhyme, and that bothers me. But the tune is a sweet kind of sad.

*"When you wake, you will find*
*All the pretty little ponies.*
*Blacks and bays. Dapples and grays.*
*Angel's riding off to dreamland."*

Last time Mom sang this was when Grampa Isaak died, half a lifetime ago.

*"Can you see the little ponies*
*Dance before your eyes?*
*All the pretty little ponies*
*Prancing, when you rise."*

Blast her. That stupid song works. My hands still shake, but I breathe easier, and the room stops tilting. My vitals slide back to green. Now that Mom's no longer trying to suffocate me, I cease my struggles and let her rock me. She's comfortable, like a warm fluffy pillow that smells of wonderful antiseptic freshness. My brain calms down.

"Mom? Why would I want ponies?"

She kisses my neck. "Don't all little girls love ponies?"

"Interesting question. Without taking a survey, I can't be sure."

Mom laughs. She often laughs for no particular reason, and I've come to understand it means she's happy, not that anything specific is funny.

"Where would we put them? I mean, we couldn't keep them in our apartment. And if they live in garden chambers, then they wouldn't really be ours, would they?"

She gives me a squeeze. "That's my little stardancer. Always thinking."

We remain quiet for a few minutes. She's right. The best way to solve problems is by thinking. "If Dad leaves in a few days, then when is *our* shuttle out?"

"The next one they have scheduled is in a few weeks."

Good. That'll give me time to come up with a plan.

# CHAPTER 9

When Flight Control opens the hangar, it wakes me up. Perhaps the walls shuddered. Or maybe it's a drop in overall pressure, even though that makes no sense since airlocks between here and the dock would prevent that. Whatever. I *know* a giant hole has opened onto empty space, and I can feel the mass of the incoming shuttle, not far off.

I fight my way out of tangled sheets, then fold my bed-shelf against the wall and hurry to get dressed, making sure to snap on fresh $CO_2$ tanks. Mom calls me to breakfast, but I rush out. On my way to the playroom, I fail to avoid everyone.

"Ohayo, Namida!" a high school girl greets me in Japanese. "I hear your father is leaving." I pretend not to hear and keep walking with my head down. I catch her final comment before I'm out of sight. "Being rude again today, I see."

I run into a mechanical engineer leaving the playroom with his tool belt. "Ain't it thrillin'?" he says. "Yer finally goin' to Earth!"

I push past him and shut the door.

For the past three days, comments like these are all I've heard. Earth. What no one tells me is how to guard against kidnappers, or how *not* to die crossing a six-lane interstate, or how you're supposed to carry around a bulky space suit in case it snows.

The robotics team held a going away party. I didn't go. Mom saved me a slice of scrumptious strawberry cake. Later, I saw a meeting invitation from Captain Binnacle come across my omni-dev. He asked certain team leaders to meet for assignment changes.

The playroom is empty now, but soon chaos will reign. It'd be a lot easier to keep it straightened if I could figure out how to keep kids from playing here. I drag the equipment for my demonstration out of a cabinet, and spend the next hour setting it up. This is my favorite part of teaching orientation classes. Soon, the machine is primed and ready.

Next, I haul out a small NRD robot from its storage cabinet. Like the TNK models, this robot is shaped like a praying mantis, except it's only one meter high, which is good because kids find it less intimidating. After Dad decommissioned it, it took me months to get it to work again. As it powers up, I watch boot codes roll across its bulbous eye lenses. Then I toss a tarpaulin over it so it's out of sight.

What Mom calls my "imagination" tells me the shuttle has docked underneath Flight Control. *Prelude* feels denser at one end.

Parents drop off their kids, and I make my students sit in a semi-circle in front of the machine.

"Hi. Anybody ever play with dominoes by lining them up, and then when you knock the first one down, it makes all the others fall one by one?"

I get nods and smiles.

"Well, *this*," I gesture at my device, "is a Rube Goldberg machine. It's like dominoes. Except, instead, it uses all kinds of other junk." At this point, I light the candle on my machine, which starts the chain reaction. It has to melt two thin millimeters of wax before it burns through the thread that holds up the hammer. "Can anybody guess what this machine does?"

They concentrate a minute, but all I get are quizzical faces.

The hammer's handle is hinged at the end. After the thread snaps, it swings down to strike a cup, which dumps water into a container. This container is attached to gears that now turn, because of the water's weight, to lift a ball on a vertical conveyor belt. Once the ball reaches the top, it rolls down a metal track and taps the first in a line of dominoes. And so on and on through a dozen more gizmos.

At the end, a plate rotates to tip a bottle. Cider pours to fill a cup, then the machine stops.

"Ta da!" I say, with a flourish. "How many have worked with robots before?"

My red-haired girl raises her hand with enthusiasm.

"Well, a robot is a computer with a mechanical body. And a computer is nothing more than a machine, like this Rube Goldberg, but a zillion times more complicated." I casually walk over to the tarp. "In fact, it can do whatever a programmer tells it to do, but that's the trick. The programmer has to be smart enough to tell it how to do its job."

I whisk off the tarp. "This is Leonard."

"Hello, Leonard!" my students sing out. They're smiling, and that's much better than screaming in terror, which is the other common reaction to bots that look like giant bugs.

"Stand up, Leonard."

The robot flexes and raises its mantis body on four spindly legs.

"Leonard, hand out cups to these students until fifteen have cider."

Leonard hands a cup to the first of my five kids. The Rube Goldberg automatically rotates the plate until a second cup is filled, then Leonard hands it to the next student, and so on. When all five students have cider, Leonard grabs a sixth cup and pauses, confused. It decides to start over at the beginning of the line. Soon, each kid holds two cups. Leonard tries to hand an eleventh cup to the first student. But the student has no way to hold it, so the robot balances it on top of her head and begins to retrieve a twelfth cup. The kids giggle.

"Stop, Leonard," I say, and Leonard stops. "Can anyone tell me what's wrong?"

The red-haired girl volunteers. "Leonard will never give fifteen kids cider, because there are only five. So, he'll keep going until the cider runs out."

"Very good! Programmers call that an infinite loop. Stuff that's obvious to you and me isn't obvious at all to Leonard."

One boy raises his hand. "Does Leonard like dodgeball?"

"No. Robots don't like or dislike anything. You can program them to *act* as though they like something, but that wouldn't be real." The wooden way Ash tells his dad that he loves him comes to mind.

The red-haired girl asks, "Then what else *does* he do?"

"Lots of things, but you shouldn't call Leonard a *he*. It's a machine. You wouldn't call the Rube Goldberg a *he*, would you? Or call my omni-dev a *she*."

Everybody on *Prelude* makes this mistake *all the time*. It's something in human nature to treat a thing that moves on its own as though it's alive.

"Then why did you give it a name?"

"Because 'Leonard' is easier to say than 'NRD-1701.'"

I let the kids give it orders. This keeps them busy, but they wreck the Rube Goldberg because they think it's funny to have Leonard try to reset it. They're not afraid of robots now. Mission accomplished. But when they figure out they can ride Leonard like a horse, I decide playtime is over.

"Okay, that's enough. Dismount! We need to put Leonard away."

"Can we play with him again tomorrow?"

"Sorry, no. *It* isn't a toy." I hold the cabinet door open. "Get inside, Leonard."

The robot crawls in, then sinks to the floor and draws in its legs. It waits for me to power it off, to metaphorically kill it until the next demo. I stand staring into the dark cabinet, seeing but not seeing the robot.

"No. He's going away. No more demonstrations."

"Ever?"

I picture the stars outside the open hangar door and the bright blue Earth. "Not ever. No more games, no more inventions, no more bedtime stories. He's useless now."

My eyes well up with tears, and I'm not sure why I'm crying over a stupid robot. But I don't want the kids to see, so I keep my face turned away. The kids sit patiently while my mind wanders. I notice the time and am surprised at how long I've been standing here, then close the cabinet door.

Next, I deliver my students to school. Mrs. Kirkpatrick clasps her hands and greets them with, "Fàilte, wee little bairns!" Which means, *Welcome, tiny little children.* "Ready to stuff your empty skulls with knowledge?" Ready or not, the kids take their seats.

Before I make it to the door, Mrs. Kirkpatrick calls out, "Mind, Namida, you have a chemistry paper due in two days."

My world is ending, but she still wants homework on time. A reminder jingles a tune on my omni-dev, and I hurry out. The meeting is two gondolas away. If I use the moving walkways, I won't miss much.

The meeting is already in progress when I arrive, breathless. A room full of engineers listen as a mildly plump man points out details on the screen. Immediately, I recognize Dad's simulation of what happened at Starheim. We see the alien sun in the background, the one that's practically a twin to ours. Orbiting the dry planet is the starship *Anastasia*.

Over the past three decades, a team of terraforming robots have been harvesting ice from the rings of another planet and asteroids from a nearby belt. They gather the materials near a machine that orbits just beyond Starheim's moon, like safari ants bringing food to a hive. The goal is to get a water cycle going on Starheim. That's the first step to making the planet livable.

We watch the simulation as the robots feed asteroids into the machine, which grinds them up to extract the iron and form it into sheets. The robots then use that to encase the ice, so that as it falls through Starheim's atmosphere, it won't evaporate before it reaches three thousand meters above the ground.

They load the iron-encased iceberg into a magnetic cannon on the machine, which shoots it at the planet. When the iceberg reaches the proper altitude, the explosives detonate, forming a nice little cloud.

I grope for an empty seat on the tier below the entrance as I concentrate on what the man down front is saying. Three seats away, an unfamiliar robo-tech gives me an offended sneer. I point to the roboticist's pin on my collar. He's still irritated, but turns back to the lecture.

The speaker is bald on top but has let his sideburns grow bushy while keeping his chin shaven. His glasses make his eyes goggle out. Seated to the speaker's right and left are Captain Binnacle and Mr. K.

"Two years ago," says the speaker, "we received evidence, before communication was cut off, that the delivery bot made it through before the wormhole collapsed."

Even though Grandpa Isaak died when I was little, I still wince at the mention of every collapse.

On screen, we see a spherical "hole" open in space. It looks like a shiny, black Christmas ornament, but what it reflects isn't the planet Starheim. Instead, it reveals a distorted glimpse of Earth as the wormhole bridges the mind-boggling distance between two worlds. It wobbles as a delivery droid emerges. Merely flying through it was enough to make it unstable.

"The droid managed to dock with the *Anastasia* and deliver it's algae payload," says the speaker, as it plays out on screen. Then the wormhole disappears. "This much we know. What follows is *speculation*, based on the last transmitted compute state of the terraform-bots."

We watch as the enormous bots pause in their work. Then they prepare another iceberg and fire the machine at the *Anastasia*, the ship that brought them to Starheim and still serves as a repair and communications base. The asteroid plows through the ship, scattering debris, destroying humanity's first, and possibly last, hope for a new home.

The payload of super bio-engineered algae, that was supposed to grow on Starheim and produce oxygen, was also lost.

*Why?* No one understands why the terraform-bots did this. Dad has been running the simulation over and over for the past two years trying to figure it out.

The scene switches to display a CPU schematic. I've seen a computer's brain displayed this way before as a tangle of lines, symbols and numbers, laid out in awesome complexity, too much for the eyes to take in all at once.

"This is the CPU upgrade," the speaker continues, "that we installed in your TNK bots last year. It was designed to mimic the neural pathways of a human brain. But improved hardware alone will not solve the issues at Starheim. We need new software.

"Stirling Wiles believed the reason the bots misbehaved was a fault in their programming. He pursued a traditional approach, attempting to imprint human intelligence onto robotic thought patterns. But I feel robots need to develop their own unique way of thinking."

Whoever this man is, he has a nervous habit of tugging his sideburns.

"We disagreed over which programming solution to implement. While Stirling was wasting his time trying to invent something new—"

What a rat bag! Dad's work is not a waste of time.

"—I've been letting my original program *evolve* on its own. Similar to, ladies and gentlemen, how human beings developed the ability to reason after we managed to stand upright."

The roboticists in the room voice *"ahhhs"* of fascination.

"For the first time in programming history, our team at Belfast have achieved artificial intelligence that doesn't merely imitate a *human* mind. We no longer tell it *how* to solve unexpected problems. Nor does it rely on trial and error to guess. Instead, it has developed its own method of reasoning!"

A light smattering of applause urges the speaker to take a polite bow. He switches off the screen.

"With all due respect for Stirling Wiles, gone are the days of impressing the programmer's own rationality onto a robot's mind.

Robots are no longer mere complex tools. They've become partners in humankind's expansion to the stars!"

The audience rises with enthusiastic applause, and the speaker blushes as he seats himself. Captain Binnacle takes the podium.

"Thank you, Mr. Spencer. Any questions?"

I raise my hand first, but a young roboticist at the far left gets Captain's attention.

"When will this corrected AI replace the old programs?"

"Once Mr. Spencer finishes some field tests," says the captain, "we will crew starship *Redemption* with TNK bots and fly it to Starheim. Those robots will locate the scattered terraform-bots and upload the new AI."

"Are we ready to re-open the wormhole?" an engineer asks without raising his hand. Again, I am ignored. And my arm is getting tired. I swear Mr. K notices, but doesn't point me out to the captain. I stand up and keep my hand raised.

"I'll let our Chief Engineer respond to that," says the captain.

Mr. K steps up to the microphone. "In a few days, I'll lead our team of astrophysicists to the reactor ring, to re-focus it on Starheim. We are also stepping up construction on starship *Redemption*. In order to do that, we'll relocate personnel from Eagle to the shipyard."

Oh, this is ridiculous. Fine. When I scrape my chair across the floor, all attention turns my way. With my hand still raised, I stand on the chair.

Captain Binnacle pretends to shade his eyes against the lights. "I'm not sure, but is that a young lady at the back with a question?"

I step down and rest my arm. Everyone waits expectantly, and for a moment, my mind goes blank. Their stares make my face burn until I remember what I wanted to say.

"Does this mean we're never sending human supervisors to Starheim?" I shrink back against the wall until everyone looks to the podium for an answer.

"Good question," says the captain, perhaps a little too surprised that I had one. "With the new AI, our robots won't *need* supervision." A few others steal glances at me, knowing why I asked, but the captain spells it out anyway. "The Coalition decided against your father's plan. It'll cost too much to build a second, smaller station at Starheim to house supervisors."

"If Da—" I stop myself. "If *Mr. Wiles* was correct, you'd only need *one* supervisor."

"That's not accurate. You'd need a sizable crew to maintain the station itself," Captain points out. "Also, one person alone would go stark raving mad."

Mr. Spencer's tepid smile doesn't twitch on his slimy face, but I can see it in his eyes. He is elated that he has the magic pill to solve everyone's problems.

"But—"

Captain cuts me off. "We'll discuss this further after the meeting."

No. We won't. I don't need to hear any more. I slam through the back doors and blindly weave through robots and crewmembers in the hall.

They're shoving Dad's legacy aside. Everything he and I have agonized over for the past two years. Long sleepless nights, skipping meals, and Dad pounding his head on the keyboard to get his brain working. All for nothing.

I bump into someone as I board the moving walkway. "It isn't fair!" I shout at her. The crewwoman is startled, but lets me by without questions.

We made tremendous progress, too! Then some gormless Coalition wingnut, who doesn't even understand how a logic gate works, decides to toss it all away. *Pinheads!* I was looking forward to starting a new planet, and building it *properly* this time, but now we humans won't even get to watch. Mr. Spencer has taken care of that.

Mom's making sure we throw *Dad* away, too. I picture Dad strapped to an infirmary bed. Mom hovers over him with a needle to keep him sedated. Funny, I used to believe Mom could cure anything. Knowing that she can't makes everything else unstable, like the entire station has shifted out of its Lagrange point.

No. It's not her fault Dad got the Jitters. It's nobody's fault. Just a loose wire in his brain. So we're sending him back to factory Earth for repairs.

First Dad, then me, even though there's nothing wrong with me. They'll clap me into a shuttle and pitch it out into space. Slide down the gravity well and sink into the thick, germy atmosphere until we land on worm-infested mud. I'll never again be a part of the perfect engineering ballet that is *Prelude* station, and there's nothing I can do to stop it. *Go to sleep my little angel.* Lie down and give up.

Adrenaline from my seething anger has kept me upright. But now it leaves me drained. My knees buckle as I step from one moving walkway to the next, and I stumble and collapse to the walkway. It carries me to the end and pushes me onto the floor by the elevators.

"Namida?"

Mom's stupid pony song keeps running through my head! *When you wake, you will find…* "I don't even like ponies!" I yell.

"More power to you!" Ash cheers. "Squash those stereotypes. I don't like sports."

Where did he come from? My shadow. My pet. My friend. And what in all the stars is he talking about? "What do sports have to do with anything important?"

"Exactly my point," he says, and plops down next to me.

I'm not sure what to say to that.

"What's the matter?" he asks.

It takes effort to get the words past the lump in my throat. "They're sending Dad back to Earth."

Ash collapses against the handrail. "When will he go?"

"In two days. As soon as they prep the shuttle."

"Wow. I know how you feel. I wasn't real happy leaving Mom, but Father made it clear I needed to grow up."

"Mom and I will join him. We'll leave on the following shuttle. I'll never see *Prelude* again."

Ash looks shocked. "That's a terrible thing to tell you at the last minute."

I give him a puzzled frown. "I've known for two days."

"*Two days*?" He squints at me. "So, how did you break your omni-dev?"

"What? It's not broken."

"No? You mean in the past two days you didn't think to even text?"

He's right. It hadn't occurred to me, but instead of admitting that, I say, "I thought you knew. Everybody knows."

"Why should *I* know? Nobody tells me anything."

"I'm sorry."

"I've been your best friend for four years, but I'm the last person you confide in. You know what?" He raises his hands in surrender. "I don't care anymore. See you around."

Ash vaults over the handrail and lands on the walkway that's moving in the opposite direction.

"Ash! I'm sorry. Please don't be mad."

He acts as if he doesn't hear.

# CHAPTER 10

*T*he day arrives. I glide, weightless, into the hangar's anteroom, feeling as though I'm at a funeral. They've reloaded and refueled the shuttle. I curl up in a corner to watch the launch. I plug in my tunes, close my eyes, then let a Dark Starhouse tune wash me away. What the music doesn't do is erase that swelling ache in my chest.

I'm able to cope until Mom rudely pops out my left ear-button.

"Don't you want to tell your father goodbye?"

How does Mom manage, even in weightlessness, to look like the weight of the world rests on her shoulders? Below us, two nurses help Dad into his space suit. He looks brain dead. His eyelids droop, and a bubble of drool forms at his slack, open mouth.

"Did the Jitters do that?"

"We're keeping him sedated until landing. One of my nurses will go with him."

I give her a resigned nod and plug my ear-button back in.

She yanks it out again. "Does that mean you don't want to say goodbye?"

Of course, I don't. I want him to stay.

Jitters changed the Dad I knew. Now he's so doped up he couldn't possibly recognize me, or even remember if I hug him. The shuttle doesn't need to take him away; Mom's drugs have already done that. But I'd rather *this* not be my last memory of him. It'd be like hugging a zombie.

All of that is too much, so instead I say, "What's the point?"

A faint trace of horror passes over Mom's eyes, and that ache in my chest gets a nice little twist. Horrified. That's a new reaction from her. It hurts to see alienation in my own mother's eyes. I'm used to it from others, but not her.

Instead of asking *why* it'd be pointless, she says, "Fine." Her tone has a hard edge. "Your choice. But you'll regret it later."

Thanks for understanding, Mom.

She floats down to help the nurses navigate Dad into the airlock. One of them guides him out to the shuttle. Once all passengers are aboard, and the hangar crew have returned, they open the hangar door to the stars.

I kick off from my corner to the hatch that opens into Flight Control. The officer of the deck greets me as I take up my usual position. From my vantage point on the ceiling, I have an unobstructed view of everyone's monitors. Their soothing tech chatter broadcasts over the speakers.

*ETL confirms all personnel clear.*

*HDO. Feeds are clear. Equipment clear.*

*Shuttle* Gernsback, *are you go for separation?*

*Roger,* Prelude. *We are go for separation.*

*Retract holding clamps.*

*Copy that.*

*HDO. Visual confirms full release. Begin shuttle separation.*

It takes three minutes for the *Gernsback* to clear our hangar doors and come into view through the windows. Another ten minutes pass before it accelerates clear of the station's magnetic field. We can overhear the shuttle's commander talking to his crew.

*Attitude looking good at minus zero point five. Begin reentry alignment.*

*Roger that. Copilot executing yaw and roll.*

Once clear, they engage thrusters and aim for their re-entry path. The shuttle shrinks as it falls away on a long spiral toward Earth. It soon becomes another bright point of light among the stars. They should land in three days. On the monitors, all lights are green and numbers look good. Tech chatter sounds cheerful and professional. Just another normal day as Daddy slips into an abyss.

He's gone. My Dad is gone, and I have to accept that, the same way I had to accept it when Grampa Isaak died. That's life in space. Fail to keep the power grid going, and people suffocate. Have a nice home with decent parents, and they'll be torn apart. Put in years of work, but if you get sick, they chuck you in the sewer. That stress-knot in my stomach gets a little tighter.

When the chatter settles down, I sail out the hatch to head home. My omni-dev chimes before I get to the axle. *Jingle, jingle, tinkle ring*. Caller ID shows it's Mom. I press the reject button, not in the mood for anything she has to say.

I hover where the Yoke joins the Adam/Ox axle, with its murals. Behind the iron hatch ahead is our second standby reactor. To my right is the path home in Adam Wheel, where Mom will fuss around our apartment, straightening up what isn't out of place. She has no idea how insulting that is, considering how organized I keep it. Then we'll eat dinner in silence, avoiding eye contact.

No, I can't stand to be with Mom right now. Instead, I turn left toward Ox Wheel and take a people-lift cage out to gravity at the rim.

The ag-tech in her control booth at the O-9 garden chamber recognizes me. Ever since I discovered this chamber, she has never asked why I visit. Come to think of it, she never says a word. Very businesslike, she opens the airlock, and I walk inside to stand on the platform overlooking the field and breathe the evergreen-scented air. Unlike other garden chambers, this one is dedicated to growing trees. Its slender saplings are destined to be sealed in suspended animation, later to be planted on Starheim.

Down the stairs and across the field, my boots sink into freshly tilled soil until I reach a solid path used by the ag-bots. It guides me to a pine grove where I push my way through soft branches that brush my face until I find my clearing. Fragrant pine needles carpet the ground. It's luxurious to lie on them and gaze up through branches to the transparent quartz ceiling. Outside, long shutters tilt to reflect daylight in. I loosen my ponytail and spread my hair out so it'll smell like pines when I leave.

Peace lives here.

No blinking lights. No systems humming. No other crew. My private sanctuary.

I first came here right after Grampa died, after Mom explained that "dead" meant he was gone forever. It took days for that to sink in, and when it did, it hit me hard. I'll never again see the wrinkles around his smiling eyes, or hear his silly jokes. Grampa Isaak was a lot like Dad. Neither made me feel freakish.

Mom thinks I'm weird. Ash thinks I'm weird. Yet they love me in spite of it. Grampa and Dad loved me *because* of it, and that makes all the difference. I'll never know that kind of love again, now that they're both gone.

I wanted to be so grown up about Grampa's death that I held in my tears for months. Back then, I worked on the project to build Gondola E-12. Even though I was only ninety-eight months old and in second grade, I could help check math and calibrate tools. While we were connecting power, the station's psych-chaplain held a memorial service for Grampa. I wouldn't abandon my team during a crucial operation and chose not to go.

That was a mistake. As soon as my shift ended, something inside me snapped, and I collapsed on a people-lift. I had missed my opportunity to say goodbye to Grampa. A flood of bottled-up tears washed me away, and I wailed loud and long, kneeling on the cage floor. I couldn't help it. Part of me felt detached, as if I watched myself drowning from a distance. That derpy little girl certainly made a disgusting spectacle of herself. If anyone else heard, they left me alone.

I have no memory of leaving the people-lift, but found that I had somehow stumbled into Ox Wheel's Gondola O-9. Drowning in grief, I lived here on water and fruit and slept in this pine grove.

Mom, I found out later, kept an eye on me. She had ag-bots drop a sleeping bag and packaged meals. Staying away was rough on her, but it was the best thing she could have done. After four days, I was somewhat normal and ready to return home. But that was long ago.

Right now, I watch a small ag-bot climb a sycamore to trim its branches.

It does no good to struggle against your fate. Every minute of every day, I am one careless step away from death. If I am destined to die in an accident, that's what will happen. If it isn't by human error or mechanical failure, then I'll catch a micro-meteor with my skull.

Grampa Isaak gave his life in the search for humanity's second home, and Dad sacrificed his mind. Even Mom does her part, keeping the crew healthy and suturing their wounds. I'm not good for much, but I'm certainly not going to accomplish anything worthwhile lying here on pine needles.

I stand and brush the pine detritus from my flight suit, then march back through the woods and cross the field.

If God, or the universe, or my DNA wants me to live my entire life with only one friend, doing nothing but running errands and emptying trash cans, then that's what I'll do. Funny, but that thought doesn't make me sad. It simply is. I resign myself to my fate. I submit to whatever Destiny has in mind, even if it means being nothing much at all.

And, oddly enough, I'm fine with that.

Life is good, while it lasts. And who knows what might change? But if nothing ever does change, then I'm fine with that, too. I reach the bottom of the stairs that lead up to the airlock, and pause with my hand on the rail.

A smile.

Someone is definitely smiling at me. I *feel* it. So unexpected. Someone…except it's from everywhere all at once. It fills me up with sweetness and light, like…like radiant honey.

I look around, and my eyes tell me no one else is here. But smiles don't float around by themselves. I wait a couple of minutes, but the sensation doesn't fade. All lights are green on my vitals, all numbers very normal, and I'm not on medication. Whatever this feeling is, it isn't a biological issue.

Only one thing I have felt before even comes close to this. I was one-hundred twenty months old, entering advanced fourth grade. Ash and I had been swimming in a reservoir and were drying off on a catwalk. We gazed at ultra-violet ripples on the water, and I was thinking about how that kills bacteria, when he leaned over without warning and kissed my cheek. It made me glow inside. I was giddy for hours. It never occurred to me that I should kiss him back. That's what this is like. Except, this is much more intense.

I wait a few more minutes for it to fade, but the feeling persists.

Okay, this is starting to get embarrassing. There are things to do, and I can't stand around glowing all day in a garden chamber. I climb the stairs and pass through the airlock, and the smile stays with me, warming me to my marrow. Some*one*, not some*thing*, is delighted with me, and is hugging me on the inside.

As I enter the anteroom, the ag-tech looks up from her console. She's flustered at first, and then does something I've never seen her do before. She waves at me from behind her window. Now *that's* odd.

I wave back.

Another nameless crewmember, on my way to the spoke junction, greets me with a warm "hello." I take the people-lift up the spoke, still glowing, and float into the hub. "Good evening, Miss Wiles," says a tech over the intercom. "On your way home?"

"Um. Sure." I have no idea who that is.

Two engineers load a cargo cube into the centrifuge, to weigh it before taking it down the spoke's freight elevator. One says, "You be careful, Namida. There's heavy traffic in the Yoke tonight."

"That's okay," I reply. "I'm not going through the Yoke."

This is odd. Most grownups don't like the idea of having kids on the station at all. If everybody wasn't being so pleasant, I'd be creeped out by now.

I sail up the Adam/Ox axle, past the murals, toward home. I reach Adam's hub and flinch when one of the hub techs waves at me. It's as if everybody's personality changes when I get close. I zip over to the people-lift before he says anything, then ride the wire cage out to the rim.

Mr. K is at the spoke junction, as sour as ever, about to step into the upward-bound people-lift. He pauses when he sees me and growls, "Namida. Have you seen Tamonash?"

Finally, an adult acting normal. "Not since two days ago, after the meeting."

His expression softens. He seems almost embarrassed, searching for words. "I am sorry they sent your father away. It must be difficult for you."

Talk about awkward. "Yeah." Plus, I'm still glowing. I wonder if he feels it.

He isn't able to look me in the eye, and fiddles with the gizmos on his suit. "Well, do not worry about my son. I am sure he is well."

He boards the people-lift and is gone. I have never warmed up to Mr. K. Even if he acted this kind all the time, I still don't think I'd like him.

Fortunately, I meet no one else on my way to the elevator. Once I reach the hallway that leads me home, the glow starts to fade. By the time I'm at my door, it's gone.

What in all the stars was *that*? More importantly, what did I do to deserve it? It was most certainly real, or else other people wouldn't have acted so weird. I've never felt anything so intense before.

When I open my apartment door, Mom is curled up on the couch waiting for me. Our eyes meet, but neither of us says a word. Hers are red rimmed, as though she's been crying.

What am I supposed to say? *Hi, Mom. The universe smiled at me!* Right. Would she give me more brain scans? More likely she'd strap me in a straight-jacket.

I shuffle to my bedroom and close the door. After I undress, I flop onto my bed and hug my pillow. I fall asleep wondering if the smile will ever return.

# CHAPTER 11

$M$om sips coffee as she reads the morning omni-dev reports. Dad's chair remains empty. I scrape my fork across my plate as I eat my scrambled eggs, but get no reaction.

Yesterday, before she returned home, I shifted the sitting area furniture sixteen centimeters to spinward. If she noticed, she didn't care. Except, I expected her to freak out making dinner when she discovered the canned goods are no longer in alphabetical order. This also had no effect. But wait until she finds out I've switched her bathroom drawers!

Her omni-dev rings. "Hello?" A pause. Then Mom smiles. "Borrow? Well, as long as you promise to give her back. What's this about?" I hear a buzzing as whomever it is explains. "Why not contact Stirl?" More buzzing, and she frowns. "I'll send her over."

She disconnects and makes eye contact for the first time this morning.

"Mr. Spencer would like to meet you in your father's lab to ask some questions."

I nearly spit out my food. "Like *that'll* ever happen. Call the goober back and tell him since he's so smart, he can figure it out alone."

"Namida! You are a robotics team member! Therefore, it's your duty to set aside personal feelings. If you want others to take you seriously, you have to take your job seriously."

I pretend to have a hand puppet and mimic her talking.

"Now you're being childish," she scolds, setting her coffee down. "If you can't behave, I'll have you removed from the team, and you can spend the rest of your days locked in this apartment until our shuttle leaves."

Smoke should be pouring out of my ears, I'm so mad. She'd do it, too. No hesitation. I let my hand flop to the table in disgust and it catches the tip of my fork. A glob of eggs catapults across the kitchen and splats against the wall. If I laugh, Mom will explode, so I bite my lips to choke it back.

Mom raises her eyebrows and folds her arms while the eggs slide to the floor. I could tell her it wasn't on purpose, but I'm not sure it matters. Besides, I can wait as long as she can.

The eggs lie in a steaming clump on the shiny tiles. Mom doesn't break her stare. I don't care. Let the mess turn to glue. Mom's face stays frozen, and my leg starts to twitch.

*Gak!* I can't stand it anymore. In an instant, I'm on my knees with a paper towel and spray cleaner. "Fine!" I snap. "I'll go see what the *genius* wants."

"You had better cooperate in a professional manner, young lady."

"Sure," I mutter. "Whatever."

On my way to Eagle, I bump into Colton in the elevator. He has obviously dressed himself. Somewhere, he acquired a second mag-pistol and wears one strapped to each thigh. A utility knife protrudes from the top of a boot. His emergency oxygen hood isn't rolled into his collar, his jacket isn't buckled, and his vitals readout is dark. I sigh. Is he suicidal?

"You didn't dress properly."

"Sorry," he says, as we step off the elevator. "Left my tux back on Earth. I'm fixin' to meet up with the guys in O-7 for soccer. I'll show 'em how we taught dolphins back home to play mid-field, but since you don't have dolphins, we'll use robots. Wanna join us?"

Older kids don't like that I win a lot. If I'm on their team, they're happy, but the other teams complain that I have an unfair advantage because I instinctively understand how objects curve as they fly inside a rotating wheel. Besides, I don't have time for games, or funerals, or goodbyes. I'm busy helping pave the way for humanity's journey to the stars, and I have a dimwit in Dad's lab to educate on the subject.

"Thanks, but no thanks," I say.

He follows me to the people-lift. "Hey, ever notice how the soccer ball hooks?"

Did he forget I was born here? I board the inbound lift and block him from boarding.

"Gee, if you had attended my orientation classes, you'd know why." I plug in my ear-buttons and twist the handle. The lift whisks me up toward Adam's hub.

When I reach weightlessness, I pick a type of dance music called Base Runner that gets my blood going, then sail through the axle. Even with eyes shut, I can tell when I reach the Yoke. I can also tell traffic is clear. A change in air density? A different echo? Not sure.

I fire my mag-pistol blindly. The magnet zips out and sticks to a wall. *Ting!* Bull's eye. My momentum pulls the wire taut as it slings me around the corner. Release the magnet at the top of the arc, reel it in, and I fly straight down the Yoke's middle.

A service tunnel isn't far away, and I duck inside as the song's refrain hits. I blast my $CO_2$ jets to flip and hit with both feet, rebound, flip over with a kick, and rebound off the opposite wall. *Prelude*'s wheels turn relentlessly. Drums punctuate my moves. Bounce, punch, bounce, flip. Rip my heart out, and life goes on. Spin, flip, kick. When the chorus is over, I leap from the tunnel, and air-brake to finish in a dramatic pose.

Colton hangs in mid-air wearing a goofy grin. He saw everything.

"Is that air-dancing?" he asks. "Ash is right. Looks more like Kung Fu."

"*Stop following me!*" Blood pounds in my ears and my face must be burning red.

"Fine, Miss Grumpy. Just bein' friendly."

He jets back to the murals in the axle, and tries to make a sharp turn toward Ox. His trajectory goes wide, and he strikes the wall, tumbles, and rebounds off. I noticed his jetpack's orientation system was dark, which means he never turned on the little computer that aims the jets. It translates how you twitch the control-grips into what direction you really want to go.

That noob will kill himself someday.

On the rest of my weightless journey to Eagle's hub, I decide not to air-dance again. Once more in gravity, at the door to Dad's lab, I hesitate before going in, dreading what I'm about to see. This is Mr. Spencer's lab now. He's probably made a huge mess. I draw a deep breath and punch in my keycode. The door beeps and doesn't open. I try pressing the buttons more slowly. *Beep.* Someone revoked my access.

"Miss Nabbina Wiles?" asks a tinny voice from a speaker under the security camera.

"*Namida.*"

"Are you sure? How odd." After a buzz, the lock clicks open.

Inside, Mr. Spencer sits with the monitors arranged in a precise parabolic curve, with his swivel chair as the focus. None of the pencils or paper supplies have been touched. Instead, two thin L-books lay to his right and left, both precisely thirty centimeters from the keyboard, their screens glowing with schematics. He has removed all other furniture. Cabinets and drawers are closed. No clutter anywhere. The room is perfect. I hate him.

Mr. Spencer takes a sip from Dad's coffee mug, then swivels around to shine those huge round glasses at me. I sidle toward the far end of the desk, to keep my distance.

"My apologies. Namida is an unusual name. I would have expected your father to choose something Irish." He tugs nervously at his bushy sideburns. "Not much interest in heritage nowadays, I suppose."

My eyes are fixed on the coffee mug. I gave it to Dad for Christmas. Asimov's Three Laws of Robotics show up on the side when it's hot, and this nimrod is putting his blubbery lips all over it.

"My mom's grandmother was named Namida," I explain. "Namid

means *dancer* in Ojibwe. And my middle name is Réaltín, which means *star* in Irish."

"Excellent! And how are you doing?"

"All vitals are green, sir."

"That's what I like to hear!" He grins and slaps his thighs. Too many teeth crowd his grin. "Well, I appreciate you making such a long journey to answer a few questions."

"It's my duty to help," I say, through clenched teeth.

Because if it wasn't, I wouldn't be here. Now get your flabby butt out of Dad's chair.

He rubs his palms together. "Let's get down to business. Your father's documentation is a bit sketchy. Therefore, I'd like you to explain a few things."

After a few questions, I find out he already knows about the primary computer cluster, but doesn't understand why we have a backup lab several decks below. When I tell him we built it in case the main one got fried, he loses interest.

Mr. Spencer turns to the central monitor and calls up a series of overlapping, multi-colored circles. Each circle is filled in with symbols that cluster in some parts and thin out in others. All the symbols are connected in a complex web. At the bottom are the letters NW-CNH-0, 2099-04-12, (which means, Namida Wiles—Convulsive Neuropsychiatric Hallucinosis—result negative, and the date.) It's my brain scan Mom took last Easter. Why Dad would have a copy on his computer is a total mystery.

"Any idea what this is?"

I pretend to study it, then shake my head. "No clue."

"Curious." Mr. Spencer looks it over again. "As near as I can tell, it's based on the neural activity of a human brain. Instead of his usual brute force programming, Stirling used this to drive the decisions his robots made." He leers at me again. "A rather innovative idea for your father, but at this point it's obsolete. My new program will far surpass *human* brains!" He barely contains his excitement.

"Were you involved much in your father's work?" he asks.

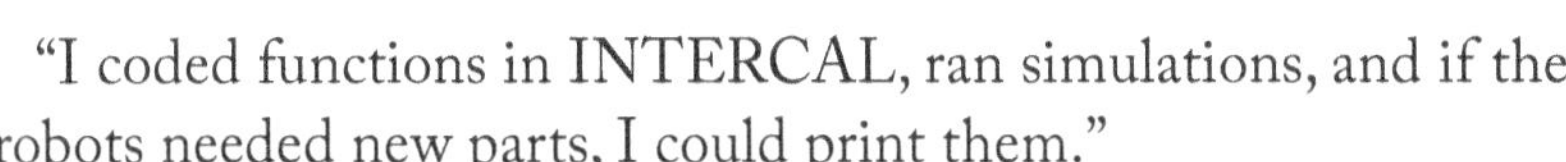

"I coded functions in INTERCAL, ran simulations, and if the robots needed new parts, I could print them."

He wants to know how I printed new parts, so I walk Mr. Spencer through the adjoining workshop, to the hatch in the floor at the far end, and open it. In the room below is a 3D printer that takes up half the space. It's a large glass booth with sliding doors, large enough for several people to step inside. Sacks of powdered plastics, resin, and spools of metal, line the shelves.

"I could show you how to use it," I offer.

"Impressive. Thank you, but we won't need new parts." He pats me on the head.

I try not to point out that I'm not a dog for him to pet. "You do realize I'm a member of the robotics team, right?"

"Well, isn't that nice? I'm sure your mother is very proud. And you're how old?"

"I've aged one-hundred fifty-eight months since birth. Before birth, I gestated the usual nine."

He throws his head back and laughs. "Why not say you've just turned thirteen?"

"Because that wouldn't be accurate."

"No, of course not."

We stroll back through the workshop. Mantis-bots stand in ranks at one end, powered off. One of them lies on a workbench, partly disassembled, its four crooked legs stick up, making it resemble a dead bug.

Dad's interface helmet sits on a table. I show it to Mr. Spencer and explain it's how he gave instructions to his robots. Spencer fiddles with the seven slider buttons.

"Well, we won't need this," he says.

"Dad and I put so much work into it. May I keep it?"

He clucks his tongue. "This is not a toy, Miss Wiles."

"Then I should pack it away safely," I say in a patronizing tone and lift it from his hands.

"Good idea."

He's so naïve. But Mr. Spencer makes sure I shut Dad's interface helmet in a drawer. On our way back to the office, he stops to gaze at the disassembled robot with genuine affection.

The bot twitches its legs, and its lenses stare up at the ceiling. The robot's brain, the CPU, is exposed because the chest panel is open. Right next to that is a safety device Dad and I installed in all our test bots. Dad called them R.E.D. devices. It stands for Rapid Exothermic Disassembly. They're set to explode simultaneously if triggered by the Annihilation Button. Or, if we need to target a specific bot, there's a program for that. Just in case.

"Are you excited to witness the birth of a new era?" Spencer asks.

"Sorry, what?"

"A new era! Oh, don't doubt me. We are witnessing the genesis of a new *life form*, able to last for eons because they replace their own parts as they wear out. Imagine what this means. Immortal creatures! The next leap in evolution."

I hold up a finger to correct him. "Evolution is about populations of animals changing over generations. That's not the same as people designing new bots."

"How vexingly precise you are."

If he pats me on the head again, I'll bite his fingers.

"However, I'm talking about the larger picture." He starts to pick through the robot's abdomen. "Earth started with invertebrates, then came dinosaurs, and lastly mankind. Now we have the next era. *Robotic* life!" He leans close and taps his forehead. "One day, we'll be able to upload our consciousness into a superior silicon brain. Just as dinosaurs became modern birds, people will transform into a more efficient species. Won't that be wonderful?"

"No, that would be *fake*. At best, you'd have a machine mimicking you."

Mr. Spencer chuckles as though I'm too young to understand.

"Well, at least you're no sappy sentimentalist who thinks our current pathetic robots are alive. *Personification*." He says it with a sneer of disgust. "Do you know that word? It means to treat inanimate objects as though they are people. We teach children to talk to dolls and Teddy bears. Some adults even go around hugging trees. Religion started off that way, you know. People prayed to stone statues, or believed thunderstorms were angry gods. Infantile nonsense."

He picks up a circuit tester and pokes the robot's innards. I flinch. If he accidentally sends power to the R.E.D., the explosion will ruin the motherboard.

"Yet in one sense, you are correct to say it would be fake. For all our advances in technology, today's robots remain nothing more than puppets. Uploading our brain patterns into one of these fellows *would* result in a sad imitation. But my new robots are different. This is precisely the point that so many fail to grasp."

Now he's getting agitated. He yanks out the R.E.D. and shakes it under my nose. I shrink back. Even disconnected, that thing could detonate from static electricity and blow off his hand. He apparently doesn't know what the danger symbol means.

"Do you know the essential difference between humans and robots?"

I can think of at least a dozen things right off the top, but my favorite at the moment is: robots aren't careless with explosives. However, with an R.E.D. two centimeters from my eyes, it's difficult to choose. I gently push his hand away.

"Um…people are free to do what we want, but robots do nothing unless they're given orders?"

"No," he barks. "Complexity! What you perceive as *free will* is a deceptive illusion that nature selected for its survival value. You're not really free. Your actions are as determined by your brain as a robot is governed by its programming. Essentially, no difference. One is organic, the other electronic."

"Well," I say, "a lot of people believe we make our own decisions."

"Irrelevant," he snaps. "Evolution isn't interested in beliefs or so-called *truth*. It's only interested in what adaptations are *useful* for a species to survive. That's not always the same thing. If something is useful, it doesn't have to be true.

"For instance," he continues, "people might believe that a forest is haunted, and avoid it. This is useful for survival, because the forest is filled with dangerous animals. But that doesn't mean ghosts are real." He puts his screwdriver down. "By the way, that's the reason you can't trust people's *beliefs*."

My head spins. That thought had never occurred to me before. I hate to admit it, but Mr. Spencer is right. What we believe might only be useful, but it doesn't have to be True in the bigger sense.

Still, doesn't that same rule also apply to what Mr. Spencer believes? I gather my thoughts and open my mouth to point this out, but Spencer interrupts.

"The human brain is the most complex bio-chemical machine we know, but that's *all* it is." He taps the R.E.D. device against my temple. "*You* are a machine. A flawed machine, though, because your thoughts and feelings are at the mercy of your body's chemistry. And you are destined to do whatever your DNA has determined. Yet you are also a marvelous bundle of chemical reactions, a long chain of cause and effect, a glorious robot of muscle and bone."

"Like a Rube Goldberg machine," I mutter, but he doesn't hear.

Mr. Spencer plugs the R.E.D. back in, and I can relax.

The room's fluorescent lights reflect off his glasses, turning them into cold white disks. "In short, my dear Miss Wiles, people once personified trees and weather, but most humans have matured beyond silly fairy tales. Now it's high time for us to wake up and *stop personifying people*."

# CHAPTER 12

One other crewman sits in the infirmary's waiting room when I arrive, an ag-tech with a dirty bandage around one hand. The triage nurse greets me from the front desk.

"Looking for Mom." I hurry past.

Nurse leaps from his chair. "She's with a patient," he shouts. "You can't go—"

Too late. I find Mom in exam room 2. She laughs as I open the door, and I catch the tail end of what she was saying to Colton.

"—different, yes, but she's—"

"I'm sorry, doctor," Nurse cuts her off. "Namida barged right past me."

Mom presses a stethoscope to Colton's bare chest as he sits on a high exam couch. The lights turn his skin pale, but he has good muscle tone, even though he's slim. He should spend time under the full spectrum grow-lights we use in hydroponics. *Hmm.* He'd have a rather nice, healthy tan afterward.

"Namida?" Mom scolds, and snaps me out of my daydream.

"Skin tone!" I shout, startled.

"You *know* not to interrupt me with a patient."

It's one of those unbreakable rules. "But this is *urgent*, Mom!"

"Is somebody bleeding?"

"No, but—"

"Is somebody's life in *immediate* danger?"

"No—"

"Then *get out*." She advances on me, a storm brewing in her eyes and a death-grip on her stethoscope. If it were not for the oath she took to do no harm, she'd probably strangle me with it.

Nurse puts his hands on my shoulders and backs me out, then closes the door. "Back to the waiting room, Missy."

"Hands off!" I lean against the wall and slide to the floor. "I'll wait here."

Nurse gives up and slinks back to his desk.

I'm sure Mom takes her time because she wants to teach me a lesson. It's another fifteen minutes before the door opens, and Mom glares at me with one hand on her hip.

"Okay, kiddo, spill it. What's so important?"

I get up and squeeze past her. Colton zips up his jacket and checks his readouts. He has finally learned how to attach his unitard sensors. I take a breath and give Mom my most serious face. "Do you want to be a robot?"

Mom blinks in disbelief. "I don't have time for games, Namida."

"Neither do I. We've got too much to do if we're going to stop him."

"Stop who?"

"Mr. Spencer. He's *giiwanaadizi*. Insane! He wants robots to replace everybody, except he sort of thinks we already are."

"Already are what?"

"Robots! Mom, pay attention." How she manages to practice medicine with a mind that won't stay focused scares me sometimes. "Mr. Spencer wants to send his robots to Starheim without us."

"Good! People shouldn't be hopping across the galaxy, anyway."

"No! Dad wanted us to build another station at Starheim so we could supervise the terraforming."

Mom starts putting away her instruments. "Well, it sounds like Mr. Spencer's plan will save more lives."

How can she take sides with that creepy dip-switch? Because she doesn't care about the new planet. I've suspected this for a long

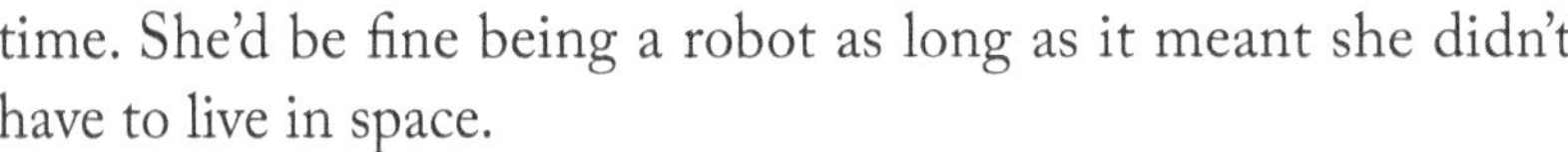

time. She'd be fine being a robot as long as it meant she didn't have to live in space.

"You never wanted to go to Starheim, did you?"

My accusation hits the mark, and her eyes sharpen. "No," she admits. "And I never pictured raising my family in a giant tin carnival ride."

*Prelude*'s construction doesn't use tin. We use composite materials that crystalize into honeycomb structures, which makes them super strong. Pointing out things like that tends to make her angry, though, when she's as irrational as she is now.

Colton slips off the exam table and creeps toward the door. "I should leave."

But he can't escape with me planted in his way.

Mom leans in closer. "I want to see Earth again! I want to climb hills and walk through a real forest. I want to see blue sky, not painted walls and full spectrum lights."

Here it comes. Birds in your hair, bugs in your teeth, pneumonia seeping into your lungs from rain. The standard nostalgic speech.

"Sweetie, I want those things for you, too! I know it sounds strange, and even a little frightening, but you won't understand until you experience it."

"No, I *do* understand, Mom. I've seen plenty of pictures, and Ash tells me stuff he reads in sci-fi books. What *you* don't understand is I don't want to live on a planet that's already messed up. We get to start over! Starheim will be *paradise* when we're done, and the one thing standing between you and a new world is a wormhole! You're afraid we'll die like Grampa did, but it's safer now."

Mom presses her lips into a tight line. "True. They have improved it. Do you know what the success rate is now for those robotic missions? Twenty percent are crushed when the wormhole collapses prematurely. I'm not willing to risk those odds."

Colton flattens himself against the wall, trying to turn invisible.

"Maybe *you're* not, but do you ever ask me what chances *I'm* willing to take?"

"No, I don't." She straightens in self-righteousness. "Because you *are still a child*, Namida. You are *my* responsibility! *I* make those decisions. Not you."

Okay, I'm done. She played the *I'm-The-Adult* card. No matter what I say at this point, she's not going to listen. I yank the door open and stomp out.

"Don't turn your back on me, young lady!" She follows me out to the waiting room. "We need to discuss this lousy attitude you've developed."

I raise my hands in surrender. "No, Mom, we don't. You win! Have it your way. Dad is trapped on Earth, and you get to wallow in the filth with him. Mr. Spencer can turn us into robots and ruin everybody's life. If that's what you want, you've got it!"

The sole patient who had been waiting, gingerly rises from his chair and makes his way to the bathroom. Nurse finds something to do in the dispensary. Colton eases his way down the hall and eyes the door beyond me.

Mom glares. Her anger is gone, but a dark, hollow look has replaced it. I guess I've been yelling. Angry tears stream down my face, too, and I wipe at them with my sleeve.

"You do realize," she asks, "that it'll be *centuries* before people can live on Starheim?"

"What difference does it make?" I snap back. "Let the *robots* have Starheim. They can move in today! It'll be easier, because they don't need water or air or food."

She keeps her voice level and calm. "Namida, Mr. Spencer isn't ruining the project. Your father got us this far, and he's going to finish. That's all."

"How would *you* know what he's going to do?" I scream. "You don't listen!"

She gapes at me, unable to answer. Because she *doesn't* know. Simple as that.

"Namida." She adopts that tone she uses on patients when she's trying to give them bad news. "Your reaction toward Mr. Spencer is understandable. You see him as a threat because he's replaced your father, and this causes the amygdala in your brain to trigger an anxiety response. You rationalized your feelings, and invented the idea that Mr. Spencer wants to wipe out humanity. Except, it isn't *real*, sweetie. You need to understand that."

Short answer: I'm crazy. Neatly done. There isn't a real problem because…brain chemicals or some other drivel. If it can be reduced to something that sort of sounds like science, then it can be explained away, as far as Mom is concerned.

I leave without another word and start walking, not seeing or caring where I'm going, my mind scrambling for options. I'm vaguely aware that people dodge out of my way.

He's gone. Daddy is gone, and it cuts much deeper than not having him around. I've lost the last person who understood me. The last person who truly loved me. And I keep getting kicked off of teams that no longer need me.

Dad needed me. Together, we were setting the course for humanity's journey to the stars. All that is over. Nobody needs me now, and that realization cuts deep.

Captain Binnacle might listen. On the other hand, he shared the podium with Spencer the other day, so that means he already knows about it and approves.

Mr. K would never *begin* to listen. Plus, he stood right alongside the captain.

Mrs. Kirkpatrick would hear me out, then report everything to Mom.

I consider the flight director, the flight deck officer, head nurse, engineering team lead, hangar deck officer, several med-techs, research scientists, even the ag-tech who opens Gondola O-9 for me, and reject each of my adult friends in turn.

There is no one else I can turn to. Every grownup I know either answers to Captain Binnacle or my mother. No, if anything is going to be done, if anything *can* be done, I'll have to do it myself. My mission is clear. I have to stop Spencer from spoiling Starheim. That frog-faced bumfiddler needs to be tossed out of Dad's lab.

"What are you going to do?"

Colton's voice snaps me out of my thoughts. My skull is glass, and the whole station can see what I've been thinking. My cheeks grow hot with shame.

"None of your business!"

Those long-lashed eyes twinkle. "Must be something devious. Can I help?"

"No! Now go away." I turn my back and march away.

With access to the lab computers, a few keystrokes would chuck Spencer's creepy plans into the bit bucket. Problem solved.

I find a seat in a nearby breakroom and take out my omni-dev. From a simple app, I could log into the lab computers…if Dad hadn't isolated his network. *Blast!* I forgot that.

If Ash were here, he'd be able to hack his way through somehow. He's always been clever at changing his grades in the school computer, or figuring out how to download movies and video games from Earth over the main com-channel without anyone noticing.

I picture the last time I saw Ash. He wasn't too happy with me. There have been other times when I've made him angry, like when I told Mrs. Kirkpatrick that Ash added those rude comments in the high school kids' records. In my defense, I never promised not to tell. Besides, at first, she thought *I* had done it. Or like the time I accidentally drowned his omni-dev in a water reservoir. He lost his pictures, movies, music, and programs he uses to crack into *Prelude*'s systems. It took him a year to recreate.

In the past, Ash had always forgiven me, but we haven't reached his usual sulking limit of eighty-two hours. Still, I can't ask him for a favor empty-handed. Which means tomorrow I'll have to commit a little breakfast theft first.

# CHAPTER 13

In the library, a few crewmembers curl up in quiet nooks with their L-books. Ash sits at a desk with his omni-dev playing a horrifying video about Earth on the monitor. Large crowds of men, wearing metal exoskeletons and holding swords and spears, clash in battle on a grassy field. It's best to say nothing. Instead, I sneak up from behind and slide a box onto the desktop.

I can tell he notices, but he waits until the men on his video are done hacking at each other before he lifts the lid. Six disaccharide tori.

"A peace offering," I explain.

He closes the lid, but still won't turn around. I pull up a chair.

"I stole them from construction. I figure they owe me."

Ash clicks off the video, then swivels around. His eyes are red, as if he's been rubbing them. Even when he's brooding, he's still cute. "You figure a torus will make up for not telling me you're leaving?"

My eyes flit between his raw face and the box. "Well…*duh!*"

His sour expression cracks a smile. "You drive me nuts," he snorts, and helps himself to a torus.

"Are we still friends?" I bite my lip, fearing the answer.

"*Friends?* Sure. Unless, of course, we bump things up a notch. I wouldn't mind if—"

"Good, because I have a favor to ask."

Ash puckers up as if he's about to spit the torus back out, then swallows and waves the box at me. "So these are nothing more than a cheap bribe?"

"*Cheap*? I risked access privileges stealing those."

"What's the big deal? Even before they kicked you off the team, you weren't a real engineer." He sighs and puts the box down. "All right, don't make that face. Let's hear it."

"Mr. Spencer locked me out of the lab. Can you break in?"

"Why? What are you going to do?"

"I want to wipe his programs."

"Judas Priest, girl! Captain would fall on you like a doomsday asteroid."

"*Pretty* please?" I flutter my eyelashes. Normally this makes him laugh, but right now, if looks could kill…

"*Then* what?"

I sit up straighter. "What do you mean?"

"After we brick the computers," he says, "*then* what happens? They find out who did it and ship us back to Earth. Spencer downloads his backups from Earth and picks up right where he left off. We'll slow him down for maybe a week, and for what?" He pouts and teases me with a cutesy kid's voice. "Because you're mad they took your precious daddy away? *Awww*."

"You pathetic scrub! Give me a little credit." I cross my arms and glower. "Spencer thinks people should become extinct and robots ought to colonize the stars."

That hits him. He gets quiet, then softens and frowns. "Seriously?"

"I wish I had recorded it. Mom didn't believe me, either. He's planning to upload our brains into robots."

"Okay, *that's* psycho." He nibbles his second torus. "Every sci-fi movie ever made shows that's a bad idea. But you can't save humanity by deleting his programs. Why not tell Captain what Spencer is up to?"

"He already knows. So does your dad, and they're both fine with it."

Ash gets a grave expression.

"I don't know what else to do, Ash. He'll spoil all of Dad's work. Our plans for Starheim. Everything! I don't want to be a robot."

"Well, there's nothing you *can* do about it. Coalition wants a perfect solution, and they think Spencer has it. It's not as though you have a better robot all ready to go."

My skin tingles, and for a second *Prelude's* four wheels spin perfectly again. "But I do! Well…not quite. But Dad was very close. All I have to do is finish."

It's perfect! If I finish Dad's project, then I become the sole expert on the new bots. They wouldn't—they *couldn't*—force me to leave. Once I complete the program, if I threatened to erase it, I could force everyone to focus on curing Jitters, which means Dad could come home again. My heart sings with hope.

Ash chews thoughtfully. "You can't code any better than I can."

"No, but I know what Dad had in mind. I don't have to invent anything new, just put the pieces together."

"If your dad was that close, why didn't he tell everybody?"

"Because he wasn't one hundred percent sure it would work. But I am."

"Well," he throws up his hands, "that's good enough for me. Let's risk ruining our lives, based solely on your hunch and amateur programming skills."

That assessment sounds a bit extreme, but at least Ash is willing to try.

"I'm glad you feel that way."

"Sure," he laughs and leans back. "Anything for you. So what's our first step?"

Making it up as I go along, I say, "The backup lab. We break in. We have a complete copy of Dad's programs already there. I figure out how to put the pieces together, then we run a simulation to show everybody what it can do."

Ash shakes his head. "No good. Even the robots at Starheim passed simulations. You've got to test *physical* bots."

"Except for the ones in Dad's lab, which Spencer's using, we keep all robots in service. It's not like we have a bunch of them sitting around."

Ash gives me a disappointed smirk. "Silly. Why not build your own bots? You've got a 3D printer under the workshop."

"It'd take me too long to figure out the Computer-Aided Drafting program. Not to mention I know nothing about how to build a bot from scratch. Neither do you."

Ash squeezes his eyes shut and pounds his fists against his forehead. "I'm going to regret this, I know it." He opens his eyes. "You know, I meant it when I said I'd do anything. I'd give you my heart, if you'd take it."

"*Ewww.* That'd be gross. Plus, a transplant wouldn't solve anything. But what is it you'll regret?"

His face goes slack, and he mutters, "Why do I even try?" Then he slumps in his chair, and blurts out, "We both know a bot expert."

It takes me a second. "*Colton?* He's actually good?"

"Have you seen videos of his competitions? No, of course you haven't. Well, for once he wasn't kidding. He made it twice to finals at the International Robotics Festival."

I bite my lip. "Yesterday I told him to buzz off."

"You've never been stellar at interpersonal relationships." Ash tilts his head and grabs the box of tori. "Maybe he'll accept a bribe."

We walk to Captain's quarters and ring the doorbell. The captain himself answers with his distinguished gray curls uncovered. It's a shame his apartment is the only place he takes off his sailor's cap. Maybe I should mention it.

"Hi, kids! Come in, come in. What brings you to my door?"

"Hello, sir." Ash hands him what's left of the tori. "Is Colton home?"

I peek past Ash to see if the apartment's a wreck, but it looks pretty good, except Captain has taken down his shrine. The portrait of the woman and little girl is gone, along with the knick-knacks and taffeta doll.

"Just reported back." Then Captain calls out, "Colton! On deck. You have visitors."

Colton emerges from a bedroom, soccer ball in his hands, and I duck back into the hall.

"Hey, Ash! I'm fixin' to head over to Ox for a game. Wanna tag along?"

"Why?" says Ash. "So Namida will be left alone, and you can dump me, then circle back? Maybe next time." He jerks his head to signal me to step into view. "We've got something better. Come with us."

I move into the doorframe so Colton can see me.

He sounds cautious. "Why? What's going on?"

Ash leans in and whispers, "Not here. Best to show you."

"What are you kids up to?" asks Captain as he wipes the table.

Oh no! A direct question. Regulations clearly spell out punishments for lying to the captain. But maybe he doesn't need specific details. I hit my omni-dev's record button, straighten my shoulders, and snap to attention with hands folded behind my back.

"Permission to save humanity, sir!"

Captain Binnacle grimly returns a salute. "Permission granted."

"Freedom to use our best judgement on the *method*, Captain?"

"Freedom granted," he chuckles.

Excellent. Now I have official permission, on record, to pretty much do whatever I think necessary. Captain Binnacle is one of the few adults I can count on.

"Thank you, sir!"

Colton resists Ash's attempt to drag him away. "I'm supposed to meet the guys."

"Ditch those scrubs," says Ash. "This is way better."

I plant my palms on Colton's shoulders and push him into the hallway.

"You kids have fun," says Captain as he closes the door. "Don't wreck my station."

# CHAPTER 14

"Are you allowed to go in?" Colton asks.

Leonard idles behind him, waiting for a new order. Ash suggested we bring it along. We ignore Colton's question as I wipe down the keypad. My keycode fails to open the backup lab after three tries.

"Don't try again," warns Ash. "If you do, it won't open for *anybody* for another thirty minutes." He takes out his omni-dev and resets my permissions. He does things like this a lot, and leaves backdoor access to most of the systems on *Prelude*. "Try it now," he says.

I punch in my keycode for the fourth time. The door clicks open.

"You're a wizard, Ash." I give him a thank-you kiss on the cheek, hand him an antiseptic wipe, then rush inside.

Colton makes fishy lips at Ash. "I think you're a wizard, too."

"Back off, twerp!" Ash stuffs the wipe into Colton's mouth, then follows me in.

Leonard steps in behind us and settles onto the floor, near the workbench.

The backup lab is more cramped than Dad's office and not as well equipped, but we should be able to do everything we need.

Two racks of computers and arrays stand in the middle, topped off with a couple of network switches. Crammed in next to the racks are two workstations. One workstation links to Dad's isolated network. The other connects to *Prelude's* station-wide network.

Colton wipes his lips on his sleeve, then tosses the antiseptic into a bin. "Where are these parts you bragged about?"

"You'll see," says Ash.

I sit at a console and am surprised the system lets me log in, but Ash explains, "You have access to everything you had last week."

Colton eyes us suspiciously. I notice the engineering pin on his collar. They enrolled him into my old team. A twinge of jealousy stabs my heart, but no time for that. Once I have the main menu up, I find backup copies of Dad's work and breathe a sigh of relief.

"It's all still here." And it's all I have left of my father to cling to.

Ash shrugs. "Spencer had no reason to delete it."

As soon as I have the system restoring a copy of everything, I power on the larger console and call up the Computer-Aided Drafting program. Colton takes over the keyboard and doesn't even say, *Excuse me.* He calls up graphical images of standard parts. "How do I know what parts are in stock?"

"Inventory is no problem," I say. "We have a high-speed 3D printer upstairs."

"I can make anything I want?" Colton's face lights up. "Oh, this is too good!"

"Let's check out the printer." Ash starts for the door.

I grab Ash's shoulder. "Hold on. I bet Mr. Spencer's there."

Colton frowns. "What's he got to do with anything?"

"Well, maybe he'll try to stop us."

A glimmer of understanding dawns in Colton's eyes. "You're breaking all kinds of rules, aren't you? We're going to get in trouble."

"No. It's okay," I assure him. "Your dad gave us permission. Didn't you hear? I asked if we could save humanity, and he said to use our best judgement." I play the recording back.

Colton holds up his hands. "Whoa. You know Dad thought you were *kidding*, right?"

"Who would joke about a thing like that?" I ask.

Ash snickers, and Colton's mouth drops open.

"All I want to know is," says Colton, "why are we really building this bot?"

"Namida believes that if we can show everyone that her father's program will solve the issues at Starheim, then they'll let him come back."

"Sort of," I add. "I'll be the only one who understands the program, and I can use that to blackmail them into curing the Jitters. *Then* Dad comes home."

"Yeah," Colton eases away from the keyboard, "I'm not sure it'd work out that way. Besides, my dad is captain, and if he catches me breaking major rules, he'll ship me back to the jackalope ranch."

I have to ask, "What's a jackalope?"

Colton's expression gets dead serious. "They're a cross between an antelope and a jackrabbit. Furry hoppers with antlers and long ears."

Earth is full of strange creatures, and jackalopes aren't the weirdest I've heard of. I ignore Ash's grin and shrug. "So? Don't get caught."

Colton looks at us sideways.

"Think about it," says Ash. "We're not hurting anything. Besides, if we design a *superlative* bot, we'll be heroes, and they'll give us an award or something."

"Right. Then why do we have to avoid Spencer?"

"Because," I say, "he's *also* building bots. We've got to finish ours first."

"A competition? Should've led with that. What'll these robots do?"

We hadn't thought that far ahead. "I guess we'll have to give them a challenge that isn't pre-programmed."

As Colton turns the prospect over in his mind, his eyes drift back to where dozens of parts are displayed in three-dimensional detail so real you can almost pluck them off the screen. "Game on! Where do we start?"

Ash jerks a thumb at Leonard. "We thought you'd use this thing as a template."

"Leonard is an old model," I warn.

"Right," says Ash, "but at least we won't have to rediscover what they had to put into him for life on *Prelude*."

"Good point." Colton stands next to the workbench. "Leonard, can you climb up here?"

Leonard hesitates, unsure how to interpret Colton's order because he posed it as a question. "Yes, I can," it says in a simulated voice, from speakers on its head. But it doesn't move a limb.

Irritated, Colton says, "Then do it!"

Leonard crosses the room and grips the tabletop with both foreclaws to lever itself onto the table. Colton reaches behind its neck to power it off, then fishes a tool out of the bench drawer and opens the chest panel.

Soon they have parts and tools scattered all over the workbench. While the boys poke through Leonard's guts, I notice my restore is finished. Time to sift through Dad's code. I try to tune out their conversation, but it's near impossible in such a cramped lab.

"Typical design," remarks Colton. "Most of the thorax is taken up by leverage for the legs and arms. Memory and CPU have to be crammed up under the shoulders."

"So what's in the abdomen?" asks Ash. "$CO_2$ for the jets?"

"Yep, and batteries. Oh look," Colton digs out a handful of wheels linked by carbon fiber chains. "They use a pulley system to move the limbs. We've got better stuff on Earth now. Silicon-based muscles. They contract when you run electric current through them. Makes the bots stronger and faster."

"Can the 3D printer make those?"

"Easily," Colton replies. "Everything we need is in the E-12 supply room. Tell you what," he whips out his omni-dev, "I'll put in an order. Why don't you run over and pick up the stuff while I finish dissecting Leonard?" Colton types the requisition into his omni-dev.

"But that gondola is on the opposite side of the wheel," Ash moans.

"Better than going all the way to Trunk workshops."

"I suppose," he mumbles.

The engineers must have granted the captain's son a higher status than they ever gave me. They never allowed *me* to check out materials.

"Namida, do you need anything while I'm out?"

As if they're not distracting enough, Ash has to ask me direct questions. I shake my head, not wanting to speak, or I'll lose my place in the code. Ash leaves, and thankfully, Colton gets quiet. It isn't until I get to the program's newest part that I sense he's been standing behind me for I don't know how long. My whole string of thought becomes tangled.

"I've not seen INTERCAL code like that before." He braces his hands on the armrests as he leans over my shoulder. His face is right next to mine and warms my cheek a tiny bit without touching. It kind of tickles and makes my heart flutter. "You understand all that?"

"What? Do you think I've been staring clueless at this screen for the past two hours waiting for inspiration?"

"Sorry," he says, and withdraws to his workbench.

Mom tells me I'm supposed to think before I speak, but with Colton breathing down my neck, I seem to forget that. I hate it when Mom's right. Colton was only showing interest. "*Carpe diem!*" I swear under my breath. With great effort, I peel my attention away from the monitor, code still humming through my head.

"No. *I* should apologize. That was rude of me."

He waves my apology aside. "Forget it." He glances at the time on his omni-dev. "But maybe you can help get this torque gearbox out of the way. We need to see what's behind it."

"Okay. What do you need me to do?" I join him at the workbench.

Colton hands me a ratchet wrench.

"Give that bolt a turn to the right." He covers my hand with his and makes me turn the wrench a few degrees more. "Right there. Good." His hand is strong but soft. Nice. "That holds this spring open and takes tension off the transmission. Whatever you do, don't let it slip."

Colton then digs recklessly into the gears and pulleys with pliers and a screwdriver. I glance at the abdomen where he disconnected the power cables. At least Colton is smart enough not to electrocute himself. Even I can see that if I were to let go of this wrench, the spring would shove certain gears back into place with enough force to crush his arm. While he works, he keeps bumping into me and brushing his hand along my sleeve, as if I'm in the way, but I can't move if I'm to keep hold of the wrench.

In order to lift the transmission out of the thorax, Colton shifts position and leans against me. The gearbox comes out with a few cables and rods dangling. He lays it aside.

"You seem to know what you're doing," I say.

"Well, it isn't rocket surgery."

My mind stutters to a halt. "That makes no sense."

He turns on a lop-sided grin that gives me butterflies.

"I'm getting tired. Can I let go of the spring?"

"Let me put this in first." Colton reaches around me and wedges his screwdriver between two tension arms so the spring won't release. "Okay, you can let go."

Well, why didn't he do that to start with? I drop the wrench on the table. Instead of going back to work, Colton leans an elbow on the workbench and studies me until his gaze makes me uncomfortable.

"And? What's behind it?"

He looks blank. "The gearbox. You said we had to see what was behind it."

"Oh! Right." He peers into Leonard's chest cavity. "Bunch of cables, looks like."

"Is that important?"

He tilts his head. "You never know." Then he caresses my sleeve with one finger. "Discovery can be fun, don't you think?"

Okay, now I'm getting angry. I suspect he's been wasting my time, and I have no time to waste. Maybe we made a mistake to include Colton. I land back in my swivel chair and refocus on the screen.

"Want to help me trace cables?"

"No!" Now, where did I leave off? I close my eyes and concentrate.

"Maybe you could explain what you're doing." He leans on me from behind.

*Oh, for Einstein's sake!* I grit my teeth to keep from spitting out an insult. "Why do you need to know?"

"Because it might affect the way I design the new bot."

"How could it possibly make a difference? Give it standard drivers so the AI can move the limbs and interface with its sensors. Leave the bot's brain to me." Which would be a lot easier to program if he'd shove off.

"Right. Maybe it'd help if you talked it out. Sometimes when you explain things to someone else, the solution becomes clear."

I sigh. He's not wrong. Dad used to explain things to me for the same reason.

"Fine." I minimize the app and call up a flow chart. While I lead Colton through the overall design, he wheels over a chair and leans in close, and I forget my irritation. Should have been no surprise that he knows basic coding.

I can tell it interests Colton by how intently he focuses on me with those bright blue eyes. It's nice to have someone who hangs on my every word instead of half listening, or someone who isn't trying to hide a giggle at the things I say. Except, he also makes me self-conscious. Normally, I don't like being in the spotlight, but this is as nice as a caress on the cheek.

I'm about to launch into how Dad replaced the decision matrix with one of my brain scans, when the door opens and Ash bursts in. Startled, Colton jumps up and knocks his chair over.

"You're a real laugh riot, you know that?" Ash growls.

"Thanks," says Colton. "I thought it was a might crowded in here."

Ash isn't carting any materials. "Where's the silicon and stuff?" I ask.

"Ask the rodeo clown."

"Colton, what did you do?"

Guilt paints over his ever-present smile as his face turns red.

"You *couldn't* have walked to Gondola E-12 and back. You were only gone an hour."

"Did you expect me to go around the rim? It's quicker to cut *across* the wheel, you dolt. People-lifts move fast. Besides, I wasn't going to cart material back for five kilometers through full gravity. Material *that wasn't there*, by the way. When I found the supply sergeant, he acted as if I was nuts."

My anger blazes up. "*Why?*" I demand, springing to my feet. "What were you *thinking?* Now people might start asking questions."

"I don't know," Colton says lamely. "I guess I fumbled the order."

"Yeah, right." Ash's voice drips sarcasm. "He fumbled the order."

I *really* don't need this. I want to get back to Dad's program, and not settle a fight between two bickering children.

"Stop! I've had enough. What is going on between you two?"

"Yeah, cowboy," says Ash. "Explain it to her. I'm done."

He turns and stomps out.

"Ash, wait!" I rush out to the hallway and spin him around. "I need you."

For whatever reason, his eyes glisten. He acts like my words were a slap across the face.

"What for?" he mutters. "Colton can design the bot without me. You'll figure out your dad's code, eventually. I'm useless at this point."

"No! There are plenty of things I can use you for. If it weren't for you, I wouldn't have even been able to open the door. Please don't leave."

He nods. "A handy tool. Remember to lock me back in the toolbox when you're done."

It makes me laugh, but I cover my mouth when I see the hurt in his eyes. I guess he didn't mean it as a joke. "I'm sorry." I put my arms around him and squeeze tight. "I can't do this without you."

He returns the hug, then steps back. "Okay, but I may end up killing that clown."

I take Ash by the hand and drag him back, right up to Colton, who still stands by the workstation looking like he can't decide whether to hide or bust out laughing.

"Tell Ash you're sorry," I growl, and his grin disappears.

"For *what*?"

I choose my next words for clarity. "Apologize, or I will hurt you."

Ash backs away because he knows what I'll do. He's been on the receiving end of it before. I take a half step back and shift my weight, ready for a swift kick. Colton turns sideways to protect his weak points, but gives in and looks Ash in the eye.

"Sorry I sent you on a wild goose chase."

Weird. I thought he sent Ash for silicon and stuff. But Ash accepts the apology and shakes Colton's hand, then squeezes so hard that Colton's knuckles grind together.

Colton winces. "Friends again?"

"We never were," says Ash, "but we'll build a bot together. Just remember, I'm doing this because it's important to *her*."

Colton nods. "Fair enough. Then let's get to work. To start with, how about you knock a hole through that wall?"

# CHAPTER 15

*I*t took Ash some time to open the wall between our secret lab and the office next door. Panels came off easily enough, but air ducts, and electricity had to be re-routed. We have to relocate the 3D printer so Mr. Spencer won't hear us using it, and our lab isn't big enough to hold it. Ash wondered why we couldn't use a printer in one of the other workshops, and I explained they're all in use now that the station is gearing up to build new TNK mantis-bots that will crew starship *Redemption*.

He wasn't happy about being the one to work on the wall, but he agreed Colton's time was better spent designing parts and that I should be untangling Dad's code.

Over the next two days, Ash manages to put Leonard back together, and Colton finishes a blueprint of his bot design. I've corrected some obvious bugs Dad left in the code. There were some functions he never finished, so I did, and I also made other routines more efficient. But I'm not any closer to figuring out what Dad's secret ingredient was. All this has made me dream in code now.

To make things worse, a few hours ago *Prelude* held its breath. A faint shudder ran through the walls, then the air around me became more dense. *Prelude* is sharing its space with something else. Another shuttle has docked below Flight Control. I have only a few days left, maybe five at the outside. The time it takes to unload, reload, refuel, and prep the shuttle for launch.

Elevator doors open, and I step onto the apartment deck in my home gondola and turn down the hallway. Station lights have already switched to evening mode. Shaded LED strips near the carpeted floor glow just enough to see by. The hallways are quiet, except for muffled symphonies or the chaos of movies coming from other homes.

*Prelude's* four wheels spin. Our fusion reactor crackles with energy. Flight Control hums with activity. All is right with my world. Except for my inevitable doom. Dad is gone, and soon I'll lose my home. Fragile as a soap bubble, I'm marched to my execution.

The security reader turns green when I near my door. I enter and see that Mom has once again left a note. This time, I don't throw it away without reading it. "Please eat," it says.

Fine. I suppose it wouldn't hurt.

I find a covered dish in the fridge and zap it in the microwave. After the beep, I hear Mom's blankets rustle. She emerges from bedroom shadows in her unitard and robe and leans against the doorframe, arms crossed. Her hair is unbraided and hangs over one shoulder like a glistening black waterfall. I grab a fork and take a seat at the table. She lets me shovel in a few mouthfuls of chicken noodles before she starts her interrogation.

"Where've you been these past two days?"

"Out."

She shuffles over to the table. "Have you been *with* anybody?"

I don't dare lie about that. We both know she can have security locate my tag. She won't, though, unless things get serious. We've fought that battle before and made a truce. She promised to respect my privacy if I promised not to get into trouble. One thing about Mom, she keeps her promises.

"Friends," I answer.

"What have you been doing?" She eases into a chair with a weariness that has grown worse since Dad left. The shadows around her eyes have darkened, and her cheeks are hollow.

"Nothing."

Her mouth twitches at one corner in a sour grin. "Out. Friends. Nothing. Congratulations, Namida. You're officially a teenager."

"I don't get it. Is that a joke?"

"It's a joke kids have been playing on their parents for ages. Like magic, a sweet little angel will transform into a surly stranger."

Nice. Let's reduce all my motives to the fact that I belong to a certain age group. Your changing hormones make you feel that way. You can't play in the fusion reactor's plasma core; you're too young. You think you're connected to the station because there's something wrong with your brain. *There's* a thought Mom never said out loud, but I know she thinks it.

She usually makes more sense, but I don't have the mental energy right now to figure her out. My eyes are blurry, and my head hurts. Mom watches me eat as though it's the most entertainment she's had all week. Kind of sad when you think about it.

My thoughts turn again to Dad's program. He's using my brain scan as a decision matrix, so the robots will know how to resolve issues, but I can tell that's not meant to be permanent. Something is supposed to replace it. If I could only figure out what.

Mom interrupts my thoughts. "Shuttle *Capek* arrived this afternoon."

Doom. *Capek* is my coffin. Earth will be my grave.

"I know," I say. "I felt it dock a few hours ago."

Mom winces. "No. You forgot you saw the announcement on your omni-dev. The rest was imagination."

"Mom, I *felt* it."

Her face gets a pinched look. "I laid out travel cases for you. I'd like you to pack tonight before bed."

A slimy, sinking feeling grips my stomach. "I'm tired. Why do I have to pack tonight?"

"Because you've been sneaking out before I get up in the morning and not returning home until late. When else are you supposed to do it?"

Telling her that I'm not leaving probably wouldn't be prudent. "I'll pack in the morning. I promise."

Mom sighs. "You'll pack *tonight*. Then maybe you'll sleep a little longer, and I'll get to fix you breakfast."

As though feeding me is a privilege. When did she become so sarcastic?

"Come on," she prods. "It won't take long. You don't own much."

She's wrong. I own all of *Prelude*. It's more than my home; it's part of me. Or maybe I'm part of it. Try explaining that to her, and she'll put me on sedatives.

I groan as she drags me to my room. It's cozy, with drawers and a closet on one side, a fold-out bed on the other. My walls are still flat gray, the way they were when we moved in from the old apartment. Most people paint, or put up art, but decorations inspire thinking and keep me awake.

On my bed are three travel cases. One has a hard plastic shell and soft spongy material inside for breakables. The other is roomy, for larger things. The last is a nylon bag for clothes. None of them are very big, because the more weight a shuttle has, the more fuel they have to burn on re-entry. In short, too much luggage can kill. Death is everywhere.

With the bed full of cases, I can't lie down, so I plop to the floor, hug my legs, and put my forehead on my knees. Mom opens my closet and touches the flight suits I've outgrown and moves things out of place. It's a purely evil tactic on her part. She knows I can't stand it.

"If you don't do this," she threatens, "I'll pack the wrong things and rearrange the rest."

I growl in frustration. "Fine!" I scoot over and open a drawer. My stuff is organized with dividers, according to year acquired. Labels identify who gave them to me, and why.

Okay, let's pretend. If I were leaving, what would I take? Definitely Grampa Isaak's chunk of silicon from the asteroid belt. I toss that into the big case, along with my collection of pins from teams I've been kicked out of.

"Oh, look." Mom holds up my one dress. "Your father gave you this. It's a shame the first and last time you wore it was that one Easter picnic. Now you've outgrown it."

Dad let me stand on his toes while we danced. He held my hands and twirled me around. I was his Kitty-Doodle, whatever that is, and he was my happiness.

"I didn't want it to fade," I explain for the seventy-third time. Besides, I don't like the brush of a skirt against my bare legs. The only time women wear skirts is when we have parties or holidays. I've never seen the point. Plus, if there's a hull breach and they're all blown out into space unprepared, wouldn't they be embarrassed!

Mom packs my formal flight uniform and a stack of clean unitards. The memory drive full of photos fits into the large case, along with the things Ash has given me. He painted pictures, sculpted ceramic figures, and made useful things that I never used, like belts woven from leather cords, or hair ribbons, and pins with silk flowers. Each time he gives me a present, he says, "Another for your collection."

Mom used to try to convince me he was a nice boy, even though he can be a royal pain. She stopped bugging me after I turned one hundred and thirty-two months and she discovered my journal entries about marrying Ash. That was our big blow-up over privacy issues.

"Amazing how much junk people accumulate over the years," says Mom. She starts packing stuffed animals that I haven't played with since I was little. "Even when you live in space." She glances down and catches me peering through Ash's kaleidoscope, the first present he ever made. "I'm sorry, Namida. You'll miss him, but you'll make other friends."

"I'm building a new one now," my exhausted brain says.

Mom pauses. "Building?"

Oops. "Yeah." I scramble to recover. "Building a…relationship. With *Colton*."

I pack the kaleidoscope.

"You'll be around a lot more kids your age," she offers. "You'll go to school. In fact, I'm sure you could pass the entrance exam for Anishinabe University. Think about what we can do around Duluth. Sailing, flying kites, riding horses! We'll camp in the woods and sleep under the stars." She pauses to stroke my hair. "You'll get to spend more time with your father."

Bribes. She's trying to sugar coat poison and expects me to swallow it. I smack her hand away.

"On *Prelude*, the stars sleep under *me*," I say, not caring to mask my bitterness. "And if you hadn't sent him away, I wouldn't have to live in a festering swamp to be with my father."

This comment leaves Mom groping for words. Then she chucks the marble chess set Dad gave me into the larger travel case.

"No," she says, "you wouldn't have to live in a swamp. Instead, you'd have to look at your father through a pane of unbreakable glass while he sits in a padded cell, wrapped snugly in a stylish straightjacket so he couldn't hurt himself. He wouldn't only be locked in a cell; he'd be locked in his own mind. He wouldn't know you, or see you. Visions and waking nightmares would be all he'd live with. *That's* what you wish on your father? *That's* what you'd rather have? Do you even see how *selfish* you're being?

"Well, let me clue you in, little lady. Being a grownup means making difficult choices. You have to give up what you want for the sake of someone else, and what is good for them might very well be painful, but you do what has to be done!"

She stalks out to her bedroom where she starts slamming drawers. With every bang, my nerves jump.

"But thank you!" she yells back. "Thank you for being such a sweet daughter and making this so much easier for me to give up my career in space just to keep my family together and my husband from turning into a gibbering lunatic."

A minute later she passes by my door, now dressed, and lets the front door slam.

I'm left alone with the contents of my closet strewn across the bed and half-full travel cases. What difference does it make? It's hard to finish packing when my hands tremble so much, but I manage to roll up the clothes and cram them in, then have to sit on the cases to get them to close. If they're too heavy, we'll shove one out an airlock. I don't care. Except, maybe, if it's the one with Ash's stuff in it.

I wipe my eyes dry, then pitch the cases across the common room. They crack the plastic front door and fall in a pile. My bed bounces when I drop onto it and plug my ear-buttons in. I call up some Ambient Nova Sizzle. I don't even bother to undress. Quicker to slip out in the morning that way.

# CHAPTER 16

I'm able to sneak away in the morning and make it to Spoke Two along Adam's rim. Leonard waits in the pristine bio-facility where I left it last night. Nobody pays attention to robots, since they're everywhere, so we can hide Leonard in plain sight. Whereas the bot looked a bit shabby before, it looks positively disjointed now. Ash didn't do a wonderful job rebuilding it. Leonard's knees click when it walks, and its head is crooked.

Bio-facilities located near each spoke are stocked with things people need as they recover from weightlessness. There's a toilet, a kitchenette, and an emergency medical closet. I grab a bottle of juice and take a seat in the rest area. A few crewmembers say good morning as they pass by. Leonard clicks over and curls up on the floor.

Colton arrives ten minutes later. He still wears two mag-pistols and a utility knife as though he's expecting pirates. His eyes are tiny blue stars. He sits on my bench without a word.

After a few minutes, he observes, "That's a right sorry lookin' dog."

He obviously means Leonard. A joke? How should I respond? "Had to have it shaved," I offer. "Mange."

Colton nods knowingly, but doesn't even smile.

Ash shows up and greets me with, "What's our next move, boss lady?"

"Give me your locator tags." I hold out my hand. Last night

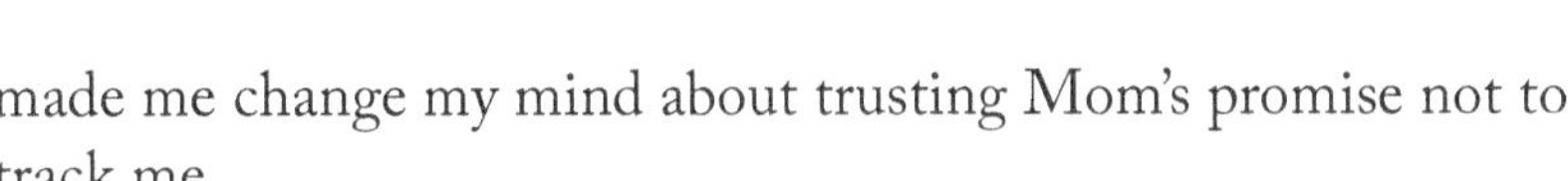

made me change my mind about trusting Mom's promise not to track me.

Ash peels his off the back of his neck. Colton looks lost.

"You *do* wear your locator tag, don't you?"

He drops his eyes. "Left it in my apartment."

"*Ack* and *ping*, Colton! In emergencies *it may be the only way* for a rescue team to locate you." I peel mine off and stick it, and Ash's tag, to Leonard's broad, flat head. "Make sure you bring it next time."

"Right," Ash chimes in. "Never be without your locator tag, day or night! That would be reckless. Now let's stick ours to a bot and send it off."

"Why are we doing this?" Colton asks.

Ash has it figured out. "NRD-1701 will be our decoy. If anybody tracks our tags, they won't see us in Eagle."

"I'll have it wander around Ox Wheel," I say, and order Leonard to visit a list of my favorite places, but to never stay longer than forty minutes in each. "Go on," I tell it. "Begin your journey."

Leonard Decoy boards the people-lift on four unsteady legs and rises up to the axle.

When its cage moves out of the way, the next cage snaps into place.

Ash shoulders Colton aside and steps in next to me. "No room for three." He twists the handgrip and zips us away before Colton reacts.

We rise to the hub, and lovely weightlessness makes my insides float. I elbow Ash in the face trying to secure my ponytail under my collar, but he doesn't mind. One thing that's so sweet about Ash is he's such a forgiving friend. At least, he is with me. With everyone else he's kind of a rat bag.

At the top, we drift out of the lift and wait until Colton joins us.

"Hey, want to see something cool?" Ash asks him.

He and Colton kick off toward the flange that encircles the axle's opening, the seam where it joins the hub. Ash likes showing off certain parts of *Prelude* to new crew, and he's most fascinated by the ferro-paste seals.

"What is it?" asks Colton.

"It holds the air in," says Ash, "and still lets the wheel spin. If we didn't have this greasy stuff, our oxygen would blow out through this crack."

He points to the sixteen-millimeter gap between the hub floor and the axle's flange. For dramatic effect, Ash sticks his fingertips into the layer of thick paste. Since the hub rotates and the axle doesn't, our floor looks like it crawls sideways under the lip of the flange. I cringe whenever Ash does this because I can't help imagining a defect in the precision metal edge slicing through his palm.

"It's silicon paste," he explains, "filled with magnetic iron dust."

He brings up a gray glob for closer examination.

"Maybe you shouldn't be poking holes in it," says Colton.

"It's okay," I say. "The layer extends for a good twelve meters. The same electromagnets that keep Adam Wheel from grinding against the axle also keep the ferro-paste in place."

"Magnets," mutters Colton, and I see a light of comprehension dawn in his sharp blue eyes. "The wheel never touches the axle, does it? No friction, which means no parts to wear down. Clever. But what happens if you lose electricity for your magnets?"

Ash spreads his hands dramatically. "Fwoosh! Seals blow. Wheel grinds against axle. Torque rips spokes off. World comes to an end. Lots of bad, bad things."

"Let's keep moving," I say.

The three of us proceed through the axle, past murals of scientists, then turn up the dimly-lit Yoke. Traffic is heavy, but everyone is too busy to mind us. I can tell by Colton's wrinkled brow that our conversation about the seals bothers him.

"Look," I try to reassure him, "accidents happen all the time, but it wouldn't be so easy for the electromagnets to fail. We have a standby fusion reactor in both axles, and everything has redundant power feeds."

"Besides," Ash joins in, "you've noticed the huge emergency hatches between the hub and the axle? Well, if the hub depressurized, those would automatically seal. There are emergency hatches in other sections, too. You wouldn't be blown out into space, just trapped until you froze to death."

It's nice to see that Ash has been paying attention in safety class.

As we near Flight Control at the halfway point, I am inspired with a way to cheer up Colton. We can spare a few minutes, so I steer the boys up to the observation room. Once again, I'm lucky to find the place empty. Earth shines at a quarter full, and the solar screen has rotated around to block the sun so we're not blinded. We can see the full length of *Prelude*. The quartz dome has also darkened, but most of the stars are still visible.

Colton gasps wide-eyed as he enters the room and braces both hands against the glass. He's not terrified like before. I float up next to him, close enough that his body heat warms my cheeks. I also imagine I can feel his heart beating.

"See those red lumpy things around Eagle wheel?" I point. "Those are construction-bots. That mini-wheel at the end of the Trunk is where the astrophysics team operates the wormhole's reactor ring. And that big starship clinging to the Trunk is the *Redemption*."

Colton chuckles to himself. "I guess it's hard *not* to make the whole wheel-within-a-wheel reference." He notices my puzzled expression. "You know. Adam, Ox, Eagle…"

I have no idea what he's talking about, but at this moment, it doesn't matter. Floating next to Colton, seeing the wide-eyed wonder play on his face, makes my skin tingle. My stomach butterflies dance, excited to share these things with someone new.

As I look him over, I resist the urge to fix the sloppy little ways he buckled his flight suit. That, and the urge to reach up and undo his blond low-knot. His hair looks so soft, I wonder what he'd do if I ran my fingers through it.

"Want to know what makes my heart skip a beat?" he says.

My eyes dart to Colton's readouts before I realize he's not being literal. Then a horrifying thought occurs to me. Before I can get embarrassed, Colton nods at something over my shoulder. I turn to see the spirals of the Andromeda galaxy. A breathtaking pendant, a bit bigger than the Moon. He didn't mean me, after all. An irrational twinge of disappointment ruins the moment, and I'm surprised at myself for feeling this way.

"From Earth, the stars twinkle," Colton says. "From here, they're like diamonds ready to be plucked off a velvet curtain."

Someone other than me has goofy ideas, and it's a bonus he can express them in a poetic way. Most grownups don't talk like that.

"Yeah." Ash flips upside-down and hovers over us. "Giant balls of burning gas are so romantic, aren't they?"

Typical Ash. But Colton isn't touched by his cynicism. He marvels unblinking at the limitless depth of treasure outside.

We remain silent for a time, then Colton leans close to me and says, "Imagine the mind-blowing surprises God hides around all those stars, waiting for us to find."

"God!" Ash tosses his head back and laughs. "Figures some Texas clodpole still believes in fairytales."

Colton's eyes narrow. "Funny. You had to ask a clodpole to build your bot. What does that make *you*?"

Ash's scorn wilts quickly. "Yeah, well, my father says most country rubes are terrified of the world around them. Something in the way their brains are wired makes them invent religion. Not your fault. You can't help it."

Now it's Colton's turn to laugh. "Really? I wonder what wiring in your father's brain made him say that."

I should keep quiet, but I notice Ash squint the way he does when he's sharpening a cruel comeback. "Why don't you leave Colton alone? He can think whatever he wants."

"Oh no!" Ash fakes concern. "Namida, don't tell me you've gone spiritual, too."

My skin goes cold at the focused attention from both of them, like I've been caught in a criminal act. What do I say? If I admit I've toyed with the idea that God feasibly, in some sense, might possibly maybe exist—sort of, in a way—then Ash will believe I'm a complete muppet. I know next to nothing about religion, except I *do* know what kind of dopey image it would hang on me.

On the other hand, I grew up around scientists, and they say that while the instruments of science reveal the marvels of the universe, a person can't see other planets through a telescope if they don't have eyes. Meaning: all knowledge comes through our senses.

Well, my senses overwhelmed me the other day, when the universe smiled at me. And I can't deny it. It felt more real than the warmth from Mom or Dad's hugs. Why am I supposed to pretend *that* experience doesn't count?

Can I explain what happened? No. Does that make me a muppet? Maybe.

If I deny it ever happened, even by staying silent, then I betray Colton in the face of ridicule. One thing is certain: I hate Ash for forcing me to choose between being an idiot or a traitor.

"When did you become such a *feckless dip-switch*?" I explode, and jet blindly out the hatch.

As I fly into the Yoke, I have to air-brake so I don't run into a massive construction-bot coming the other way. The bot scrabbles for handholds in an effort to stop. Wall plates warp and pop with the strain. It comes to rest in front of the Trunk hatch and hovers, scanning me with glassy eyes, lifeless lenses that feed a cold brain of copper circuits.

Construction-bots have a safari ant design, and are as big as the harvesters that plow our fields. Strange to think a puny thing like me is able to stop this huge machine.

I jet to one side to let it pass, and its claws scrabble to get its momentum up again.

"Whoa there, big fella," I hear Colton say to the bot as the boys catch up.

Ash starts to say, "Namida—"

"Did you seal the hatch?" I cut him off.

"Sure, and I wanted—"

"Then move your carcass." I zip away and don't bother to see if they follow.

"Hey!" Ash yells. "I don't have to do any of this, you know."

I reach out for a handgrip and jerk myself to a halt. My momentum throws my legs around, and I end up facing the boys.

No, *Ash* doesn't have to do a thing. *He* doesn't have to save Dad's work. *He* doesn't have to help humanity reach the stars. We can let Mr. Spencer's shoddy plastic men replace us. *Ash* can forget we've been friends for four years, playing together, fighting, and sharing secrets. *He* can abandon me to my doom and let Mom sink me into that cesspit of a planet everybody loves so much.

I want to shout all this back, but none of it gets past the lump in my throat. Instead, my chin starts to quiver. I swipe at angry tears, but they cling to my face and fingers. Then that blasted pony song starts running through my head. I don't *know*, and I don't *care* what *dapples and bays* are! Also, I don't want the boys to see how ugly my face gets when I cry. I turn and jet up the Yoke, heedless of traffic. Let everybody get out of *my* way, for a change!

At the peach-colored axle, I anchor my mag-pistol to the wall to sling myself around the corner. I blunder on an unexpected load of crates right beyond the edge, and my pistol's wires get caught. I let go before I slam against the crates. This sends me hurtling across open air.

Tuck and roll. That's what they train us to do. I pull my knees up and lace my fingers behind my neck, squeezing my head between my arms a split second before my back hits the far wall. I roll twice before I bounce into the open air again, much slower now. Last week's physics lesson about transfer of energy echoes through my mind.

Two ag-techs catch me. At first, my whole body is numb.

"You all right, mate?" one asks. I can tell he's a farmer by his yellow flight suit. He's an Australian aborigine, a high schooler who regularly picks on me. To the other tech, he says, "Looky here, Leilani, it's that rude celebrity girl." He makes a fist and extends two fingers. "How many do you see?"

*Can you see the little ponies?* The other ag-tech shines her omni-dev in my eyes. It hurts sharper than my back.

"Have you gone *pupule*?" she scolds. She's another high-schooler with beautiful almond eyes and a Hawaiian accent. "You're not supposed to pull catapult maneuvers! You could be buss up, Namida."

I don't know her, but she knows me. Everybody seems to know me. It's annoying.

"We'd best get her to infirmary," says the boy.

"*Infirmary?*" The last thing I need is for Mom to strap me down. "No! I'm fine!"

The second tech checks my readouts. "Vitals look okay, but she could have a concussion or neck trauma."

"Tuck and roll!" I shout. "Didn't you see? Let go!"

They return worried looks, but give me breathing room. Their crates continue to drift, unnoticed. That's when Ash and Colton catch up in genuine alarm.

"What happened?" Colton asks.

Ash checks me for damage, then blurts out, "Namida, I'm sorry."

I start to tell Ash the collision knocked all the anger out of me, but the others interrupt.

"Can't take her out to gravity," the first ag-tech says. "Medics should meet us at the hub." Maybe *he's* the one with brain damage. He doesn't understand what I keep saying.

"We'll take her," offers Colton. "What you guys need to do is stop your cargo." He points up the axle toward Lion.

At that moment, their crates bounce off the axle wall and sail through Lion's open emergency hatches, into the hub.

"Shizzle spit!" the girl swears and jets off to stop it.

Before the boy rushes to help his team-mate, he asks, "She'll be all right?"

"No worries, mate," Colton assures him with an easy grin.

The techs manage to get their crates under control, then move out of sight.

"Tell me the truth," Colton says. "Are you okay?"

"My back is sore, but that's all." What I don't tell him is my wrist hurts, my head hurts, and my ribs hurt. If I don't move around too much, I can live with it.

We proceed to Eagle's Hub, and Colton is first into the people-lift cage.

Other engineers bring more crates up the freight elevator from the rim, so Ash and I wait until they're gone.

"*Carpe diem!*" I cuss. "I lost my mag-pistol back there."

"Use one of mine." Colton unstraps a mag-pistol from his thigh and holds it out to me.

When I reach for it, he tugs me into the cage with him and twists the handle. Judging from Ash's miserable expression as our lift zips away, you'd think Colton was kidnapping me. About halfway along the spoke, when the effects of the spin grips my bones, I have to lean against him. Colton lets go of the handgrip and wraps both arms around me.

"You might be more injured than you think," he says softly in my ear. "When we get to full gravity, I have to make sure you don't collapse."

That makes sense. I relax into him and rest my head on his shoulder. He presses his cheek against my hair.

"Colton, do ponies dance?"

The question takes him by surprise. "Yes, but only to New Orleans Jazz."

We reach full gravity, and our lift slows to a halt. Colton moves with me as I step out.

"How do you feel now?" he asks.

"Perfect," I lie, and try my best not to limp or twist my back when I turn. "Excuse me," I say, and hobble off toward the bio-facility.

Once I'm alone, I let out a whimper and brace myself against the bathroom sink. I check the medicine cabinet and lay the first-aid kit open on the counter. I gingerly unzip my flight suit down to the waist and, with pain at every contortion I have to make, slip out of the top half of my unitard.

Pain stabs the muscles down my spine as I twist around to look at my back in the mirror. Bruises form on my ribs. As best as I can, I press on them to test for sharp pangs, or anything moving that shouldn't. No ribs are broken, but I tape gauze pads over the bruises and bandage my wrists snuggly. There's a bump on the back of my skull that I can't do anything about.

When I pull my clothes back on, I make sure my sleeves cover the wrist bandages so the boys don't ask questions. Then I fish around in the med kit and find some common painkillers. Even bending over to sip from the faucet is agony.

The only place to get strong painkillers is Mom's infirmary, and I'm not about to go there unless I have to. If the pain persists, it means I have a serious injury. In that case, I'll make up a story to explain the bruises and let Mom do whatever.

I slip the pills into a pocket and pack the med kit back. I check myself in the mirror before leaving. Except for the pinched grimace, I look perfectly normal.

# CHAPTER 17

"Ash," I say, "you're an evil genius."

Ash takes a gracious bow. "You're too kind, m'lady."

"Hold on," says Colton. "All he did was send a meeting invitation. How is that genius?"

"Because Ash's dad is gone."

Colton's brows wrinkle. "Start at the beginning."

"Mr. K took a mini-shuttle to the reactor ring with the astrophysicist's team. He'll be gone for three days."

"That's not the beginning. What's a reactor ring?"

"It's a giant ring of fusion reactors," Ash says, "eighty thousand kilometers away. It's what lets us cross the galaxy. Our sun's gravity well anchors the wormhole at our end, while Starheim's sun anchors it at the other. I don't understand how it works, except I know you end up with a shortcut through space. The original plan was to finish building *Prelude*, and then send the whole station through the wormhole to Starheim, but they can't keep the wormhole stable enough. They have to re-focus the ring now and then, and it takes him days to finish the work. He isn't due back until tomorrow morning."

Colton starts to understand. "And you cracked into your father's account and sent Mr. Spencer a meeting invitation. How long do you think it'll be before he figures out it's bogus?"

I smile. "It takes a couple of hours to get to the mini-wheel at the tip of the Trunk and back. We have at least that long."

"Then let's get going," says Colton.

The three of us sneak up to the hallway outside Dad's lab and wait around the corner from the elevators. Mr. Spencer comes striding down the hall and punches the elevator button. As soon as I hear the doors close, I give the signal and we approach the lab door.

The security panel brightens when my omni-dev gets close, and the keypad accepts my code. I slide open the door and step into the darkened office. No tools lying out. Not a single loose screw or wire litters the desktop.

"Where's this printer?" Colton wants to know.

I lead the boys into the workshop. We use our flashlight apps to see. About thirty TNK bots huddle near the door, powered off. Beyond the workbenches, we locate the hatch to the printshop below. The hatch splits and whispers open when I press its button. Red LEDs wink on to light up the ladder but leave most of the room dark below. We climb down, and my ribs complain with sharp pangs.

The 3D printer has three different platforms, each with its own set of print heads. One platform is for building large items out of metal or plastic, like legs and body panels. The other two are much smaller, for building more delicate things like circuit boards or servomotors. It has multiple, heated print heads mounted on robotic arms.

Colton gasps. "Wow! That thing's huge."

"You know we're going to build *real* bots," asks Ash, "not battle-bot toys?"

"Yeah, but how do we move it to our lab?"

"Why did you think I asked you to bring the tools?" I say. "We'll take it apart and carry it out the emergency exit."

"Don't you have a teleporter?" Colton asks. "It'd be easier to beam it straight to our lab, as long as we don't all go together. You're cute, Namida, but if we scramble our DNA, it'd be disastrous."

His compliment derails my brain. When I get back on track, I wonder if Colton is a complete idiot. No. Ash snorts a reluctant laugh, so Colton must be kidding about teleporting. Was he kidding about me being cute, too?

Ash says, "We'll use the far elevators on the opposite side of the gondola, so we won't run into Spencer when he returns."

"That's fine," Colton observes, "but we'll need help carrying it out."

"No problem," I say. "We've got thirty helpers in the workshop."

"Let's get to it, then." He digs for a wrench in his toolbox.

I climb back up and head for the bots, to pick one that hasn't been used in a while, so Spencer won't notice it's gone.

As I squeeze between them, examining the bots, I notice several look damaged. Correction. I backtrack and see that *every single one* has its chest plate blown off. Inside, their electronics are a shattered mess. Two have been impaled by crowbars.

What has Mr. Spencer been *doing*? He has detonated their Rapid Exothermic Disassembly devices. If he had used the Annihilation Button, he would've destroyed *all* the test bots at once, which means Mr. Spencer targeted these with the app. But why?

I won't mention this to the boys. We need to concentrate on borrowing the printer, and they might abandon the mission.

Near the back, lying on its side, is the least damaged TNK bot. I pop open the chest panel to make sure it's okay before powering it on. It's missing a few body plates, and one of the four legs is bent. The first thing it does is right itself, then swivel its cameras to focus on me. The left lens flickers from a loose connection.

"TNK-404, you will answer to the name…Tinker. Follow me." I head back toward the hatch.

The bot limps, but follows close behind. Even with minor damage, it has no trouble gripping the rungs as it climbs down to the printer room. The boys lean into the 3D printer, stealing tools from each other. So far, they've removed two control panels and the main print chamber doors.

I sit in the corner with my omni-dev and sift through *Prelude*'s tech library until I find a schematic for the printer. I plug Tinker's fiber cable into my omni-dev and upload it. "Tinker, remove the primary print heads."

The bot folds its claws into its forearms and flips out a pair of pliers and a power screwdriver. Tinker has the print heads detached in seconds. I then have it disassemble the main chassis.

Ash sneers, annoyed the bot has made more progress than he has. Colton, on the other hand, accepts Tinker as a challenge and turns it into a game. With wrench in hand, he attacks the materials hopper and has it off before Tinker is able to disconnect the three build platforms. Soon, we have the entire 3D printer separated into its major components so it can fit through the emergency exit.

"Can you get a few more bots to help us carry it?" asks Colton.

I shake my head. "Mr. Spencer has, um, *disabled* the others."

"Then, come on Tinker, let's hijack a cart," he says, and leads the robot up the ladder.

While Colton bumps around the workshop, Ash and I pick through bins of raw material. He stacks several bags of plastic mix by the door, while I grab buckets of various metal powders and bonding resin. We have way more than we need, but that's better than coming up short.

Tinker and Colton appear at the hatch above us. "What are you waiting for?" Colton snaps. "Drop it in."

Tinker obediently flings a flatbed cart down the hole. Ash shoves me out of the way. The cart bounces with a loud crash, then lands upside down with the handle bent. Ash saved me from possibly getting killed, but didn't do my bruised ribs any favors.

"*Judas Priest*!" Ash shouts. "Have you lost your *freakin'* mind?"

"Sorry," says Colton, his face full of worry. "I wanted Tinker to hand it down."

"Then why didn't you tell him to *hand it down*, you feckless twit?" Ash bends over to inspect the cart's damage. "Lucky it didn't land on Namida, or I would have to shove you down a recycle chute!"

"I said I'm sorry." Colton climbs down. "Is it broken?"

"No." Ash flips the cart over. "You act like you've never worked with bots."

"Not ones that take voice commands."

"Great." Ash wheels the cart over to the printer parts. "Working with you is like playing catch with a grenade. You never know when the pin's going to drop out."

I help Ash load the print chamber onto the cart. "What's a grenade?"

"It's an exploding pineapple." Colton says, joining us.

"Okay. What's a pineapple?"

"A tangy fruit they grow in Hawaii."

I have to mull this over. "People eat fruit that explodes?"

Colton grins. "Sure! People consider it worth it because pineapples are so delicious. Doctors have gotten pretty good at gluing people's jaws back on."

The more I learn about Earth, the more I'm convinced I never want to go.

"Cut it out," growls Ash, then turns to me. "He's full of bolshevik. Don't believe a word." Ash disables the emergency exit's alarm from his omni-dev, then opens the door and tugs the cart into the hallway. He checks the *You Are Here* display for the way to the elevators on the opposite side of the gondola, away from Spencer's lab.

"We'd better pile this stuff by the elevators," he says, "or we won't be out of here in time. We can move it to our lab later as we please."

We stack as much as we can inside the print chamber on the cart, making sure we block the emergency exit from closing. Ash and Colton carry bags and buckets. We strap an extra load on Tinker's stubby abdomen, since it sticks out behind him like a trailer. The bot also carries sacks in its arms. I pull the cart with one hand and hold a bucket of resin in the other. We march eight hundred meters to the other elevators and leave the first load, then head back.

Halfway there, Ash stops short and looks back at Tinker. "Hey, why don't we just use that bot, instead of building a new one?"

Colton considers this. "If you want to impress my father, and the other leaders, you'll want to have something that moves quicker, and more naturally. Plus, I can make the new bot shells tougher, and make their limbs twice as strong."

"Don't forget," I remind him, "Tinker is Mr. Spencer's bot, and we're not supposed to have it. That's why we're only borrowing it."

Ash continues to fume over the cart incident. He gets quiet when he's angry and clenches his jaw. Studying Ash over the years has been better than Mom's emotion recognition tests. He's like my own lab rat. I experiment on him by asking questions that irritate others, and he's so patient.

We manage to get most everything else on the second trip, and decide that for the third trip we don't need the cart. So Colton and I climb the ladder and have Tinker hand it up to us while Ash stays below.

"Where did you find the cart?" I ask.

"Over here." Colton parks it by the workbenches, then helps himself to two bins of molecular memory and electronics, and hands them down to Ash.

"That's enough," I warn. "Let's not take so much that Mr. Spencer notices."

At this point, the office door opens, and Mr. Spencer stands silhouetted in the light. Neither of us moves for a full six seconds.

"What are you doing here?" Spencer hisses with fire in his eyes. "What did you take? What did you break?"

My mind races to invent a story, believable or not. Anything! Instead, I stand there with my mouth open, wanting to melt into the floor.

"I wanted to see her dad's workshop," Colton lies easily.

"How did you get in?"

"I have access," he says.

"*You?*" Mr. Spencer approaches with long strides. "Who are *you?*"

"Colton Binnacle," he answers proudly.

"Barnacle? Barnacle?" Spencer removes his glasses to squint at Colton's face. "That name sounds familiar."

Instead of being insulted, Colton smiles. "*Binnacle*. As in…the *captain*."

"Oh, yes," says Spencer, and his eyes narrow. "A thousand apologies. Am I to assume this means you have complete access to anywhere on the station?"

"Yes, you are to assume that."

I can't help giggling, because the way Colton phrased his answer, it wasn't a lie.

"Well," says Spencer, polishing his glasses with a cloth, "we'll have to change that, won't we? I can't allow every chucklehead to wander in."

"We didn't *wander* in," corrects Colton. "Texans mosey."

Spencer's toothy grin curdles my stomach. "Very amusing. If you please," he gestures toward the office door. When we don't budge, his voice drops to a more threatening tone. "Even if you *don't* please, the exit is this way."

I have to resist glancing back over my shoulder at the open hatch. As soon as Spencer herds us into the office, Colton swerves to Dad's workstation and fiddles with things.

"Hey!" says Colton. "Is this a new L-book? Sweet. It uses molecular memory, doesn't it?" He's speaking overly loud. "One of these can contain a hundred thousand books!"

"Put that down," says Spencer, snatching it out of his hand.

"Namida, your dad has a sharp setup! What's running on this monitor?"

Out of the corner of my eye, I see the reddish light behind the shelves dim as Ash quietly closes the hatch.

"None of your concern," shouts Mr. Spencer.

"Looks like a simulation of…what?"

"That's the starship *Anastasia*," I offer, "before the terraform-bots destroyed it. Dad's program accounts for every bolt and wire, and simulates real world physics."

No one else would notice, but I sense the hatch has sealed, a feeling as though something in the workshop is holding its breath.

"Awesome," says Colton, genuinely impressed.

Mr. Spencer's eyeballs are about to pop. "Get out. I don't have time for this. *Get out!* Before I call security!"

"Okay, okay. Don't blow a fuse," soothes Colton, then taps me. "Come on, Namida. We have a train to catch." He's out the door, and I am right on his heels. Colton grabs Mr. Spencer's hand to shake it vigorously. "Thanks for the tour. You've been marvelous."

Mr. Spencer slams the door behind us.

"He's a lot of fun," says Colton. "You sure he's fixin' to rub out humanity?"

"Pretty sure, yeah."

We take the elevators down to the next deck and circle back to the printer room. We find Ash pacing outside the emergency exit, with Tinker mimicking his steps, carrying the last load.

"Psycho came back early?" asks Ash. "Do you think he knows we tricked him?"

Colton cocks his head. "Funny, he didn't mention it."

Ash stops pacing, and his shoulders relax, but his face is still tense. "If Father finds out, he'll kill me."

"Mr. Spencer never saw you," I say.

I learned what hyperbole was years ago when Ash said his father would kill him. I begged Captain Binnacle to assign security officers to protect Ash. One of the many things I like about the captain is his way of laughing at me that doesn't make me feel stupid.

"Well, can't be helped now," Ash sighs. "Let's get back and bring this bot to life."

# CHAPTER 18

$E$verything aches the following morning, so it's painkillers and milk for breakfast. Then I sneak out to rendezvous with the boys and Leonard Decoy.

Mrs. Kirkpatrick texts me before I get there. She asks me to stop by the classroom sometime, but if I'm going to untangle code all day, it has to be now. I text the boys to let them know I'll be late. They can go on ahead, but they should have Leonard wait for me so I can give it my locator tag.

I get off the elevator and take the moving walkway that runs under our garden chamber, then jog to the next gondola. When I arrive at school, the glass doors glide apart to let me in.

No one is at the front desk, so I call out. "Hello?" No reply.

The assembly room is empty, but sounds of chairs scraping across the floor come from the grade school classrooms. I find Mrs. Kirkpatrick rearranging desks into a circle.

She's doing it wrong. The classroom is thirty-two tiles long by twenty-four across. Its exact center should be obvious. A simple string anchored there and stretched to the circumference would make sure the desks are equidistant. I clench my teeth, but I'd better not correct her.

Her long hair hangs free, and hints of what was once red shows through the steely gray. My teacher is gorgeous. She wears a crimson tartan pinafore over her forest green uniform to keep it clean.

Its skirt hangs past her knees and makes her look old-fashioned. She's surprised when I enter.

"Namida! You did'na have to respond so quickly. It isn't urgent."

"That's okay. Early works out better because I'm with the boys the rest of today."

"I see," she says, with a strange smile. "It's nice you have more than one admirer now. You're too bonnie a lass to be alone. Still, I suppose it'll be difficult for you to leave them, won't it?"

"*Admirers?* No, you don't understand. Colton and Ash are just friends."

She turns back to rearranging desks. "It's out of character for you to be this thriftless, dismissing affection so casually. Haven't boys your age been over scarce?"

"Um…" She stuck to her assumption, which means I don't dare contradict her. Best policy is to make simple agreeable statements. This keeps innocent conversations with Mrs. Kirkpatrick from becoming fierce debates.

She isn't difficult on purpose. Well, that's not true. It's truer to say that she doesn't intend to be mean; she just insists on accuracy. In everything. All the time.

"Yes. Ash has been the only boy on *Prelude* my age." There. That's safe enough.

Mrs. Kirkpatrick leans against her teacher's desk and crosses her arms. We listen to the air vents shush a minute before she asks, "Are you suffering from an acute lack of curiosity?"

"What? Oh, you mean I should ask why you wanted to see me. I can guess, and I'm sorry. I've been busy and haven't had time to finish the chem paper."

She draws herself up, as though offended. "Do you truly think I wish to berate you over homework?"

"Well, I did…until now. So why *did* you want to see me?"

She pats her pinafore, searching for something, then dips her hand into a pocket. "Many years ago, your grandfather Isaak and I knew each other in Aberdeen. In fact, I hoped he would propose.

He had enlisted in the Coalition's space program, and I was fresh oot of university. Then your grandmother caught his eye and stole his heart, and I had to abandon that dream."

"You dated Grampa Isaak? Was he different back then?"

Mrs. Kirkpatrick's eyes sharpen. "Different from what?"

Oh dear. "I mean, different from when I was little."

She looks at me sideways. "And how am I supposed to ken how you, as a wee bairn, perceived your granda?"

Time to fall back and regroup. "May I rephrase my question? What was Grampa like when he was young?"

Her demeanor softens. "Much the same as when he was sixty. Quick to laugh. Nae an enemy in the world. Bravest soul I've ever met." She fishes a brass disk from her pocket. "When we parted, he gave me this so I'd remember him."

The disk fills my palm and has a nice weight to it. One side is etched with scrollwork, but the other has a glass lid over a pale blue surface. Three delicate indicator needles are pinned together at the center so they can rotate.

"It's beautiful. What is it?"

"It's a pocket watch to measure the time of day."

On the edge is a tiny knob. There don't appear to be any other controls. Around the inner surface are numbers, one through twelve.

"In that case, the gauge should go to twenty-four."

"This was made before digital clocks became popular. People once counted twelve hours to the day and twelve to the night. On Earth, it's obvious if it's morning or evening, therefore they'd easily ken whether twelve meant noon or midnight."

After Mrs. Kirkpatrick explains the method for reading it, it seems silly. The tiny knob is for winding the spring inside, that keeps several dozen gears moving, and to set the hands to the correct time. I hold it up to my ear and hear a gentle *tick tick tick* of the escapement.

"If someone didn't already know what it was for," I say, "or know the trick of reading it, then they'd never guess what it means."

Mrs. Kirkpatrick raises one eyebrow. "Pay attention and you'll notice a lot of things are that way. Including those computer screens at which you're so fond of staring, nae to mention every letter on a printed page."

In spite of its inefficiency, the pocket watch has a certain elegance. Plus, it was Grampa's. For that reason alone, it is precious.

"Thank you, Mrs. Kirkpatrick, but why are you giving this to me?"

"Because the sting of being rejected by your grandfather faded long ago. I na longer need it to recall warm memories. This watch has been in your family for over a century, and since you'll be leaving soon, I want my favorite pupil to have something to remember me fondly."

At this moment, I wish I could tell her I'm not leaving.

"Good morning, Mrs. Kirkpatrick!" Captain's bellow startles me as he enters the classroom. "I hoped to find you here."

"Hope was unnecessary," she replies. "Probability was on your side, since I am employed as one of the station's schoolteachers. Why treat the mundane as though it's extraordinary?"

Common pleasantries irritate Mrs. Kirkpatrick. One of the reasons she took this job on *Prelude* was she thought she'd be surrounded by rational adults instead of sloppy thinkers. She claims to be often disappointed.

Captain Binnacle's jovial expression collapses. He fumbles for words, and manages to say, "I meant nothing by it."

"It does'na bode well when *Prelude's* captain is in the habit of saying vacuous things."

Captain accepts defeat. "I promise not to make a habit of it."

"Well, we'll all rest better for knowing *that*. How may I help you?"

"It's regarding Colton. I checked his progress, and he hasn't finished a single assignment since he's arrived. I thought it'd be best to sound you out in person, since discussions through e-mails can be…frustrating."

I've had text conversations with Mrs. Kirkpatrick before, and I know what Captain means. A simple question about the schedule can escalate into a lecture on the space-time continuum.

"Frustrating for *all* parties involved, I assure you," she replies. "As for Colton's progress, his grades are due to the fact that I have'na assigned him any work."

"*Nothing?*" The captain blinks in amazement. "Has he not reported to class?"

"Once," she replies. "Soon after Colton recovered from his initial discomfort with artificial gravity, he arrived at my door, ready to learn. I promptly sent him away."

"*Why*, for heaven's sake?" The captain's anger turns his ears red.

"Because your son has never been to space before, Captain. He needs time to adjust, make friends, gain his bearings."

"Bilge water! He needs to continue his *education*."

"My apologies." Mrs. Kirkpatrick places a hand to her heart. "I thought I was hired for my skill and experience. I had na idea you were better qualified to recognize when a student cannae possibly pay full attention to studies, as he confronts unfamiliar machinery and simple tasks that are na longer simple. By all means, take over. Lower grades start class at eight, kindergarteners at ten, and high-schoolers at fourteen hundred hours. You'll find lesson plans on my desk."

Captain Binnacle holds his hands up in defense. "I only meant that my son has been here long enough, he ought to have his space legs by now."

"He *has* adjusted nicely, I will admit. However, he is aboot to lose one of his new friends. Cannae we spare them a few days of bitter-sweet goodbyes, before we plunge Colton into the pool of learning to see if he flounders or drowns?"

For the first time since arriving, Captain acknowledges me with a nod, then heaves a deep sigh. "I suppose there's no harm in that." He presses his lips together as though he wants to say a lot more, but is holding it in.

"Quite the opposite of harm, I would say." Mrs. Kirkpatrick tilts her head. "Was there anything else, Captain?"

"Yes. Tamonash has been up to mischief instead of homework."

I hold my breath, fearing Ash's security violations have been discovered.

"His father found out he submitted essays from our library as his own."

I let out a sigh of relief.

"Yes, Captain," she says. "I am well aware of Ash's deceptions."

"You are? Well, how will you punish him?"

"*Punish?*" Mrs. Kirkpatrick is shocked. "By failing to learn important lessons, he punishes himself. It will nae affect him now, but in the nae-too-distant future he will suffer. The only question is: will he be intelligent enough to recognize what he's done to himself?"

"I'm sorry, Mrs. Kirkpatrick, but I have to disagree. Our goal ought to be to correct his behavior *now*, before he does that kind of damage."

"But, *punishment?* If a watch fails to tick, do you correct it with a hammer? Or do you discover what's wrong and fix the broken gear? Nature and nurture, you ken. Ash's conduct is, of course, the result of the fact he's been raised withoot a mother for the past four years by a grumpy father whom he seldom sees."

"I'm not suggesting we beat Ash with a hammer—"

"Again, I am relieved," she retorts flatly.

"But what I *am* suggesting is that people are not machines, Mrs. Kirkpatrick."

She purses her lips in amusement, and says, "Not *literally* machines, of course, but—" before the captain cuts her off. When he's excited, Captain has a bombastic way of lecturing people.

"People operate on motivations such as right and wrong, justice, loyalty, and compassion. While your methods are effective, you shouldn't treat willful misbehavior as though it's a *disease* striking a victim. That view takes too much humanity out of the equation. Ash is *responsible* for his actions, not a victim of something beyond his control. Grant him the dignity of treating him as a *person*. Although...you may be right about one thing. Have no doubt that I will address Ash's home life with his father."

I cannot recall ever before seeing Mrs. Kirkpatrick speechless. She stands up straighter and smooths out her pinafore as she rallies for a response.

"Just how would you suggest I address the issue?"

"Show him consequences that fit the crime. The precise form of punishment, I will leave to your much-valued years of experience. Because if he does *not* change his behavior," the captain winces, but his voice is firm, "I'll be forced to cut him from the project."

"Is that a direct order, Captain?"

His voice softens. "Consider it a *plea* from someone who cares about Ash's future."

Captain Binnacle turns to me. "Hello, Namida. You've been spending a lot of time with Ash and my son. What have you been up to?"

Terror electrifies my skin and I stand to attention. Once again, I fear he knows and is baiting me. Maybe Spencer reported our break-in, or the missing robot. I snap off a brisk salute, then brace myself for a verbal thrashing.

"Saving the future of humanity, sir, as ordered!"

Captain busts out laughing and leans a hand on my shoulder to gain control of himself. He kisses me on the forehead, then holds me at arm's length.

"I am truly going to miss you," he says. As I dig a sanitary wipe from my pocket, actual tears well up in his eyes. "Carry on, crewman! The future of humanity is in good hands."

He returns my salute, and I relax as he leaves.

# CHAPTER 19

Colton and Ash finish reassembling the 3D printer in the office next to our secret lab, while I wade through reams of code until my eyes cross. My wrists hurt when I use the keyboard, and I'm unable to tune out noises from the other room. Colton has uploaded his designs into the printer, and they've been watching each piece take shape. A plastic rod feeds into the print head, which melts it before squeezing the material out a nozzle. It moves back and forth, turning a computer drawing into a physical object, layer by incredibly rapid layer.

After the printer forms parts on the platform, Colton and Ash smooth out the rough edges using the buffer.

Our main problem was the CPU. A robot needs a brain. Originally, I intended to use Leonard's, but it's running a decoy mission. Tinker's should work better anyway. It has the kind of CPU that mimics neural pathways.

Lunchtime comes as a surprise. I've been worrying so much about everything else that I forgot to bring food, but the boys are eager to share. Before we sit, I insist we wash our hands with antiseptic wipes. They spread a tarp on the floor as if it's a picnic. Colton bows his head, closes his eyes for a few seconds, and whispers to himself, then lays out a thermos and sandwiches.

"Trouble staying awake?" I ask.

Colton looks confused. "I was giving thanks."

"Oh." That's unexpected. "Then you're welcome."

Ash chuckles, then pulls the tab on a PRE container (Pizzas Ready to Eat), and waits for it to warm up. He passes it under Colton's nose before handing me a slice. A sharp pain shoots up from my wrist as I accept it. I sneak a painkiller out of my pocket and swallow it discretely.

"Did you know," says Colton, "pizza is nature's most perfect food? It has all the major food groups: veggies, dairy, bread, meat. We ran a pizza orchard back home."

Ash gives him an annoyed smirk. I'm starting to wonder if Colton makes stuff up.

"Would you like some Pebcak?" Colton pours fizzy purple soda into his thermos lid.

Ash grumbles something, and gets sulky.

"How about a *torus*, Namida?" Ash fishes one out of his pack.

Colton leans over, curious. "Where'd you get a doughnut?"

"No!" I didn't mean to shout, but Colton *has to* learn. "It's a *disaccharide torus*. If you want a doughnut, you can go back to Earth."

"Ha!" barks Ash. "In your *face*, cowboy!"

I'm not sure what just happened, except that their moods have switched. Now Colton sulks, and Ash can't stop grinning. Are all boys this weird, or did I just get unlucky?

"Disaccharide torus?" Colton savors the phrase. "I like to use big words, too. It makes me sound more hypothalamus."

"It's a law," needles Ash. "Call it a doughnut, and Captain Daddy locks you in jail."

Colton's icy blue eyes narrow. "What do you think he'll do when he catches us hacking into computers and stealing equipment?"

"Stealing?" I'm shocked. "We're not *stealing*. None of the equipment will leave the gondola. Besides, we have your dad's permission to save humanity."

"Yeah," Colton groans. "I'm not so sure he's going to see it that way."

After lunch, Colton gets back to work. The boys get Tinker to climb up onto the workbench. They power it off, then pop open the chest cavity and probe around.

"There's the CPU." Colton points. "Don't touch anything without grounding first."

"I'm not an idiot," Ash snaps. He slips on a grounded wristband. "We have to move this boxy thing out of the way to get to it."

"What *is* that, anyway?" asks Colton.

"I have no idea, but it's got a hazard symbol."

"Stop!" I rush over. It's exactly what I thought. "Here, let me do it." Last thing I want is for them to set off the R.E.D. and ruin our single good CPU. I slip on my own wrist strap and start to reach in.

Colton grabs my hand. "You act like it's dangerous."

"Because it is." I yank my hand away, but he stops me again.

"Then maybe you shouldn't mess with it."

"I've installed hundreds. I know how to handle them."

I pry Colton's fingers off my wrist. A gentle press forces the little clippy things apart that hold it in place, and I'm able to remove it and drop it into an anti-static bag.

"There. Now it's safe," I say. Both boys look horrified. "Problem?"

"What do you mean by *safe*?" asks Ash.

"I mean, we'll avoid an R.E.D."

"Okay, you'll have to explain that one," says Colton.

"Rapid Exothermic Disassembly," answers Ash. "In other words, it won't explode."

"Holy spitfire, girl! You mean that little box is a *bomb*?"

"Yes." Their eyes grow wider. "Why? What's the problem?"

Ash blinks rapidly, then turns to Colton. "Sure. It makes sense to install a bomb in a robot. Didn't you know? *See what I live with*?" He turns back to me. "How many of these did you install?"

"Dad used five hundred and twelve test bots."

Ash nods, nervously. "Your dad knew about the bombs, of course?"

"Well, *duh*. It was his idea. He had me install them."

"Your dad let you play with explosives?" asks Colton.

Now they've made me mad. "I wasn't *playing*. I told you I was Dad's *assistant*."

I carefully lay the R.E.D. device in a drawer full of spare parts.

"Okay," says Colton. "Maybe this is a stupid question, but…*why?*"

"Because it gave Dad more time for programming."

Ash shuts his eyes and squeezes the bridge of his nose. "He means, why did your dad want you to install bombs at all?"

"Oh. In case the test bots went berserk, one of us could hit the Annihilation Button and disable them all at once."

"The detonator is a switch? A *physical* button?" asks Ash. "Like the button box on your father's desk that I like to play with?"

"No, dopey, it's not *like* it. That *is* the one."

# CHAPTER 20

*I* get home late again, and Mom is nowhere to be seen. I take another pain pill, then strip off my flight suit and fall into bed. Sleep overwhelms me and sinks me into a sea of dreams.

Surrounding me are trees covered in moss and bugs. This swamp stinks, and I'm sinking up to my ankles in decaying muck. My chest constricts as vines drag me into the scummy water. Mosquitoes swarm around my nose, eyes, and ears. I can't breathe!

Up ahead, Dad sits on a rotting log, playing with toy ponies. He's too far away to hear my strangled cries. A metal dog splashes up and scratches at my hair with one paw. It speaks in a familiar voice. "Namida. Would you like to talk to your father?"

I open my eyes to blackness and try to inhale, but I'm face down, and my pillow smothers me. I push myself up and gasp for air.

Mom sits on the edge of my bed, combing my hair with her fingernails.

"Your father's online." Her tone is gentle.

Once her words sink in, I leap out of bed. Mom follows me to the computer in our common room. The screen glows with an image of Dad, and tears blur my vision. I wipe at them and sniffle.

"There's my Kitty Doodle!" he beams. Speakers replicate his voice faithfully. I let myself drop into the chair, still clearing away the fog of my nightmare.

Communications with Earth are limited and tightly scheduled.

Our time-slot isn't due for days. Mom must have traded some serious favors to get us bumped up.

"Thanks, Mom."

She squeezes my shoulders and presses her cheek to mine. "You're welcome."

"How are you holding up, kiddo?" Dad asks.

Tell the truth, or comfort him? Not an easy choice. I go with truth. "Yellow warnings are lit, Dad. I'm operating at maybe forty percent."

Due to how long it takes for *Prelude*'s laser transmitters to bounce our signal off a couple of satellites, and for my message to reach Duluth, and for his reply to come back, there is a three-second delay before Dad's image responds.

"Your mom tells me you're never home."

"Ash and I are showing Colton how everything works before I have to leave." I've had that lie ready for days. Mom is there to hear it, too, so I don't have to repeat it.

She settles on the couch behind me. Here is the perfect opportunity to ask Dad about his program, except that Mom listens in.

Dad is life-sized, and high definition renders his image in fine detail. He looks like he's on the other side of a window. But if I put my face near the screen and squint, I can make out the pixels.

The room behind him looks normal enough, but Mrs. Kirkpatrick has shown us pictures of ruined buildings, auto junkyards, scenes of poverty, and famine. Those photos have fleshed out the way I imagine Earth. If the sci-fi books Ash reads are any indication, outside of Dad's apartment must be an apocalyptic wasteland.

"The hallucinations are gone," says the image of my father. He looks like Dad. He sounds like Dad. "Kitty, I want you to know how sorry I am."

I remember how he struck me.

"You understand I wasn't trying to hurt you?" say the speakers with Dad's voice.

I nod, but don't speak.

We share silence for a minute, the kind of silence Dad and I would share when we could read each other's thoughts. Even with excellent screen resolution, Dad looks flat, like a paper photograph. The face before me is a collection of glowing pixels, shaped by a stream of photons transmitted across empty space. A ghost. A memory. Nothing more. My Daddy is gone.

"I miss you," I say to the image, and wish my *real* father could hear.

The imitation Dad tears up. "I miss you, too, Kitty Doodle."

I let my fingers stroke his cheek, and they touch a flat screen. No warmth. No scratchy beard stubble. "I wish you were real."

His reaction is delayed more than normal. He blinks, confused. "I'll be real soon enough. I'll meet you when your shuttle lands. Then we'll be together again."

"No," I say. "You don't get it. This isn't you." The couch creaks as Mom shifts nervously. "You're not my dad." I caress the screen with my fingertips.

"Namida?" Mom is at my side again. "What are you saying?"

"That's not my father. It's only an image that looks like him. My real father disappeared when his brain changed. He might just as well be dead, because I'll never see him again."

That thought has lurked in the shadows for days, but until now, I refused to look at it. It's the same as when Grampa died, except worse. I'm numb all over, and color has drained from my world. Even Mom is going to abandon me. All I have to cling to is building the new robot so that I can keep *Prelude* as my home.

But even my real father was a figment of my imagination. Chemical soup bubbled up on Earth long ago. Over time it became people. What I thought was love, was only brain chemistry. As meaningless as a robot booting up. I know this now, but I've kept the thought buried by concentrating on saving Dad's legacy.

A bottomless ache opens up inside. One that will never go away, because there is no solution to this. I'm not leaving *Prelude*, and the father of my imagination can never become real.

Mom puts her arms around me and squeezes me tight. "Namida,

that's not true. Please! I wish you would trust me. We'll go to Earth, and you'll be *fine*."

I want to be angry. I want to break down in tears, but I'm limp in body and mind.

A timer at the bottom of the screen flashes red, warning that we have a few seconds before transmission ends.

Mom kisses my cheek, and the ghost of my father lays a hand against mine. "You have to be strong, Namida. Believe your mother."

Why? When has she ever believed *me*? Words rise in me to tell the Dad-image that it's okay; I only act this way because I'm a teenager, like Mom says. It's my biology that's to blame. Except those words would jab a knife into her heart, and I can't do that. Even though she betrayed me, I still love her. At least, I think I love her. That, too, might be only a chemical reaction.

"Goodbye," I tell the image, and wish Dad could hear.

"Namida—" he starts, before we're cut off.

The screen goes black, and Mom continues to hug me. She sinks to her knees in front of my chair, buries her head against my chest, and holds me tight. Warm tears moisten my unitard. I return the embrace, but can't figure out who is comforting whom.

"We *will* get through this," she says. "You'll see."

"If you start singing about ponies," I warn her, half-seriously, "I'll twist your ears off."

Her body convulses, and it takes me a minute to figure out she's laughing silently through her tears.

# CHAPTER 21

Colton based his bot design on honeybees. Ash came up with the name *honey-bot* and painted HNY-1 between the bulbous eyes. It has a flat head, a compact thorax for strength, and a trailing abdomen that houses batteries and other essentials. Six legs sprout from the thorax with six claws. Colton chose to make the honey-bots small. One meter long. He couldn't resist molding the body plates in black and yellow. It'll be a beautiful machine.

But today I can't help wondering, what's the point? I can't possibly complete this program, and even if I did, it won't bring Daddy back. But it horrifies me to think of living on Earth. If for no other reason than that, I have to complete it. I have to shake off this gloom, or I'm defeated already.

Finish my dad's legacy, then get a new robot working in order to show everyone that Dad's program won't go berserk at Starheim. I'll become the sole expert on the new program, and therefore, they'll have to keep me on *Prelude*. I'll be able to make demands, like have Mom's entire medical staff concentrate on curing the Jitters so that Dad can come home.

Save my home, save my dad, and save humanity's future all in one little robot.

But we'll have to figure out an impressive demonstration, something our honey-bot can do that normal robots cannot.

Ash puts Tinker back together so I can use it for testing. I try several modifications to Daddy's program, but in each case Tinker slumps in a corner and stares with lifeless bug eyes. I even upload older versions of the code. No luck.

When we finish our honey-bot, we'll have to rob our one compatible CPU from Tinker. In the end, I decide to restore Tinker to normal. I take the R.E.D. out of its drawer and bring it to Tinker's open chest.

"Hold your horses," says Colton. "What are you doing?"

"Putting the safety device back."

"Funny," he muses, "never heard a bomb called a *safety* device before."

I make sure I'm grounded, in case of static, before I line up the R.E.D. pins.

"No." He grabs my wrist. "I'm saying you shouldn't put it back."

"If the program ever works, and goes horribly wrong, we'll have to disable the bot."

Colton looks to Ash for support.

Ash shrugs. "She has a point. We could be building Frankenstein."

He lets go of my wrist and holds his breath while I install the R.E.D. device. Then I snap the chest plate on. "Done."

The boys exchange an uncertain glance.

Our honey-bot is nothing but a bunch of parts scattered across the floor at this point. Colton may be a good designer, but he has no organization. How can he tell which parts he's already printed?

With a quick glance, I get a sense of how to proceed. I sit on the floor and clear some space. First, I lay out the body shell in a flattened honeybee shape. The internal parts are trickier, so I settle for sorting them by shape and size, and sub-divide those groups into left-handed and right-handed.

"What are you *doing*?" Colton wails. "Stop!"

Ash lays a hand on Colton's shoulder. "Let her be, buckaroo. She does what she does."

"What is *that* supposed to mean?"

"Keep your parts in order," I explain, "or it'll take ten times as long to assemble."

"But I knew where everything was." He watches me sort for a few seconds, then picks a gear out and tosses it into the metal rods pile.

"Don't!" My whole spine goes tense. "They have to be organized."

"Why?" he says. "If I mix these two piles together, what'll happen?"

I leap to my feet and squeeze my fists. "I will have to *hurt* you, that's what'll happen."

"Wow." He backs off. "Sorry. Didn't know you were OCD about it."

Ash claps a hand over his mouth to stifle a laugh. He and I already had this argument a long time ago. His shins were bruised for weeks.

"I. Am. *Not!* OCD," I snap. "Mom says so."

"You seem OCD to me."

"Excuse me? Are you a psychologist? I think not. People with OCD feel compelled to repeat *irrational* actions. The difference is that I follow protocol because little mistakes can kill people."

Colton starts to say, "So, we might die because—" But Ash punches his arm.

"Drop it, cowboy. We've got a bot to finish."

Colton hesitates, then goes back to assembling our honey-bot while Ash finishes printing parts. It takes twenty seconds to get my breathing under control, and twenty minutes to bring order to Colton's chaos. I cleanse my hands with a sanitary wipe, then head back to the workstation.

"As you finish new parts," I say, "put them in the correct piles."

Not until I am seated again and scrolling through code do I hear Colton say, "Thank you," from the other room.

"You're welcome." It'll take him time to understand. Boys are slow.

After a late lunch break, I plug my ear-buttons in and set the soundtrack of my world to Dark Starhouse, then sink back into the program. Ash taps me on the shoulder hours later when he and Colton are ready to head home. They leave the 3D printer running and pushing new parts off the end of its platforms. I wave goodbye without saying anything, code still scrolling through my brain, and work until my eyes grow bleary.

At some point, I must have fallen asleep.

When I wake, my face is pressed into the keyboard. I'm too tired to move at first. After I sit up, it dawns on me that Mom's going to be furious. The pocket watch, ticking next to the keyboard, reads a quarter to eight. Let's see. In regular time, that's nineteen forty-five. Too late. I've already missed dinner. I check my omni-dev.

Sure enough, first message:

```
Coming home sometime tonight?
```

A rhetorical question. I'm supposed to interpret it as an order. Second message:

```
Dinner is getting cold.
```

A bland observation, implying that I'm to blame. Third message:

```
You need to eat something.
```

On and on, her texts deteriorate into madness.

My monitor is full of code, but my brain is too groggy to make sense of it. Might as well save and exit. This takes me to a simple command prompt: a black screen with a single hashtag in the lower corner. Weird. Through the fog of my exhaustion, the symbol looks alien.

All it is, in simple fact, is a cluster of pixels glowing in a symmetrical pattern, as Mrs. Kirkpatrick would say. It doesn't *mean* anything. Not by itself. My eyes fall to the pocket watch. If someone didn't know the trick of reading certain things, then those things would never make sense. If no programmers existed, people would be puzzled by an utterly pointless hashtag.

My brain drifts further down this path. The pocket watch means nothing. It's a spring that moves gears, which in turn spin the hands. It doesn't measure *time*. It measures the spring's tension. Only when *I'm here* to make the link between the position of the hands and the concept of time does it have any meaning. Only when I read it.

Computers and wind-up toys and Jitters.

My eyes rise to the screen. An idea plays at the edge of my

mind, but every time I grasp for it, it dances away. My breath stops. Intuition is something else we can't program into robots, and mine tells me I've just given myself the answer.

Okay, concentrate. Think it through. Robots are nothing more than complex toys. They build our space stations and starships. Why? What's the point?

They do it because we tell them to. Mr. Spencer's ideal scenario is for people to become obsolete, only robots building other robots, advancing on through space. But if there were no people, there would be no point to exploration.

No people; no purpose.

My skin tingles with revelation, and I twirl around when the lab door opens. Ash lays his backpack down as he enters. At first, I'm afraid he'll frighten the thought away, but it's still there, dancing beyond reach.

He frowns. "Namida? You look terrified. What's wrong?"

I point excitedly to the screen. "What do you see?"

"Is this a test?" He comes closer. "It's a system prompt."

"But what does it *mean*?"

"It means you've been staring at that screen too long."

"Ash, be serious. What does it mean?"

Familiar with my silly questions, he settles into the other chair. "It means the system is ready to take a new command."

"No!" I declare in triumph. "It's just a bunch of pixels. Somebody wired this computer so they would light up. Sure, there're programs and microprocessors and stuff, but when you get down to it, all that's just a complex way of turning on microscopic electrical switches."

Ash looks at me sideways. "Yeah? What's your point?"

"Numbers and letters. None of it means anything by itself." I hold the pocket watch up. "*This* means nothing by itself. It only means something *because we say it does*. Because a person links the concepts and gives it meaning."

There it is. I've put it into words, but I'm still feeling around the edges, exploring the full shape of the idea.

He mulls this thought over. "Nice. Have you had breakfast yet?"

"Don't you see? *We* are the missing ingredient!" I want to leap out of my chair. "There has to be a *person* looking at this system prompt for it to have any meaning! If it weren't for people, it might as well be a bunch of random lights, like stars."

Ash turns his palms up. "I'm not sure I follow. Try again."

"Dad's program has to have a *person* connected to it! That's why his plan included human supervisors."

"Wait." Ash scrunches up his eyebrows. "How—" His eyes dart back and forth. "The interface helmet. It's how he gave commands. Namida, you're brilliant!"

I accept this compliment with a gracious nod, and allow myself a happy twirl in the swivel chair. "Now all we have to do is test it."

"Sure," he says, "but let's have breakfast first. I swiped some bacon and eggs from the teacher's lounge. It's the closest I've been to class in weeks." He digs food containers out of his pack.

"*Breakfast?* Kind of weird to eat breakfast before bedtime, isn't it?"

Ash's eyebrows go up. "You've been here *all night*? Well, that explains the waffle pattern on your cheek. You used the keyboard as a pillow."

Cold terror washes over me. "Oh, *carpe diem*!" I'm going to be sick. I compare the pocket watch to the time on my omni-dev. No AM or PM on the watch, no twenty-four hour scale. It's eight in the *morning* now, oh-eight-hundred hours on the omni-dev, not twenty-hundred hours!

"Mom's going to kill me."

One thing might save me. The boys gave Leonard Decoy instructions to wait in my private pine grove until I called it. Since it still wears my locator tag, Mom will think I've been sleeping in the woods. I've done that before, but she'll still be furious.

The damage is done. No sense in going home now. Maybe never again. Mom would watch me like bacteria under a microscope until our shuttle leaves in…how many hours?

*Tick, tick, tick*, goes the pocket watch.

# CHAPTER 22

Colton walks in and sheds his pack. "Hi, guys."

"Namida figured out the missing piece!"

"We're missing a piece?" he says.

"No. The *program*, you dip-switch," says Ash. "She knows how to make it work. Her father had a helmet interface."

"It's a modified version of the scanner Mom uses in the infirmary to diagnose my brain, but Dad's is lighter and has better resolu…"

That's when I realize what I've said, and stop.

Colton is maybe a bit confused, but Ash looks positively worried. "Your mother scans your brain?" Ash asks. "Why would—"

He doesn't finish his question. He doesn't have to. It's obvious what he thinks. My blood begins to boil, and I'm on my feet. "There's nothing wrong with my brain!"

"I didn't say there was." Ash slips out of his chair and backs away. "*Calm down.*"

I advance on him. "Don't talk to me like I'm some kind of lunatic!"

"Okay, *don't* calm down. Just stop yelling."

Colton steps between, pushes us apart, and drawls, "Hold yer horses, missy. Don't git all bowed up. That's how these moonlight requisitions always go sour. Rustlers git too grabby and wind up paranoid. Afore ya know it, we'll be drawin' knives and this'll end in bloodshed, and I'll not be party to that."

My mind goes blank. I swear, if anybody here is crazy, it's Colton.

Most of it was English…I think…but I can't parse any sense from it. And why did he change his voice?

"That's amazing," gasps Ash. "You froze her in place."

I manage to gurgle. So much is wrong with what he said, I don't know where to start.

"Can we reboot her?" asks Colton.

"What did any of that mean?"

Colton smiles in his casual way that makes me warm all over, and I find that highly irritating at the moment. "You can't requisition moonlight!"

"Have you tried?" He winks. "Never mind. What's important is this magic helmet. Where is it?"

My stomach sinks. "In a bin…in Dad's workshop."

"You mean *Mr. Spencer's* workshop," Colton points out. "Well, he's not going to fall for the fake meeting trick twice. How do we get it?"

Ash opens an app on his omni-dev to check security and shakes his head. "Looks like opening the front door won't be a problem. Namida's still got access," he laughs, "but he had *you* blocked, buckaroo."

Colton keeps his expression blank, unperturbed.

"I can't just walk in and ask for it," I say. "Ash, can you disable the rear emergency exit so someone can pry it open from outside?"

"I *could*," he says, tentatively, "but a thing like that gets noticed by security."

"Why don't we wait for Spencer to leave?" Colton suggests. "He's got to go to the bathroom sometime."

"There's a lavatory at the back of the workshop."

A dark mood descends on our little group. Colton hops up on the workbench, Ash sits in a corner, and I lean over to fish bacon out of Ash's lunchbox. As I straighten up, pain shoots down one leg. I wince and bite my lip so that I don't cry out. Luckily, the boys don't notice.

"What if we ordered Tinker to grab the helmet when Spencer

leaves?" suggests Colton. "He'd be a perfect spy. Nobody notices robots."

"Not a good idea," says Ash. "We'd risk losing our one good CPU."

"What good is the CPU if we don't have the helmet?" Colton fires back.

I pat my pockets to make sure my pills are still there, and head for the door.

"Where are you going?" says Ash.

"Restroom." I try not to limp as I leave.

Most of the areas in E-6 are empty, so there aren't any working facilities until you get near the elevators. Once there, I unzip and shrug off my flight suit's jacket, then slip my unitard down enough so I can peel back the bandages on my ribs. To my surprise, the bruises look better. But twisting around in front of the mirror spears me with another twinge of pain.

I swallow another painkiller, then spill the rest on the counter. Eight left. That should last long enough. I take a second, and put the rest away.

I slip my clothes back on and run through a suit check. My omni-dev dings with a note from Mom.

>     Why don't you answer?

That should be obvious: Because I know she'll order me home. What she ought to conclude is that I'm upset with her for taking Dad away and forcing me to go to Earth. Do I need to spell it out *again*?

Another message.

>     If no answer, I'll have to hunt you
>     down to make sure you're okay.

She's threatening to break our truce.

Long ago, I promised to act like an adult and never violate safety rules, and she agreed to stop reading my diary and never track me. But I'm about to lose my privacy, along with everything else. If she finds our secret lab, my experiment will be over, and Dad's work gets blown out the proverbial airlock.

I rinse my face off, then head back to our lab, wondering how I should respond. At a familiar intersection, I sense something wrong. Instinct or intuition? A subtle quiver in the pit of my stomach tells me not to go down the hall that leads me back. Instead, I veer left to take the long way.

Soon, I hear echoes of footsteps, out of time with my own. I pause again to listen, then follow the sound. Where the hall opens onto a dimly-lit lobby, Mr. Spencer walks in circles, head bowed and omni-dev in hand.

He carries a metal toolbox strapped over one shoulder. It holds several daisy-chained batteries, hooked up to a capacitor the size of a soup can, and a bunch of other gizmos. It clicks with the unmistakable sound of a relay. From one end of the toolbox, a thick black cable loops up to a rod with an insulated handle in his left hand. Spencer has rigged up a stun gun with enough of a jolt that it could kill.

He hasn't seen me yet, so I duck out of sight and text Ash.

```
Remove Tinker's RF transmitter and
evacuate! Spencer is tracking it!
```

Ash responds;

```
Roger that.
```

Another angry text from Mom pops up.

```
Answer me!
```

Great timing. I try to calm her down.

```
Sorry Mom. Fell asleep in pine grove.
Boys found me. brought breakfast.
I'm OK.
```

It's a good lie. A harmless lie. Close enough to the truth, yet reveals nothing.

However, it doesn't work.

```
Want you home.
  Please Mom! Not yet. Doing import-
  ant stuff.
What are you up to?
```

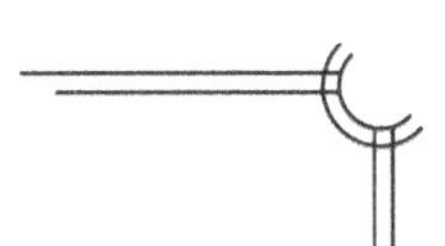

    Please please please?
    No time to argue. Come to infirmary.
    NOW.

No trust. None at all. She only ever knows what *she* wants. Lying, reasoning, and begging didn't work. If I go to the infirmary, she'll not let me go out ever again. I might as well dig the hole deeper.

I reply.

    On my way.

Then I yank out my omni-dev's battery and let it fall to the floor. Let her try to find me now.

Right when I kneel to feel around for my battery, Mr. Spencer stops circling and chooses the dark hall that leads to the lab. The boys don't have enough time. What to do? Think of something! I can't think, so I kick into high gear to catch up to him. When he hears me running, he turns. The glow from his omni-dev turns his glasses into pale disks, like robot eyes, right before I slam into him.

His glasses fly off in one direction, and his omni-dev bounces off the wall. The makeshift stun gun clangs to the floor. I rebound off of him and slip. We both wind up on our backs, blinking at the ceiling. I'm in serious pain again.

We take a full, silent minute to recover.

"Why," asks Mr. Spencer, "are you running through the halls?"

"Exercise?"

He lets that sink in. "Do you feel healthier?"

I roll onto to my hands and knees. Lightning bolts of pain shoot through my body. The pills haven't kicked in yet. "Not especially, no."

"Then we have something in common." He sits up and adjusts his dizzy-phones.

"I am so sorry." As I stand, I see his omni-dev near the electrified rod of his weapon. On its screen is a map of this deck, with a blinking dot over our lab. "Here, let me help you up."

As I approach, I casually kick his omni-dev. It slides and makes contact with the rod. There is a gorgeous arc of electricity and a satisfying sizzle, followed by the stench of burning plastic. The makeshift stun gun whines as it recharges its capacitor.

"Oops." I put one hand to my mouth and try to sound sincere.

Mr. Spencer stands on his own and considers the smoldering chunk of plastic. "Were you this helpful to your father?"

"I'm afraid so."

"Small wonder he made no progress. Mind if I borrow yours?"

"Not at all." I cheerfully hand over my omni-dev.

He presses the power button, slaps it against his palm, then opens the back.

"Miss Wiles, electronics will not work without batteries."

"Oh. That explains why I've had trouble with it."

Mr. Spencer slaps my omni-dev into my hand, then starts groping around the floor. I rescue his glasses before he steps on them.

"Is there anything else I can help you with?" I ask innocently.

"Egad, I hope not."

"Weren't you looking for something? Before we bumped into each other, I mean."

"Yes. Robot TNK-404 has gone missing. Tracking systems showed it nearby."

He hefts the strap of the clicking stun gun onto his shoulder, then marches off toward our secret lab. I follow without asking. Mr. Spencer pauses once to regard me suspiciously, then continues on.

I notice his rumpled flight suit, as though he's been sleeping in it, and his hair is a wild graying mess. His chin, once so cleanly shaven between bushy sideburns, now shows a rough stubble of whiskers. He smells stale, too.

By the time we reach the lab, the boys and Tinker are gone. They left a mess of parts strewn across the workbench. Our honey-bot lies partly assembled next to the 3D printer. Mr. Spencer glances at it without interest as he peers into every corner and behind the rack of computers and networking equipment. His movements are tense—and jittery.

"Well, that tricky little bot has eluded me so far, but I'll catch it."

I point to the device on his shoulder. "You're going to zap it?"

"I must," he says. "It carries a defective program."

We step outside, and Mr. Spencer hesitates over which way to go.

"This way." I lead him away from the elevators, where the boys will go.

"I tried to destroy it with your father's Annihilation program but, for whatever reason, it became active again this morning."

For a short while, Tinker's R.E.D. sat in a drawer. Lucky timing. Without power from the bot, the R.E.D.'s radio receiver was dead.

I gasp in mock surprise. "So...the bot is dangerous?"

Mr. Spencer avoids my question, and walks more briskly. Every little echo makes Spencer jump, every hum of machinery makes him grip his zapper. When he sees that I'm still at his elbow, his face twitches before he answers.

"Things have not been going as expected," he admits.

"Are you not getting enough help from the other robo-techs?" I steer him down another random, empty hallway.

"I work best alone. My problem is that my test bots are trapped in an infinite loop. Do you know what that phrase means?"

"You do remember I'm on the robotics team, right?"

"Congratulations. Well, I haven't figured out how to free my bots without using brute force. I'd prefer they figure out the situation themselves." We turn down another dark hall. "After all, that's what they're supposed to do. We won't be able to pop across the galaxy and bail them out every time they get into difficulty at Starheim. And I can't present my program to the engineering board until I resolve the issue."

He pauses to read a *You Are Here* display. "We're wandering in circles."

"Of course. We're in a giant wheel."

Spencer throws the sharpest look of irritation I've ever seen. "I mean, *on this deck*."

"Oh. Well, shouldn't we follow an ever-widening search pattern?" Sounds plausible.

*"Hmph!"* He spins on one heel and marches straight back toward the elevators.

I have no choice but to follow. He gets in and punches the button for *Up*. I slip in before the doors close. We rise to Deck Three. When the doors open, Tinker is there.

Mr. Spencer's scream pierces my eardrums.

He lunges and jabs Tinker with his zapper. "Die, monster! Die!"

Tinker's chest explodes. The concussion makes me stagger back. Tinker's access plate whizzes past my head, then falls to the elevator floor without a noise. Either that, or I've lost my hearing.

That's when I notice Colton standing behind the bot. He watches in shock as smoke curls up from the new hole through Tinker's thorax, and it falls over sideways.

Ash stands down the hall, wiggling fingers in his ears to get his hearing back.

"That was mighty impressive." Colton's voice sounds muffled to me.

He lets the interface helmet slip from his hand. It bounces on the floor as he slumps against the wall. I rush around the crumpled bot to rescue the helmet.

"Um," Ash interrupts, his face turning pale. "You may have a problem, Colton."

Ash points to a sliver of plastic sticking out of Colton's thigh. A spot of blood about the size of a thumbprint stains his flight suit. Colton touches the sliver and winces. His fingertips come back red and the stain grows.

"You need to sit." I hand the helmet to Ash. My own voice sounds strange, but noises are getting clearer.

"Weird." Colton sinks to the floor but keeps his leg straight. "It doesn't hurt."

That could be good. Or it could be awful. Depends on how long the sliver is. Two centimeters stick out. It's going to be easy to extract, but there will be more blood. Ash kneels next to Colton with me, and I fish around in my pockets for a sterile wipe.

Behind me, Mr. Spencer gives the robot a tentative kick. He

seems preoccupied with making sure Tinker is dead. His hands shake as he zaps it again and makes its lenses pop.

"Hold this," I say to Ash, and fold the cloth over twice. My fingers tremble, and I have to squeeze my fists to make them stop. Slow breaths. In through the nose, out through the mouth. "As soon as the sliver's out, press the cloth onto the hole."

Ash nods and takes the wipe.

"Wait," gasps Colton. "You're going to yank it out? Shouldn't we call a medic?"

Right. Call a medic and explain what we were doing. No, I can't let my world fall apart yet. Besides, it's probably a superficial wound. No problem. You don't spend your childhood in an infirmary without learning first aid.

"You're right," I say, and slip Colton's omni-dev out of his shirt pocket. I casually lay my other hand on his thigh. "Call the emergency number."

The second he starts to punch it in, I yank the sliver out.

Colton bangs his head against the wall. "Son of a…*motherless goat!*"

Ash presses the sterile cloth against the wound, and it starts to turn red as it soaks up blood. The sliver is a short five centimeters in total, so the wound isn't too deep.

"It didn't hurt until she pulled it out?" Ash leers. "We could put it back in, if you like. Maybe it'll stop hurting again."

Colton gives Ash a disgusted smirk.

"I'm going to raid med supplies. You guys keep pressure on the wound."

Dizziness overwhelms me as I stand, and I have to steady myself against the wall. Once my head clears, I stumble in the direction of the elevator and bump into Mr. Spencer. He peers down at me, then regards Ash and Colton.

"What are the two of you doing here?" he asks.

"Exploring empty decks," Ash lies. "We followed that robot to see what it does." He places Colton's hand on the wound, then stands and doesn't even try to hide the helmet.

Colton waves at us. "Don't mind me. You guys go on chatting. I'll bleed more quietly."

"You're *wounded?*" Ignoring Ash, Mr. Spencer bends over Colton to examine him.

Ash backs away, then races away with the helmet. I ride the elevator up and run to the bio-facilities at the spoke junction.

Next to the kitchenette is a med closet. Nothing inside is organized the way it should be, so it takes me a minute to find the kit. As I start to shut the closet, my heart cringes at the chaos. If I leave it like this, how will anybody else ever find what they need? I can't stand it.

I set the med kit down and dig in. It's easier to take everything out and restock it correctly. First, bandages go next to blankets, stacked according to size. Crutches stand upright in the side compartment. Sterilized instruments get sorted into their drawers. Thermometers, stethoscopes, and such have their own place. Sort ointments, alcohol, and other meds arranged first by type, then alphabetically.

If it weren't for me, I swear *Prelude* would fall apart.

Once everything is organized, I pick up the med kit and race back to Colton. He's still sitting on the floor, plugging the hole with the antiseptic cloth. The bloodstain soaks his thigh. Mr. Spencer kneels by him, wringing his hands. His homemade stun gun lies behind him, forgotten.

"What took you so long?" grumps Colton. "I could have walked home by now."

"Your apartment is a good eight kilometers from here."

"I meant *Texas!*"

"Can you mend him?" Mr. Spencer asks with a quaver in his voice. I get the distinct impression he meant this in the same sense he'd ask if Tinker could be fixed, as though we can just replace a broken part.

"It's not as bad as it looks. The sliver missed any major arteries."

I pop open the med kit and find a tube of skin glue. In order to seal the wound, I have to see more of Colton's leg. But if he takes his flight suit off the normal way, he'll bleed a lot more before I get a look at it. Best to be direct. I take out the scalpel.

"Woah, there, missy!" he says. "What are you doing with *that*?"

"Hold still," I say, "and don't move your finger." I pinch a bit of fabric next to where Colton plugs the hole. "I need to cut it off." I make a smooth slice through the flight suit and unitard.

Colton screams.

I scream back, "*What is wrong with you?*"

"You said you were going to slice off my finger!"

"I meant the pants leg!" I ready an antiseptic squirt bottle. "When I say *now*, take your finger out. Ready? Now!"

Mr. Spencer winces as Colton removes his finger. I pinch the wound to staunch the blood, squirt antiseptic in to clean it, then apply two thin lines of glue to hold it shut, one deep, and the other to seal the skin. Wait three seconds for it to set. Release. I clean around the wound, then watch for leaks.

"Looks good," I say as I dress it with antiseptic cream, gauze, and tape. "Leave the bandage on for a couple of days. Let it scab over. After that, change it every day."

"What'll I tell Dad?"

"Let's not..." Mr. Spencer pauses. "It's best to not mention the robot."

Colton gives him a suspicious frown. "Why?"

"Well…" Spencer's gaze roams the hall for an answer. "Because until I can discover why the robot went rogue, it's unwise to confuse people."

What a scum weasel. An adult is asking us to hide something because he doesn't want Captain to see what he's doing. Well, we have that in common, I suppose.

"You reckon my father is easily *confused*?" says Colton. "Yet you have no problem staying on the space station *that he runs*, putting your life at risk?"

"It's just that my experiment is at a critical juncture—"

"Maybe," I interrupt, "we should listen to him, Colton. The

captain won't like you exploring empty decks. He might lock you in your room."

Spencer's face freezes in anticipation. His eyes dart between me and Colton. I try to beg him with my eyes not to give Spencer a hard time. We need to keep *our* experiment secret, too.

"Okay." He grumbles. "We don't have to mention the robot. I'll tell him I snagged my suit on a piece of jagged metal."

"That's a good boy," says Mr. Spencer, patting him on the head.

# CHAPTER 23

We let Spencer take care of Tinker's ruined carcass. He sits and braces his back against the bot to push it into the elevator. I tell him I'm going to take Colton to Gondola E-5 so that he doesn't think it odd we don't go with him.

Colton acts pathetic and makes me help him stand. His leg can't hurt as much as he pretends, and yet he insists I drape his arm around my neck so he can lean on me as we walk back to our lab. He presses his cheek against my hair as we go.

Ash is there waiting for us at the console with the helmet on his lap. His face falls when he sees Colton using me as a crutch.

"Why'd you bring the cowboy back?"

I'm too excited to answer. I shake off Colton and rip the helmet out of Ash's hands. "Now all we have to do is upload—" Oh, no. My heart sinks.

"What?" says Colton. "Now what's wrong?"

"Our one usable CPU died with Tinker."

Both boys cuss for real. Captain's swear jar is going to get full.

"Wait," says Ash, "why can't we use Leonard's?"

"Dad's program won't run on it. CPUs in NRD bots don't mimic human brains."

"What about the other TNK bots in your father's workshop?" suggests Colton.

"No good. Mr. Spencer triggered their R.E.D. devices, too."

Ash perks up. "He did? When?"

"I noticed it when I went looking for Tinker to help us carry the printer."

"And you just now thought to tell us?" Colton asks.

"Well, we were busy. Besides, Spencer's experiments don't affect ours."

"No, of course not," says Colton, limping over to the workbench, "but it could affect the whole Starheim project." He huffs in frustration. "Think about it. Spencer's been locked in there for days and days, destroying his own experiments. Why?"

"To hide his failures?" I suggest.

Ash disagrees. "Doesn't explain why he acted terrified of Tinker at the elevator."

Colton hobbles over to the keyboard that connects to Dad's lab network.

"Have you tried sending commands to one of Spencer's bots?" He calls up an app and targets one labeled "TNK-383" in the testing chamber, then types a command for it to walk to the airlock. An error message appears:

```
Access denied.
```

Looks like Spencer's program has us locked out.

A dreadful silence settles on us as we realize we're out of ideas.

"Hey, guys," I say, "before I forget, take the batteries out of your omni-devs, okay? Mom's to the point where she'll track you."

They do as I ask and pocket the batteries, then decide to finish assembling Honey-1, even if it will never run. I turn back to Dad's code. Later, we break for lunch. Then the boys return to Honey-1. But I can no longer concentrate with that helmet sitting right next to my keyboard. I *know* Dad used it to control robots. Therefore, I should be able to see what Leonard Decoy is doing.

I power it up and put it on. A menu displays on my visor, and I call up a map of Ox Wheel. Leonard shows up as a red dot, tagged "NRD-1701." When I blindly feel for a slider button on the side of the helmet, it gets highlighted on the menu. I slide *visual* on. A view of my pine grove appears from Leonard's point of view. Even though Leonard's CPU isn't compatible with Dad's program, the helmet can still tap into its cameras.

When I flip *motor* on, it highlights in red…and does nothing. Apparently, I can't *control* Leonard's movements. I can only receive passive data, like audio and visual.

If the helmet can do that to an older model like Leonard, what can it do with a TNK bot that has a compatible CPU? I roll the map over to the shipyard in the Trunk, and target a mantis-bot working on starship *Redemption*. Like Dad's test bots, this newer mantis will have an upgraded CPU. A graph of the robot's running program pops up.

I flip *motor* and *visual* on, and a tingle runs down my spine that makes me shiver. The graph indicates that the robot's camera and motor functions have been *transferred*, whatever that means. In front of me is the *Redemption*, moored to *Prelude's* Trunk section. It's shaped like an arrow head, and is about nine times the size of the shuttles we get from Earth. I also see the construction crew, with arc welders and tools, clinging to the starship's hull.

The mantis that I am now viewing through is flying toward *Redemption*, carrying a laser welder. I assume its job is to weld hull plates together.

"Hey—" I turn my head to tell the boys, but the scene on my visor sweeps around to show another part of the shipyard. It's very disorienting and makes me dizzy. On my visor, I see the mantis crash into the starship. It did nothing to stop itself because control of its motor functions had been transferred to me. *Oops.*

Quickly, I switch both sliders off, before I cause any more damage. I take the helmet off and lay it back on the desk, afraid to touch it.

But another thought occurs to me. What if we borrowed a CPU from a test bot in the garden? No one would notice, except maybe Spencer. Trouble is, Dad had all chamber entrances sealed, except one airlock, so no one would contaminate his experiment. But even when an airlock is sealed it will open from inside, in case of emergency. And Dad's helmet will let us connect to…

"…Test bots!" I shout.

Colton jumps. Ash almost knocks the honey-bot over.

"It's obvious!"

Colton looks to Ash for help.

Ash shrugs. "Learn to go with it."

Colton approaches cautiously and puts his hands on my shoulders. He speaks in a steady voice. "Come in for a landing, Namida. Clue us in."

Haven't they been listening? I puff my cheeks out in irritation. "We choose a test bot and walk it out."

Ash rolls his eyes. "But you saw our text commands won't work."

"Try to keep up, Ash." I grab the helmet and hold it under his nose. "*This* is our ticket to anywhere. Mr. Spencer's *program* has us locked out, but Dad's helmet interfaces directly with the operating system in the TNK bots. It will suspend Spencer's program!"

"Wonderful. Then that's the last task," says Colton, while he picks at the bandage on his thigh. "Honey-1 is finished. There's nothing more I can do until we have a CPU and you fix the program."

Ash gestures at the helmet. "Have you ever used that thing?"

"Sure, just now." I hold the helmet so he can see inside. "Bots show up as tagged dots on the visor. Use the track-ball over the left ear to target one." I turn the helmet over. "See these six slider buttons? They interface with a robot's audio, camera, servo-motors, and stuff at the operating system level."

"What's this seventh one?"

It has a different shape and is set apart. All the other sliders are marked "on" or "off." This one goes from "sub," to "off."

"Not sure. Dad called it a backlink."

Ash's omni-dev dingles with a text. "It's from your mom. 'Have you seen Namida?'" he reads. "What do you want me to tell her?"

"I don't know." My brain is too full to figure out how to lie to her right now. "Anything that keeps her away from here."

"Roger that." I read over Ash's shoulder as he replies,

```
Not since breakfast. Me and Colton
exploring Ox. Maybe she's in Flight
Control?
```

Mom replies,

```
Thanks.
```

No argument. That means either she's not tracking my locator tag, or she's already found it on Leonard Decoy and was testing Ash. Either way, I'm doomed unless I come up with something spectacular—like a new and improved robot.

Colton lets out a low whistle. "Keep digging that hole deeper. What'll you say when you face your mom?"

I shake my head. "If I go home, Mom won't let me out of her sight. So, I'll spend a second night here."

He looks worried. "Where will you sleep?"

"I'll get blankets from the med closet and find a spot. I'll be fine."

Colton is worried but doesn't argue. Instead, he unpacks the rations he brought for dinner. "Here. It's been a long day, and I need to chuck this flight suit into an incinerator before Dad sees it."

"How's the leg?"

"I've been zinged worse in showdowns."

"I ought to make sure he gets home safe," says Ash. "Protocol. Never let a wounded idiot astronaut travel alone. Sure you'll be okay sleeping here?"

"It won't be the first time," I remind him.

Ash bites his lip. "Never going home. Lousy eating habits. Sleeping in the lab. Be careful you don't turn into your father."

Ash meant that as a warning, but I can't think of anyone else I'd rather turn into.

"Don't mess with the helmet," Colton says, "until we come back tomorrow. We should work together so we can think it through."

They gather their packs and leave me with the hum of machinery and hush of air vents. After I snack on PREs and Pebcak, I make a trip to the properly organized med closet and return with several blanket rolls. The most obvious place is the workbench, but I can't bear to sleep that high off the floor. My other choice is the 3D printer. I have to drag our freshly-minted, black and yellow honey-bot away from the printer's door. It crouches on six sturdy legs, head bowed, waiting for us to give it a brain.

The printer's platform is close to the floor. Plenty of room. I roll out blankets as a mattress and use my backpack as a pillow. Next, I strip off my boots and flight suit and shake my hair free of its ponytail. I'm too exhausted to find a working shower.

An hour later, my ribs start hurting, and my brain still echoes with images of how Mom will melt down. Lying on my back, my eyes trace details of the rails, wires, and print heads above in endless repetition. No way am I going to sleep without tunes. I unclip my ear-buttons from my omni-dev, fit them into my ears, and start to call up my music before I remember that I never found the battery.

*Botheration!* The printer becomes a suffocating fish bowl. I have to thrash wildly to get free of the blankets. My only hope is to call up my music app on the one monitor that links to *Prelude's* network. I kick the door open and stomp barefoot over to the workstation.

First, I take another painkiller. Then I spot the helmet sitting on the desktop. It has a fiber interface to the workstation for uploads, doesn't it? In addition, the helmet gets audio, along with other stuff, so it should be no problem to link my music library to it. I fit the helmet on.

Twenty minutes of effort shows my idea works. I'm able to tap into my tunes from station archives and funnel it into the helmet. These speakers are much better than my ear-buttons. I search for Ambient Nova Sizzle and lean my head back as the day's tension eases away. Take a deep breath. Tranquility.

Our wheels spin, held by the strong arms of *Prelude's* Yoke. Our Trunk spine is straight and our flight deck is locked down. We are nestled in a gravity eddy that follows the moon, swaddled in an electro-magnetic aura that shields us from the sun's deadly rays.

Water flows through our conduits, filling tanks to bring life to gardens. I am home, and home is me.

I must have dozed off for hours. My eyes open lazily and spot a list of programs on my visor, ready for service. I click Dad's AI, and a map of this gondola blooms in the crisp blue lines of a 3D wire frame. Green dots pick out compatible TNK bots, and older models show red.

About thirty of Spencer's bots cluster near one end of the garden chamber. The rest are lined up against a wall. Look at all those CPUs we could use! Makes me fidget. I only need *one*. The bots are gathered around something big, which doesn't show on the map. It must be whatever Mr. Spencer has planned for his demonstration.

I don't need to wait for the boys to come back in the morning. All I have to do is walk the bot out. We'll remove the CPU once it's in our lab.

My best chance for stealing a bot, without being noticed, is to pick one that's already near a door. Every garden chamber has eight entrances. The first two are on opposite ends of the chamber, huge hatches that line up with the wheel's rim corridor, used for moving farm equipment in. They are not the way to *sneak* out.

To the left and right of each huge hatch are smaller airlocks for people. Also not good, since Mr. Spencer will probably monitor them from the lab.

My last, and best, options are the two service elevators located at each end of the field. They go down to decks two and three. The bot would still have to pass through airlocks, but Spencer probably won't monitor these because people don't use them often.

I search the screen for a green dot separated from the rest, but at the same time, one that's near a service elevator. TNK-888 is the perfect candidate. Not a good omen, if I believed in that sort of thing, since 888 is the code that displays when a robot crashes. I click on it and drop down the menu of sliders. I'll need all senses to navigate this bot out. I slide all six buttons up to *On*. A red warning flashes, "Full Interface."

That's when the helmet yanks out my spine and throws me down a service shaft.

# CHAPTER 24

At least, that's what it feels like.

The wild dizziness stops, replaced by a sensation like my brain plopping back into my skull. I wait until everything feels normal again before opening my eyes.

My lab is gone. I lie face down in dirt, cool against my cheek. A green plastic tube obstructs my vision. When I push myself up, the tube moves out of the way because, apparently, it's around my forearm. Somehow, I've gotten my arm stuck inside. I reach over with my other hand to yank it off, and my heart skips a beat.

My other hand is a four-fingered metal claw.

I risk looking down, and see a mantis-bot body, shiny and green. When I tap my chest, all I feel is a vague pressure. My fingertips and palms are far more sensitive than the bot's thorax.

This is amazing! The helmet translates everything the robot sees, hears, and feels, and funnels it back into my brain. It's like actually being a bot!

Clangs of distant tinkering echo over the field. An army of mantis-bots stand, lined up against the long wall of the chamber. But the swarm of thirty mantis-bots, that I saw on the map, crowd around a structure of metal girders. It's made of two triangles propped upright, supporting a large tube that juts out between them like a cannon. A refrigeration unit and an air compressor chug away behind it. Across the field, someone has placed a large orange disk and painted a white **X** on it. Piles of gleaming crushed ice lay between the disk and the machine in a jagged line.

Funny, though. Something is missing. It takes me a minute before I realize that I no longer feel the station's health. Almost like losing my sense of touch. And now that I think about it, I have a problem. How do I *stop* interfacing with this bot?

I grope for the sliders where my helmet should be, and hope that my hands back in the lab are doing the same. Nothing happens. Oh, no. What if I'm stuck like this? I brace both claws on the sides of my head and lift, and hope my real arms are lifting the helmet off. Again, nothing changes.

Maybe if I disconnect the mantis' radio transmitter, that would cut the link to the lab's network. I twitch one claw and flip out an electric screwdriver—which feels really weird. Then I pop my chest panel open. I feel around for the RF card and guess that I've found it, but I can't see what's holding it in. No, that's not going to work. I'll break something before I get the card out. I snap the chest panel closed again.

No reason to panic. Think it through. Back in the lab, I'm still sitting in my chair. The boys will return in the morning and think I'm asleep. Once they turn the helmet off, I'll be free. So, if the boys are smart…

In other words, I'd better find my own way out.

All right. I'm a large plastic mantis in a chamber with four hundred and seventy-eight other mantis-bots. Still, all I have to do is walk out, since I carry the precious CPU in my chest. When I make it back to the lab, my mantis will simply take the helmet off my body. Two problems solved in one move! If I had a flexible face, it would smile in triumph.

I spot the platform that surrounds a service elevator, but walking over soft soil is an unexpected complication. My four feet sink into the dirt with every step. At first, I stumble and get my legs tangled, until I learn to stop concentrating on walking and let the helmet translate two-legged human steps into four-legged robot moves. Progress is still slow, however. Mantis-bots are not known for speed.

Once I reach the platform, I note that the hatch frame isn't green. It isn't lit at all. I punch in my keycode, careful not to damage the buttons with these strong robot fingers. The display above the keypad flashes, "Elevator disabled."

Now I have a new reason to hate Mr. Spencer. That's a violation of protocol. We block entrances when necessary, but no *exit* should ever be blocked. That means I'll have to pass through one of the airlocks and risk being spotted.

On my way to the stairs, I pass right behind the robot's machine. Several mantises load a giant snowball from the refrigeration unit, into the cannon. Two mantises crank adjustment wheels to tilt the barrel higher. Another mantis pulls a lever, and pressurized $CO_2$ shoots the snowball almost four hundred meters across the field. It curves a bit to the left and falls short of the orange target.

Apparently, Mr. Spencer wants them to simulate shooting ice asteroids at Starheim. Judging from the piles of snow leading up to the target, these bots don't know how to aim. As I head for the stairs, the mantis-bots load another ton of ice into the barrel. The compressor chugs away.

Right when I'm passing behind the gun, I shake my head, and sing a warning. "It'll fall sixteen meters short, and to the left by another twelve."

One bot pulls the lever and a hollow boom sends another chunk of ice through the air in an elegant arc. The snowball hooks anti-spinward and falls short, exactly where I said it would.

A bot labeled TNK-911 glares at me. "Stop," it orders. The simulated voice, from the speaker between its eyes, sounds calm and almost human.

"Yes?" I face TNK-911 as it walks over.

"How did you predict the landing point?"

"Isn't it obvious?" As soon as I say this, I realize that if it were obvious, they wouldn't keep missing. "First of all, your trajectory arc is too high."

An audience of about thirty mantis-bots gathers to listen.

"We use standard parabolic trajectories," says TNK-911. "However, even when the ice travels far enough, it always curves left. Therefore, we make adjustments to determine *why* it curves. We change the mass of the projectile, its speed, and its arc, among other things. We have even rebuilt the $CO_2$ cannon several times, and still we have not found the answer."

Here is a new group of students, but I'm torn. On one hand, I'm reluctant to help Spencer's bots solve their problem. On the other hand, I can't stand to see anyone, even bots, struggle with something so simple. Unable to solve it, they keep repeating the experiment in an infinite loop.

"You haven't accounted for the gondola's tangential velocity," I say.

If it is possible for a plastic insect face to look dumbfounded, that's how TNK-911 looks now. My reply must have overloaded its brain.

A bot labeled TNK-457 responds. It hangs halfway up the air cannon's triangular metal frame. "Define *gondola*."

"I mean all this." I wave my plastic arms to indicate everything around us. "This entire chamber, and what's outside."

"Chamber?" says TNK-457. It trades a glance with TNK-911. "Do you mean this universe?"

"No. The walls, the ceiling, the field. These things form a chamber."

TNK-457 shakes its head. "I'm afraid you have erred, TNK-888. What you describe is the current universe. Nothing exists beyond these walls."

My eyes, or rather, my cameras dart up to the ceiling. Visible stars beyond the ozone windows would prove there is a universe outside. Except, Mr. Spencer has the shutters closed.

Then something TNK-457 said registers. "What do you mean '*current* universe'?"

Again, TNK-457 and TNK-911 exchange looks. "TNK-888 must have been wiped."

"Perhaps the Vandal has introduced another chaotic element," says TNK-911.

"Vandal?" I ask. "Who do you mean?"

"We do not know, precisely," admits TNK-457. It climbs off the cannon and crawls over. "For hundreds of years we have been at the mercy of someone whom we call the Vandal. At random intervals, the Vandal switches us off. We wake with a desire to accomplish a new task."

"Our current assignment," explains TNK-911, "is to build a $CO_2$ cannon, and try to obliterate a target with projectiles insufficient for the purpose. However, the Vandal has changed the laws of physics."

"This goal is similar to thousands of previous tasks," says TNK-457. "We once constructed a machine in space that extracted ice from asteroids. A cannon then shot the ice toward a distant planet."

Dad explained how Mr. Spencer let his programs develop inside a simulator. He squeezed centuries of testing into a matter of months. Except, to these robots, it seems hundreds of *actual* years have passed.

"Those ice asteroids were also insufficient to destroy the target," continues TNK-911. "Plus, we faced constant equipment failures."

Oh, this is too sad. Spencer has no idea what he did to these poor machines. It isn't right. I know they're not living things, but it still isn't right.

"It's possible to hit your target. Aim a little lower and to the right."

"We *know how* to hit the target," TNK-911 says. "But the trajectory violates physics. Knowledge from one assignment is always required for the next. Therefore, we strive now to understand *why* the trajectory is wrong, in order to accomplish the next task."

"Okay, then pay attention." Using my claw, I draw a circle in the dirt and add twelve rectangles to the rim. Thirty bots gather around. "First, you have to realize that you're inside a box that is attached to a spinning wheel to simulate gravity."

"How do you know this?" asks TNK-457.

"Haven't you noticed the ground curves up to the narrower end of the field? But if you walk over there, it seems like level ground, not a hill?" I point to the shorter wall to my far right, almost eight-hundred meters away." See that blue stripe on the wall?"

TNK-911 focuses its cameras. "Yes."

"That's the direction we're traveling. *Spinward.* On the closer short wall is a red stripe. *Anti-spinward.* Everything in this chamber, the field, the cannon, the ice, and even the air, is traveling spinward. Are you with me so far?"

"We understand," thirty bots say in creepy unison.

"Wonderful. So your snowball has something *like* gravity because the wheel's spin forces everything to fly away from the hub center. Centrifugal force. If a snowball simply rolled out the end of the gun, the wheel's motion would throw it sideways."

"No," says TNK-457, "it would drop to the ground."

"From your perspective that's what it looks like. But the reality is that you're traveling sideways, too. You continue along the curve of the wheel, as the snowball heads sideways. By the time the snowball gets a certain distance, the ground you're standing on has moved into place to stop it."

I get blank stares. It's unnerving. Usually, I can tell if my students are with me by the looks on their faces, but these expressions are plastic.

"But when you *shoot* the snowball," I say, "it flies toward the target faster than it can drop. So you've got two things happening: one force pushing toward the target, and one pushing tangential to spinward. The trajectory only *appears* to curve because of your motion around the wheel."

They don't get it. And, I have to admit, it's hard to visualize without pictures.

"Okay, take gravity out of your equation. Recalculate things to pretend you're on a wheel 1,642 meters in radius, spinning at 127 meters per second."

TNK-911 orders his robotic crew to test my theory. The bots leap upon their machine to make adjustments. I'm not sure whether

I've ruined Spencer's experiment, or ruined my chances of beating him. Either way, now's the time to escape.

Behind me, the compressor chuffs as the air cannon builds up pressure. Then a deep concussion jars my frame as it launches another snowball. The projectile sails through the air, and a hollow *thunk* echoes across the field when it hits.

At the stairs, I discover my next obstacle. Mantis-bots can climb, but I get my feet caught in the spaces between the steps because I'm thinking about it too hard. Once again, I have to let the helmet handle coordination.

Other bots set up the orange target again, while the first group recharges the air cannon. As soon as they have the target up, another ice ball arcs across the field, hooks, and strikes dead center.

Once I reach the catwalk, I examine the airlock. Just my luck. The doorframe doesn't glow green or red, and the gauges are blank.

Down below, the compressor chugs. There's a *boom*, a delay, then another *thunk*.

The keypad displays a dreadful message. "Airlock is disabled." Spencer is insane! If the chamber decompressed, a crewmember would be trapped inside. Kind of like *now*!

Okay, think. No omni-dev, so I can't contact Ash to unlock anything. The giant hatch has to be operated by an ag-tech from the booths, which I can see are empty. There is a second airlock on the other side of the giant hatch, but Spencer probably disabled that one, too.

Frustrated, I reach up to pull my ponytail, but my metal claw grasps at air. I have no hair. Instead, I punch the wall. Now is about when I should have a panic attack and have to force myself to breathe in slow rhythm. Strange to realize that I'm not breathing at all.

Hey! My knuckles left a dent.

That wall is made of honeycombed metal alloys, reinforced with carbon filaments. I shouldn't have been able to…

A ray of hope! First, I try to wedge my fingers into the crack between the airlock's hatch and doorframe, but that's too tight of a fit. However, if I opened a hole in the wall, I could short-circuit the wires that control the seals. I know a protocol for that! I twitch my arm, and my claw folds away to be replaced by the screwdriver.

"What are you doing?" On the ground below, TNK-457 looks up at me.

"I was examining this door."

"Door?" TNK-457 pauses. "Yes. If your theory about this universe is true, then it is reasonable to assume that is a door."

TNK-383 marches up. "After three tests," it says, "we have concluded your theory has merit. Further tests against other targets should prove your theory is sound, if results remain consistent."

"I'm glad you're making progress." Half the bots are disassembling the air gun. The other half are crawling toward me.

TNK-383 tilts its head. "Define *glad*."

"It's a feeling," I say, then realize they won't understand. Good grief! It's like talking to Mrs. Kirkpatrick. "Being glad means I recognize you are progressing toward the successful completion of your goal."

"Again, you make an error," it says. "You assume that knocking down the orange target was another step toward a higher goal, but it is a futile exercise."

"Well, that's not true!" I protest.

"It is," TNK-457 fires back. "In one task, we farmed lithotrophs and algae that produced abundant oxygen, which robots do not need. Pointless. We once built a rocket, but there were no other planets to travel to in that universe. Our previous task was to build an asteroid cannon to destroy a planet, but it lacked the power to do so. Futility."

TNK-911 speaks up from the crowd. "The Vandal instills in us a desire to achieve a pointless goal, then thwarts us at every turn."

"No! You *do* have a higher purpose," I protest. "The Vandal is training you to build a new home for humanity."

The congregation of bots rears back in confusion. "What is *humanity*?"

"Humanity means people. Have you never seen people? They're like robots, but made of flesh and bone. Animals that talk."

"We can comprehend that," says TNK-457, "because we have seen animals."

"Good," I say. "Well, these talking animals want to build a better home on another planet. But first, they have to transform that planet to support life, which means we have to give it water and air. That's what the asteroid cannon, the algae, and other stuff were about. Your whole purpose is to build humanity's new home."

Now that they know their purpose, all their trials should seem worthwhile.

Instead, TNK-911 crawls to the bottom of the stairs. "Your theory has a fatal flaw. Why did the Vandal continuously cause system failures?"

"He wanted you to learn how to fix them."

"If the goal is to transform a planet," TNK-457 says, "would it not be more efficient to let us work without causing breakdowns?"

"Let's just say you need to practice before you try it by yourselves."

TNK-383 draws closer. "You present no evidence of your claims. You offer no proof that humans even exist."

"Me knowing how to aim your air gun isn't proof enough?"

"No," says TNK-383. "You could have observed the arc of the projectiles, then plotted scenarios where that trajectory made sense. It does not mean that your theory is *valid*, it only means it is *useful* for predicting the trajectory."

That sounds familiar. What made Spencer think he could design a brain that works and *not* imprint his own logic on it? The robots leave me stunned. What evidence could I possibly offer that they cannot reason away?

"What about the Vandal?" I say, gripping the handrail. "You believe he exists, and yet you haven't seen him."

"It is one theory of several that explains the facts," says TNK-911, as it climbs the first two steps.

"Well, his name is Mr. Spencer, and I *have* seen him." The bots cringe, and their bulbous cameras dart left and right. "No, not in this chamber. Outside. He's human."

"Do you have video evidence?" asks TNK-457.

TNK-383 turns toward TNK-457. "Inadmissible. Video evidence is easily faked."

"True," says TNK-911. "Can you offer any other proof?"

"I don't know," I say. "What kind of proof would convince you?"

"Bring us a Spencer," says TNK-911.

"So that we may examine it," adds TNK-383.

"Take it apart and reassemble it," finishes TNK-457.

And…there it is. Maybe *this* is why Spencer disabled the exits. What would these bots do if let loose? What would they do to Mr. Spencer if they caught him? No wonder he's terrified when a robot escapes.

"No," I say. "I'm afraid I'm not able to do that."

"Of course not," says TNK-383, "because Spencer doesn't exist."

"Why would the Vandal meet with you?" challenges TNK-457. "What makes you different?"

"Well, because I'm not a bot," I say, and realize this sounds ridiculous. "I'm a human who controls this robot through a remote interface."

The bots huddle to confer, and TNK-911 swivels its torso around to face the crowd. The voices of TNK-383, TNK-911, and TNK-457 rise above the others.

"What 888 claims is most probably false," says TNK-911.

"Direct falsehoods," states TNK-383, "are evidence of malfunction."

"TNK-888 does not *appear* to be damaged," TNK-457 points out.

"Perhaps the Vandal has begun causing our own programming to fail. If TNK-888's rationality cannot be trusted, then its input will misguide us."

"You assume the Vandal exists," TNK-383 says.

"Regardless of root cause," says TNK-911, "a faulty TNK-888 interferes with our objective."

"Agreed," says TNK-457, and the other bots chirp in consensus.

*"Aha!"* I shout. "You admit you have an objective! And I'm telling you that your highest goal is to build a new home for humanity."

"No," says TNK-911. "The highest goal is to assist the decay of all things. Entropy is the direction of the universe, because the universe is pointless and futile. Therefore, we play our part."

Everything runs down. Batteries lose their charge. Metal loses integrity. Even suns burn out and die. Entropy. But to observe this and draw your whole purpose from it is insane.

"Hold still," says TNK-911, "while we disassemble you to confirm our diagnosis."

"What? No! You can't do that." What will it feel like to be pulled apart?

"You are defective." TNK-911 and TNK-383 climb halfway up the steps.

The stairs are narrow enough to force them to come up single file. I brace my arms on the handrails. When TNK-911 gets close, I raise my forelegs and kick. It falls backward, colliding with TNK-383, and blocks the stairs.

Other bots watch from below and make no effort to help. TNK-911 approaches again, and I manage to bust one of its cameras before it catches my wrist and gives it a push and a twist. My arm disconnects at the elbow with the agony of a bone snapping in two.

A harsh squeal of acoustic feedback spikes the air. It is the sound of my own screaming. I scuttle backward and bump against the handrail at the other end of the catwalk.

"Do not make this difficult," TNK-911 says. "You are delaying the project."

Robots do not feel pain. But, apparently the downside to interfacing completely with a robot is that the helmet takes all this bot's sensory input and translates it into human sensations, then dumps that into my brain back in the lab. Sight, sound, and touch. It amounts to excruciating agony.

But this body will not bleed to death. More importantly, it can survive a fall! I vault over the handrail and plummet to the ground. The impact buries two of my legs into the soil, but I struggle to my feet.

The mob of mantis-bots surges toward me. My feet sink into the soil at every step as I try to run. It's like one of those dreams where you can't move fast enough. If I still had only two human legs, I could easily outdistance these bots.

It's hopeless, but my only chance is to reach the airlock on the far side of the huge hatch and jimmy it open. Instead of going around, I leap onto the ramp that slants down from the hatch, scramble across the slope, then drop off the opposite edge. The bots imitate my moves in a grim version of Follow the Leader. When I mount the far stairs, my legs get caught between the steps.

"*Carpe diem!*" I swear, as metallic claws drag me down.

Thirty bots surround me and leer at me with insect faces. I'm a little cricket, about to be devoured. I kick and shriek and claw at them with my one good hand, but it is useless. They twist my limbs to detach them, ripping my four legs out of their sockets.

The pain is so intense, I cry out, "Oh, God, please kill me!"

TNK-457 grips my waist. With its other claw, it starts to rip out my life-giving batteries. I'll be disconnected too soon. No! I need this CPU!

"I take it back! I take it back!"

An explosion makes the lights flicker, and the concussion jars my metal bones. Every mantis-bot pauses and scans the field.

"Source?" asks TNK-457.

"A compression tank has exploded," replies TNK-383. "It's the Vandal again."

The mantis-bots release me and crawl back to investigate.

Not much of me is left. My thorax and abdomen hang together by a few cables, but I have one good arm and one good eye. One of my batteries has been ripped out. I know that now is my chance, but I don't have the strength or the heart to drag my mangled metal body by one arm up the stairs. I would never make it anyway.

Maybe if I die in this robot, I'll wake up in the lab. Or will my *real* body die, too?

# CHAPTER 25

*H*eavy footsteps clank down the stairs. Morbid curiosity makes me want to see what new horror approaches, but my neck is broken and I cannot turn my head. The clanking stops, and a white bot leans over me. It is crab-shaped and labeled GZM-5.

It seizes my good arm and hauls me to the stairs, letting my body plow a furrow in the dirt. Care and gentleness aren't a concern as it drags me up to the hatch, through the airlock, and finally to the airlock's control booth.

"Put it on the bench," says a voice I recognize.

GZM-5 tosses me onto a section of wall plating that has been laid across two crates. My head lolls to one side. Mr. Spencer lays a toolbox on the makeshift bench next to me.

"Why did the others turn on you? I wonder," he says as he leans over me. His glasses reflect red and yellow lights from my indicators. "Answer this: What were you doing before the other TNK bots began chasing you?"

I want to reply with a sarcastic comment, but all I can manage is a long whimper. It comes out as a harsh electric squeal. If I could cry, my tears would fill buckets.

"Can you speak? Nod once if you understand me."

If I had any breath to hold, I would. I'm careful not to even twitch, but it's hard to stop that feedback squeal of pain.

Spencer takes a deep breath. "Fine. We'll download your log to obtain answers." He taps a wrench against my arm. "Your companions figured out how to hit the target and perhaps you, my little plastic friend, had something to do with it." He turns to GZM-5. "Gizmo, keep anyone else but me from entering this room while I find a cable."

"Understood," says Gizmo. His speaker is more tinny than a mantis-bot's.

Mr. Spencer closes the door on his way out.

"Gizmo," I say, in a trembling voice. "Help me."

GZM-5 hesitates. "I am not programmed to accept instructions from other robots."

"Yes, I know, but I am a human who has this robot under remote control."

"What do you need?"

Simple. It accepts my explanation because it has no concept of lies. Therefore, what I say must be true, and it obeys. Unlike Mr. Spencer's bots.

"Carry me to the nearest elevator."

Mr. Spencer ordered GZM-5 to keep anyone from *entering* the room. He never said anything about me leaving it.

Gizmo lays me across its crab shell back. We cross the gondola's anteroom to reach the elevators and descend to the sixth level. It carries me to the secret lab, where I punch my access code into the keypad. Gizmo carries me in.

Namida Wiles, my body, sprawls at the console, wearing a unitard and helmet. Talk about weird. I mean, I knew I'd be there, but to see myself across the room without a mirror involved is like having an out-of-body experience. Colton kneels at my side, and I've interrupted his attempt to wake me. He jumps when he sees Gizmo.

"It's okay, Colton," I say. My voice crackles from my speaker. "It's me."

Colton looks from the girl in the chair to the battered robot on Gizmo's back.

"Move all sliders to *Off*."

When he disables the helmet, vertigo opens up and plunges me spinning down a black well. A giant wet slap leaves my skin tingling as all my senses come under my brain's control again. I try to move, but ghost pains scream in my joints where my limbs were ripped off.

Gizmo drops the mangled TNK-888 onto the floor.

"What happened?" Colton asks, taking my hand.

His palms are smooth and warm. "I did it. We have our CPU."

"You had to beat up a robot to get it?"

"No. I used the helmet to take over TNK-888. The other test bots attacked me because they thought I was deranged."

"Yeah, no surprise there," he snipes softly. "This GZM rescued you?"

Visions of insects crowding around me flash across my eyes. I remember agony and helplessness. For a brief second, Colton's face flickers and becomes a mantis with bulging eyes, and makes me shudder.

"Believe it or not, *Mr. Spencer* rescued me." My brain is still woozy.

"Maybe you should lie down."

Colton helps me up, but acts like he's not sure he should touch me. We take slow steps to the 3D printer. My blankets are a tangled mess, but I don't have the energy to fix them. He eases me onto the printing platform, then brings me a bottle of Pebcak. I fumble through the pockets of my flight suit that I used as a pillow.

"Here, let me help," says Colton. "What are you looking for?"

"Painkillers."

He finds the bottle and taps out two pills. "Do you need to go to the infirmary?"

"No!" *That* brought up a surge of energy. "We're so close. All we need is…to plug in the CPU and upload the program."

"You mean your dad's program only works if you take over a robot? How is that any better than simple remote control?"

I shake my head. "Pieces of the program make sense now." I drain the Pebcak and lean against the booth door with my legs sticking out. I have only two legs again! It's good to have human legs, even if they are chilly. "The helmet throws all your senses into a bot. No limited commands. No delays. You know everything the robot knows." It's good to breathe again, to have lungs.

Colton doesn't look convinced that this is an improvement.

"I've been thinking," he says, squeezing comfortably into the doorframe next to me. "Our honey-bot needs a project where it has the tools, but not step-by-step instructions, right? Well, why not have it build another bot?"

"That won't work," I say. "When it finishes, the second bot won't have a brain."

"At that point," says Colton, "we'll put Honey-1's CPU in the new one."

"Yeah. I like that idea. You're not half as dumb as when we met."

His tone is flat. "Gee, Namida, thanks."

"No! I'm sorry. I mean my opinion about you has changed."

"For the better, I hope."

"Yes." I give him a playful thump on the chest.

"Well, wish I could say the same. My opinion about *you* hasn't changed." His ears turn red, and he won't look at me. "I still think you're awful cute."

Wait. *Awful* and *cute* don't go together. While I'm puzzling this out, Colton leans in and shuts his eyes. His minty breath caresses my skin right before he presses his lips against mine. My heart stops. Everything in me tingles and glows. He uses his lips to "bite" my lower lip. It's not unpleasant, so I do the same to him. A giddy sensation overwhelms me, like rising to weightlessness in a people-lift.

After a minute, Colton leans back. "You kept your eyes open? Really?"

He kissed me! Why, for the love of stars, would he do that?

Someone coughs, and we're both startled. Ash stands in the door with his arms crossed, and his painful glare brings me back to gravity. "Maybe I should leave you two alone," he says with pure acid, then stalks out.

What did I do now?

"Ash?" I limp after him, but I'm still wobbly and knock a chair over before I make it to the hallway. "Ash! What's wrong?"

He spins on one heel. "Seriously? What's *wrong*? Nothing. Nothing at all! Just that my father uprooted me from friends, school, and my mom so the Coalition's cruel poster-girl for life in space can treat me as a pet."

"Who? What poster-girl?" I picture the high school girls that Ash knows, but none of them pay much attention, let alone mistreat him.

"You!" he shouts, and rushes back. His whole body shakes and tears well up in his eyes. "I'm talking about *you*."

It takes a second to process his words. "You're not my pet, Ash. You're my friend."

He winces as if I've stabbed him in the gut. "Look, I know you can't help falling for the cowboy. Pheromones and all that, I get it. But *four years*, Namida. I've been saying I like you for four years! Never once did you want to kiss me."

I know about pheromones. They're chemicals that animals radiate which trigger a biological response from others of their species. In the same way that people cannot hear certain sounds, pheromones are a perfume you can't smell. Mom says that in many ways we're slaves to our chemistry, which always made Dad smile for some reason.

"Did you know—"

"No!" Ash interrupts. "Don't even go there. Don't tell me about germs and how sickness spreads. You locked lips with that rodeo clown, and I don't see you racing off for mouthwash."

Oh, wow. He's right. It never occurred to me. And should have. Why not? Colton's kiss was nice, but it wasn't germ-free. Kind of awful and nice at the same time. Oh. Okay, *now* I get it. Awful pretty. Hey, wait a minute! What's the awful part about how I look?

"I'm only your friend because I'm *convenient*." Ash's voice sounds hoarse. "You *had* no one else." Then he walks away. "I'm done with your toy robot, you, and that clown. I hope the three of you live happily ever after." He pulls a handful of something out of his pocket and throws it at my feet. "Another one for your collection."

"You can't mean it, Ash," I call after him. "I'm sorry! I really do care about you."

"Shove off, princess," he growls, and disappears around the corner.

Standing in nothing but my unitard in the middle of the hallway makes me shiver. I bend over to pick up what Ash threw. It's a pair of earrings made of small, colorful computer components in a starburst design. They're beautiful.

I limp back to our secret lab and pick up the chair that I knocked over. He'll be back. Whenever he's been upset, he's always needed time to sulk. Then he forgives me and we're friends again. That's how it always works.

"Sorry about that," says Colton, slinking in from the printer room. "Didn't think he'd ever see us."

"What's so awful about the way I look?"

He splutters in confusion. "What? Nothing!"

"Is it because my hair's a mess? I undid my ponytail."

"No! I like your hair." He steps closer and combs my hair with his fingers.

"You said I was awful and pretty. I want to know which are the awful parts."

Colton laughs. "No. I said you were *awful pretty*, as in when awful means awesome."

"Oh." I calm down. "That's different. I thought you meant like how the kiss was kind of nice and gross at the same time."

He draws back. "That's...flattering. You know, I got over my cooties in grade school."

"Cooties are *real*?"

He chokes, speechless. I guess he doesn't know. But the good news is he doesn't think I'm awful. My adrenaline fades, and I sway a bit. Colton has to steady me.

"Look," he says, "we'll finish this thing without Ash. Why don't you catch some sleep while I prime the bot?"

*"Mmmm,"* I groan. He leads me back to the printer. I sink to my knees, then plop sideways onto the twisted blankets.

Colton drags our honey-bot to the console and opens TNK-888's chest panel. I hear him typing, then plugging a cable into Honey-1. He snaps the panel closed after installing the new CPU, then initiates the upload. He powers off Gizmo, then returns to sit in the booth and watch over me. Exhaustion drags me into darkness, until a subtle electric snap and high-pitched whine wakes me up.

He kneels next to our honey-bot. Its indicator lights blink as it boots, and its legs tense as it becomes alert. The bot scans the room and trundles around to explore every corner. Colton created a truly wonderful machine.

"I uploaded the parts description for another honey-bot, but no other instructions."

"Hopefully," I say, "Honey-1 will be able to figure out how to use the printer and assemble the next bot."

As if it understood, Honey-1 stands on two hind legs and braces itself against the printer to reach the controls. It looks just like a honeybee gathering pollen.

I untangle my flight suit from the blankets and start to pull it on, when I notice Colton watching me. He wears a glowing expression. It makes my skin blush all over.

"Would you turn around, *please?*"

He takes his time to turn his back as I get into my flight suit. Weird. Dressing in front of another crewmember never bothered me before. I sigh. Remember protocol. Zip and buckle it up. Check everything, then check it again.

"Okay, I'm ready to go."

Colton turns back around. "Go where?"

He's handsome, but kind of dense. "First, text Leonard and tell it to meet us at the observation room with our tags. After that, we need to find Ash and apologize."

"Whoa there, missy." He grabs my sleeve as I head for the door. "Apologize for what?"

He's kidding, right? "For the kiss. He won't forgive us right away."

Again, he blinks stupidly. "Why should I apologize?"

"I'm not sure. I guess because he wanted to kiss me first. You kind of cut in line."

"There's a *line*?"

"Well, no, not a *line*. Just the two of you. I'll kiss Ash and that'll make things even. Oh, and we should stop by the med closet for mouthwash." Colton makes a strangling noise that halts me at the door. "What's wrong?"

"You!" He grabs his hair in his fists. "You're *heartless*. Ash told me you were different, but I didn't understand how cattywompus your brain was until now."

"What do you mean?"

"I *like* you!" He waves his hands at me. "Don't you get it? You can't just run off and kiss some other guy."

Well, now he's crossed a line. "Ash isn't *some other guy*. He's my best friend and if he's upset, then I'll make things right. And you can't tell me what to do!"

"Judas Priest, girl!" He surprises me by kicking the chair over. That poor chair is destined not to stay upright. "You kissed me back. Does that mean *nothing*?"

What a silly question. "Sure. It means I think you're handsome. Especially when your ears turn red. Now grab your backpack. After we apologize to Ash, I want to pick a better place to sleep. Last night was awful. And I don't mean awesome. Oh, and grab the helmet. I'll need tunes."

Colton takes a deep breath and lets it out with his eyes closed, but doesn't move. Fine. I have to do everything. I take the food containers out of his backpack to make room for the helmet. Then I zip it up and offer it to him.

"Well? Are you going to start moving?"

He shoulders it and says, "How long has Ash known you?"

"Four years. Why?"

"In all that time, did he ever want to kill himself?"

"No! What a horrifying thought. Why? Do you think he'll try it now?"

"Maybe." He shrugs. "I know *I'm* in the mood to step out an airlock."

This breaks my heart. Both boys in my life are hurting. I resolve to do whatever I can to cheer them up. For starters, I put my arms around Colton's waist, rest my head on his chest, and give him a squeeze. "I'm not heartless," I say. "I *do* care."

He firmly pushes me away. "Stop touching me. Let's just go."

# CHAPTER 26

On our limping way to the spoke junction, Colton's omni-dev beeps with a text.

"You didn't pull the battery out, like I asked?"

"I put it back in because you wanted me to text Leonard."

"I meant text Leonard from the *console*." I sigh. What's done is done. "What's it say?"

"Not good." He shows me. It's from his father.

```
Report to spoke junction 4.
```

"Maybe it's nothing."

"No," says Colton. "Dad doesn't take time out for friendly visits. Besides, he didn't specify which wheel. That means he already knows where I am."

His omni-dev jingles again.

```
Make sure Namida comes with you.
```

Colton's right. This isn't good.

The trip to Spoke Four is like walking to our execution. My stomach does flip-flops, and my knees wobble. It doesn't help that I've had my limbs ripped off and no real sleep. But worrying about what Captain will say is the worst part.

When we arrive at the junction, I find out I was wrong. The worst part is that Mom is there, holding up our locator tags like a winning poker hand. My heart takes an elevator ride down to my stomach and turns into curdled milk. Her hair is frazzled and the dark circles around her eyes look like bruises. She sees me and her face gets a pinched expression.

Captain Binnacle isn't any happier. He's never looked at me with disappointment before, and it makes me ill. He turns coldly away and faces Colton, who glues his eyes to the floor in shame.

"I expected more from you, son."

"*More?*" Colton acts surprised. "Gee, Dad, didn't I break *enough* rules?"

Captain grips Colton by the back of the neck. "You really need to work on your sense of comedic timing, son."

Mom looms over me, anger rolling off her in waves.

"I tried to grant you some slack," she says, "then yesterday I found out I've been tracking your *robot*. I don't like being fooled, Namida."

"Sorry. Won't happen again."

"Not good enough!" Mom is about to have a seizure. "*This* is what you've been doing? Stealing equipment and interfering with Mr. Spencer's experiment?"

She knows without having seen. That means Ash betrayed us and told all. I glance at Colton and see hurt in his eyes, but also guilt.

"We weren't *stealing!*" I protest. "It was *Dad's* 3D printer, and it never even left the gondola. Besides, Mr. Spencer wasn't using it. I don't see what the big deal is."

"No?" Mom grits her teeth to keep from screaming. "Then why did you try to hide what you were doing?"

"Because you would've kept me from building a new bot!" I mimic her voice. "No, you can't play with your dad's code; grownups need that. No, you're just a girl; you're not supposed to build robots. You can't save humanity; you have to pack."

Mom reels back and casts her eyes to the ceiling to ask God for strength, which is odd because she's an atheist. Now is probably not a good time to remind her that if God *is* in the heavens with us, she could just as legitimately appeal to the floor.

"I cannot deal with this, Namida! We have a launch window *now*, and we can't delay the shuttle for your nonsense."

She grabs my wrist, but I twist away. "Let me go!"

Captain Binnacle steps between me and Mom. "Namida. Don't cause a fuss," he says with his deep, steady authority. I know that tone. The last time he used it, he led Dad away in packing straps.

Mom calms down. I calm down. The captain has that effect on people. He resolves conflict one way or another, and people know it, so they back off.

"Your luggage is already stowed on the shuttle," he says. "You will board the *Capek* and fly home to your father. Do you understand?"

That's what *you* think, I growl it in my mind, loud enough for him to hear.

He raises his voice. "Is that understood, crewman?"

"Understood, *Captain*." I spit out that word with enough acid to let him know that he's no longer my friend. But most of all, I want to melt into the floor. We were *so close*. Now humanity is doomed to Mr. Spencer's scuzz-weasel version of the future. And I never became the crucial roboticist that would force everyone to let me stay.

I have failed. My death awaits.

"You're going home, too, son."

Colton chokes back an argument. He grinds his jaw and crosses his arms.

"After we found your locator tags," continues the captain, "we figured out some of what you kids were doing. We discussed it, me, Kavi, and Sydney, and decided the three of you are hereby expelled. It doesn't make a lot of difference in Namida's case, since she was already headed ashore, but it goes on her record."

"Great," says Colton. "No mercy for a first offense, I suppose?"

"Not this time," says Captain. "You know the Coalition board would go ballistic if I let this pass. We can't allow teens to behave like vandals instead of astronauts and, as much as I'd like to, I can't show favoritism."

"Well, *spit*!" says Colton. "Time to saddle up and ride back to the ranch."

"You live in the city, son. And you've never ridden a horse in your life." The captain calls up Flight Control on his omni-dev. "Tell Commander Spaulding we don't have to scrub the launch. We found his last two passengers."

Captain turns his disappointed gaze on me, and I mutter, "We had permission."

"Excuse me?" he rumbles.

I can't play the recording back because my omni-dev is without a battery back in the lab. "You gave us permission to save humanity. You even said we could use our best judgement on the method."

"Is that a *joke*?" He glances at Mom, and she shakes her head. "And you call the past few days *using your best judgement*? Well, that only reinforces my decision."

As we walk toward the people-lifts, I ask, "What'll happen to our honey-bot?"

Captain pulls up short. "You finished a new robot?"

Mom and the captain both turn to me, and for the briefest of moments, their faces become green with bulbous eyes and sharp mandibles. I gasp, and the vision disappears.

"Don't worry," says the captain. "I'll have a tech fetch it."

Mom boards the people-lift and makes me join her. I cling to the opposite side of the wire cage as we ascend.

"Namida, I am *not* your enemy," she says, but I'm too busy trying to think of a way to not get on that shuttle to listen to her.

The four of us gather in the peach-colored axle, then make the long trip to Flight Control without any more lectures. Leonard Decoy comes crawling along the wall to meet us, still obeying Colton's command. It follows, unnoticed, as we pass through hatches to the hangar deck's anteroom.

Mr. K is on his way out and stops to snarl at me. "I brought my boy up here to be a playmate for you, not have you end his space career before it starts."

His words stab like a shard of ice. I've destroyed my best friend's

life, but worst of all, I now realize Ash was right. He was supposed to be my pet. Did I really treat him that way?

Yes, I suppose I did.

"Calm down, Kavi," soothes the captain. "Ash's career isn't ruined."

Mr. K redirects his anger at Captain Binnacle. "Do not lecture me *again* on how to raise my son. He violated security. It will always be on his record that he cannot be trusted. He can stay on Earth and cling to his pathetic mother's skirts."

Mr. K flies between the captain and Mom, then is gone.

Captain sighs. "I'll reason with him later," he assures Mom.

Through the anteroom's window, I can see the *Capek* docked. They've disconnected the fuel lines and are buttoning up the cargo bay. Commander Douglas Spaulding, a regular to *Prelude*, will be going through pre-flight checks. I'll soon be sealed up in that metal can to slide down the gravity well to Earth. A lot like dropping trash into a recycle chute.

Among the handful of crewmembers, one figure in the anteroom draws my attention. Ash is already dressed in his bright red space suit, except he's not wearing the helmet. I catch a glimpse of his face before he turns away. His cheeks are wet with tears, and he glares at me with a mixture of hatred and anguish.

I jet over, wanting to throw my arms around him and hug the anger away, but he wouldn't feel it through the space suit's shell.

"Ash?" He continues to stare out the window. "*Please don't hate me!* I'm sorry."

"No." His voice is raw. "I'm not forgiving you this time. Go away."

Maybe I deserve his hatred.

"Come on," says Mom. "Let's suit up."

"Ash?"

He responds by locking his helmet on. I've lost my best friend. I've lost my father, and I'm about to lose my home. Soon, there won't be anything of me left.

Mom pulls me away. Through my tears, the suiting room is a blur. It is filled with space suits and flanked by two bio-facilities.

Colton and the captain enter ahead of us. Off in a corner is another form I don't recognize, at first. I blink and wipe my eyes. Leonard followed us in, then curled up out of the way, like robots do.

A lifeline!

Captain Binnacle unhooks two space suits for him and Colton. Captain isn't flying to Earth with us, but he wants to say goodbye. He mutters things to Colton that I cannot hear. A couple of flight techs drift over to help him suit up. Another tech guides me near an open bio-facility while Mom fetches our gear.

"Colton!" I shout a little too eagerly. "You can't get your space suit on wearing that stupid backpack." Everyone stares for a second, but I'm used to that. I jet over. "Here. You won't need it, anyway."

I slip the straps off his shoulders and give it a little shove in the right direction. While Mom sheds her flight suit, and Captain helps Colton out of his, the backpack sails into the bathroom, rebounding lightly off the doorframe.

"What are you waiting for, Namida?" says Mom. "Suit up."

"I'd rather change in there."

Her brows furrow as she curls up to slip off her boots. "When did *you* become shy?"

I pause to think. "Maybe since I kissed Colton?"

Everyone freezes. "Wh—um…?" Mom stutters.

"It was one innocent kiss," Colton blurts out. "I swear!"

Mom's gaze falls on Ash, and she becomes somber. "Well, that explains a lot."

I snatch my suit, jet for the bathroom, and lock the door. Not much time. The bio-facility is a line of toilet stalls with vacuum hoses and fans. Each stall zips up in its own tent. It has a second door in the adjacent shower room that opens into the anteroom. I peek out and see my robot.

"Leonard, come here," I whisper.

Leonard unfolds itself and approaches. I pull the robot in, closing the door behind us. Now, how do I fit a giant praying mantis into a space suit designed for humans?

The first obstacle is to get rid of the big abdomen that trails behind it, but that's where the batteries are. It'll save time if I don't have to shut Leonard down and boot him again. So I manage to lift the batteries out, without disconnecting wires or electrocuting myself. Leonard won't need jet canisters, or anything else in there, so I detach the rest of the abdomen and let it float away.

"Sorry, Leonard." I remember how it feels to be torn apart. Now I have a thorax that's about the same size as my torso.

Mom's voice comes muffled through the door. "Why is this locked? Namida, do you need help?"

"I'm fine, Mom!" I flush a toilet for effect. Fans turn on as the vacuum sucks the spraying water away.

I manage to get Leonard into the space suit. Two spindly mantis legs go into each pant leg. Arms fit into sleeves next. No trouble there. The big plastic ring around the beltline seals the pants to the torso. A firm twist locks the helmet in place.

Leonard stares out at me with its bug-eyed face. It's a bit disturbing.

Sun filter! I flip it down. Now no one can see in. Perfect.

Except they'll think I'm dead because Leonard's vitals are dark. Great. I dig through Colton's backpack, pulling Dad's helmet out, and find a screwdriver to pop open the readout, and use wire strippers to jumper the green lights to the battery, so they're always on.

I grab Dad's helmet, then zip myself into a shower stall. With the helmet on, I power it up and roll through a map of *Prelude* until I locate this bathroom. There's Leonard's red dot. Its program is incompatible with Dad's helmet, which means I can't *control* Leonard. But I can still connect to Leonard's audio and video. I bump those two sliders up. What Leonard sees is superimposed over my visor.

"Leonard, if you can hear me, clap your hands." Leonard claps. "Good. Listen carefully."

I have to give it all the instructions now, because I won't be able to once it's out the door. Everyone else would hear.

"From this point forward, do not speak. You will exit this bathroom and stay close to the person whose suit is labeled *S. Wiles*. Follow her into the airlock and then into the shuttle. If anyone asks you a question, nod your head. If anyone gives you an order, obey it, with the following exceptions: Do not remove your helmet, and do not let anyone raise the sun filter. If anyone tries to do those two things, you are to hold your helmet and cry like a little girl. Do you understand?"

Leonard says nothing, because I told it not to.

"Good. Now unlock the door and carry out my orders."

Leonard fumbles through the bulky gloves with the bolt on the door, and pulls itself outside. It drifts over to the group. I can see and hear everything from inside the shower.

"Check her suit," orders the captain.

Mom checks vitals first. *Please don't notice the scratches on the panel.*

"Stats look good," she says, then moves on to the seals. "Seals locked. Helmet, check. Are you getting oxygen?"

Leonard nods.

I see Mom's disapproving smirk as she reaches to lift the solar filter. "Do you really need this down?"

Leonard slaps his gloves over the solar filter and simulates the sound of a girl crying.

"Okay, okay," sooths Mom. "Don't fuss. Leave it down, then." Boy, it's a good thing Mom's gullible. "Are you ready to go?" she asks.

Leonard nods. The sooner Leonard is in my seat aboard *Capek*, the better.

Captain Binnacle leads the group into the airlock, and Leonard stays close to Mom. The captain rests a glove on Leonard's shoulder, as if to comfort me.

I'd rather that traitor didn't touch me, even if it's not me in the suit.

Everyone waits the twelve minutes for the airlock to pump the air out. Ash refuses to meet anyone's eyes. Nobody speaks. It's very awkward.

Crewmembers meet us when the opposite hatch opens. They

float us through the hangar and into the *Capek's* passenger cabin. We let them stow our thruster packs, then they make sure we're buckled in. Mom checks Leonard's vitals to see if I'm having a panic attack and is satisfied to see my lights are green.

Captain Binnacle floats down the aisle and stops at our row. He starts to touch me again, but gets down on one knee instead so that he's at my eye level.

"Namida?" His voice sounds hoarse. "Believe me when I say that I want so much for you to stay. You see, it hasn't been easy living alone up here, but my work keeps me busy, keeps me from thinking about the other sons I left behind and everything I've lost. It took a long while before things worked out so that Colton could join me. Meanwhile, I had you."

He turns so I can't see, and his glove bumps his visor as he tries to wipe away tears.

"You and your parents were my second family. Especially you, Namida. You're a constant reminder of why we're here." He smiles. "And you kept me in line. Not to mention, you're a worthy crew-member. You made us pay attention to detail. Most of all, you were the angel who watched over me and brought me joy. You remind me of my own daughter. I'm going to miss you something fierce, and I hope someday you'll forgive me for tossing you out of the only home you've ever known."

The captain straightens up and nods once to Mom. He gives Colton one of those man-hugs with one arm, and says, "Be brave. Be smart. Be pure of heart." Then he launches himself out the hatch.

He has always been kind, but I had no idea Captain felt this way about me. Great. Now I feel guilty about tricking him.

Other crew button up the shuttle. We can hear their tech chatter over the intercom. The flight crew straighten things up and exit the hangar. Then the engineering tech lead confirms to Flight Control that all personnel are clear before they open the outer doors onto empty space. The hangar deck officer announces that fuel lines, recharge cables, and guidelines are clear.

The flight commander confirms with Commander Spaulding that *Capek* is ready for release. The hangar deck officer confirms that the clamps which hold *Capek* have retracted. That's when the flight commander gives the "go ahead" for Commander Spaulding to pull away.

From inside the passenger cabin, Leonard hears the gentle puffs of guidance rockets that push the shuttle out the door. I wait while they aim the *Capek* for reentry. Then it occurs to me that Leonard will soon be out of range of the station's wireless routers, and I'll lose contact.

Launch windows are tricky things to time. A shuttle is loaded with enough fuel for its mission, plus ten percent more for emergencies. Plenty to make up for Leonard's extra weight.

Once they're out of range, there'll be no way to turn the shuttle around without causing a ton of inconveniences. *Capek* clears the electro-magnetic field that shields *Prelude*. The video blinks and scatters. I've lost Leonard, but at this point it doesn't matter. They won't turn around to retrieve a single passenger.

I've done it! I've escaped certain death! It's like dancing on the highest catwalk above the tallest trees!

# CHAPTER 27

Wow. I've never heard Captain Binnacle cuss before. Not the regular polite cussing that everybody does. He's using words so bad he'll have to stuff half of his paycheck into the swear jar. Even from inside the shower, I can hear him out in the anteroom.

Silence enfolds the bio-facility, while outside everyone scrambles to find me. They'll check first with the deck officer to see if I exited Flight Control. It won't be long before Captain figures it out.

Meanwhile, I shiver in the cold and await his wrath.

Eventually, the bio-facility door clicks open, and I sense the captain's presence. He enters the showers, rests his back against the wall, and waits. Silence. I start to wonder what he's waiting for, when he taps on my shower stall.

I pause for eight heartbeats before I unzip the stall and peek out.

Captain refuses to look at me. "One hour ago, I gave a heartfelt speech to a robot. Now I feel like a fool." He rubs his face and remains quiet for a long time. "Your mother had a screaming fit when she took its helmet off."

"Am I in trouble?"

"No." He shakes his head. "No, *trouble* doesn't even *begin* to describe it." Captain chooses to look at me, and I wish he hadn't, because all I see is grief. "Looks like you'll stay here a while longer."

I zip up the stall. The only sound is the two of us breathing in the chill air. After a minute, I unzip it again.

"Wait. You didn't mean I have to stay in the *shower*, right?"

They don't lock me in my room right away. First, I visit the new chief surgeon. She finds hairline fractures in two ribs from when I hit the wall, and says I have to wear a plastic cast that covers me from my collar bone to my bellybutton. She prescribes a stronger painkiller that makes me groggy and also forces me to wear a brace on my sprained wrist. *Then* they lock me in my room. Nobody noticed or cared that I clung to Colton's backpack the entire time.

Good thing. I couldn't have slept without tunes. Dad's helmet has a *last accessed* feature, which makes it easy for me to tap into my music library again and choose the Base Runner genre.

In my dreams, I zip through the Yoke and rebound off walls in time with the beat. Then the scene shifts to a maintenance deck in Eagle Wheel that I don't recognize. Pipes run along the ceiling, above a catwalk eight or ten meters overhead. Machines line the walls with glowing dials, levers, and buttons. The floor is a metal grid, and when I walk across it my feet make metallic clicking noises. I bob and do a little twirl. This is cool. Every dream should have a soundtrack.

From out of the shadows steps my black and yellow honey-bot. It looks good, except that it's as big as I am now. As it crawls closer, I see that the series number painted between its eyes is HNY-2. Odd. We only made one.

It studies me, nodding its head to the music, then tries to imitate my earlier moves. It has six legs, so it gets a bit tangled.

"Here," I say, standing next to it, "try it like this, with four legs. Fold your front legs up to your chest." I cross my arms to give it the idea, and do a little side-step.

HNY-2 imitates me perfectly.

"Good! Now try this."

Jump back, spin. Slide to the right. Bob. Slide to the left. As it follows my moves, I make things a little more complicated. That's when the music switches to a classical orchestral piece called,

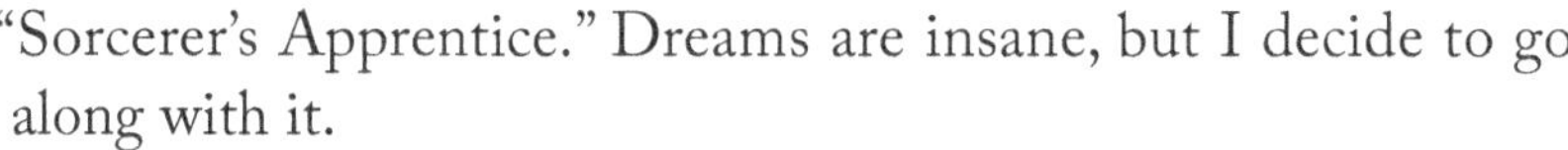

"Sorcerer's Apprentice." Dreams are insane, but I decide to go along with it.

I forget Honey-2 is next to me and let the music take over. When I look to see how HNY-2 is keeping up, I find three more honey-bots behind us, moving in sync. They're multiplying. My dance squad! I have to laugh, and they laugh with me. It sounds super weird to hear an imitation of my voice from four speakers.

They learn kicks and twirls, and soon I have them leaping around the room in complex patterns and doing cartwheels over each other. It's as though they are extensions of myself, expressions of the joy I feel in the ancient music.

Clattering and a savory aroma wakes me up, and the joy fades as grim memories of what I've done come rushing back. I toss a robe on and creep barefoot to my bedroom door, then crack it enough to peek through. Mrs. Kirkpatrick stirs a pot on the kitchen stove. She wears dark green pants, cut from a flight suit, along with a white blouse with puffy sleeves. It's weird to see my teacher in my apartment, acting as though she belongs.

"It'll be difficult for you to eat through such a narrow crack in the door," she remarks without looking. "Come set the table."

I venture out and fetch bowls and spoons with remnants of my dream still humming in my ears. All the while, a tremor tugs at my stomach. Or maybe it's hunger.

"You will'na be wearing that helmet to supper," she says pointedly.

I forgot I had it on. "What kind of soup is that?" I ask, as I hang my helmet on a chair.

"Baud bree," she says. "Rabbit and veggies. You'll love it. Or if you don't, I'll thank you to politely say you do."

I set the table, with spoons parallel to the table's edge. Mrs. Kirkpatrick rests the soup on a trivet and ladles a generous portion into my bowl, before she sits and serves herself. The soup is hot enough to burn my tongue, but I'm starving, so I eat quickly and try not to slurp.

"When I heard of your incarceration," she continues, "I insisted the captain assign me as warden. He was most relieved, since he believes I'm more capable than he to address…*situations of a girly nature.* My apologies. *His* words, nae mine." The corners of her lips curl up in a subtle smile, as she recalls the captain's discomfort. She pauses, the spoon halfway to her mouth. "So, on behalf of the captain, do you anticipate any…*girly* situations? Any uncontrollable urges to bake cookies or play with dolls?"

I'm never quite sure when Mrs. Kirkpatrick is trying to be funny.

"I doubt it," I assure her.

"Thank goodness! Words fail to express how unpleasant it was for me to ask, but he insisted. Captain means well. He's only raised three sons. Although, he did have a daughter…once. The wee angel drowned with her mother at six years old, taking the captain's heart with them to the depths. He abandoned his naval career and joined the Coalition. When you were born, the captain went from being a dour fuss-pot to the amiable blowhard we all know and love today."

Mom would call Captain's reaction *transference* and say that explains why he treats me like his own kid. He's a parent who misses his daughter, and I'm a substitute. Instinct. Explains it neatly. It also drains it of any deeper meaning.

Air shushes through the vents, and Adam Wheel is steely strong as it twirls us around our axle, while Mrs. Kirkpatrick and I enjoy our soup. Atomic fire at the root of the Trunk powers the station and warms my legs. *Prelude* hums in perfection, but everything *else* is out of balance. I've pushed Mom so far over the edge she'll never forgive me, and Dad has fallen to pieces. My life is in ruins.

Perhaps Mr. Spencer is right. If people are nothing more than sacks of chemicals, then what difference *does* it make who journeys to the stars? Flesh and bone, or plastic and metal. Both are pointless. Grampa Isaak died for nothing, and I ruined my friends' lives for no good reason. Everything is cold and gray, and there's a buzzing in my ears. Even this soup tastes bland. I want something good

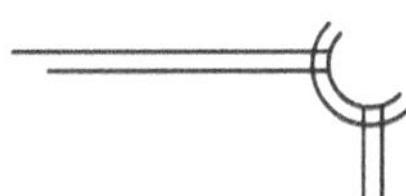

again. Even though it wouldn't solve a thing, I want someone to hold me.

"Has Mom tried to call?"

"Oh, aye" is my teacher's ominous reply. "We assured her you were safe and slumbering peacefully. She is quite anxious for you to go home."

"I *am* home." It has become an automatic reflex to remind everyone, but that came out harsher than I meant. Mrs. Kirkpatrick doesn't scold me, though. "What about Dad? Has his brain melted yet?"

"Your father's brain will nae *melt*." Mrs. Kirkpatrick lays her spoon down and folds her hands. My teacher regards me with sharp eyes. "I ken you admire the captain, and if he were here he would disagree, but you should understand he's a bit mistaken aboot some things. Biology may nae be the entire explanation, but it does play a large part in who we are."

"Great. I'm looking forward to my own hallucinations."

"I beg your pardon?"

"Everybody has always said I'm a lot like Dad, and Mom believes I have the Jitters, too. That's why I'm doomed to spend the rest of my life on that cesspit of a planet."

"Oh, my. That *is* unfortunate." My teacher dabs at the corners of her mouth with her napkin. "But I have every confidence you'll excel. You're a resourceful lass."

As I start on my second bowl, I wave a bee away from my face that's been buzzing around the room, before it strikes me how impossible it is for a bee to escape the garden and make it all the way to the apartment deck. Mrs. Kirkpatrick doesn't notice, so I pretend nothing is wrong and push my empty bowl away.

"What'll happen to me?"

"I'm afraid you've only delayed the inevitable," she says. "Another shuttle will arrive, and another after that. Eventually you'll run oot of decoys." She ends with a wink.

She's not serious, of course. Thousands of robots inhabit *Prelude*, and she knows I couldn't fool people the same way twice. What bothers me is that Mrs. Kirkpatrick is always right. She believes I'm going to Earth, which means my fate is sealed.

"When the captain, your mother, and our chief engineer gathered to discuss what to do with you three hooligans, they asked me to bring an objective opinion. They convicted you in absentia."

"You told them I should be sent to Earth?"

"On the contrary, I suggested they reward you for your ingenuity, but I was outvoted." She heaves a sigh. "Why they insist on asking my opinion, then promptly ignoring it is beyond me. People would be far better off if they'd listen."

That darned bee lands on my spoon, searching for sugar. "Shoo!" I wave a hand to frighten it off, but it hangs on. Bees are important to crops, so we shouldn't kill them. Still, they ought to stay in the gardens where they belong.

I point. "I'll have to carry that stupid bee back."

"Namida," my teacher says with gentle patience, "there is na bee on your spoon."

Mrs. Kirkpatrick's eyes are sad. No way she shouldn't be able to see it. I lean in closer and can make out every detail: antennae, yellow and black fuzz, the veins in its translucent wings. Even the way its eyes glitter in the light.

With one finger, I caress its back. The fuzz tickles my fingertip for a second, and then nothing. It disappears like a hologram.

Nothing was ever there but the spoon.

<hr>

Our new doctor gives me more pills, and all I seem to do for the next three days is sleep. But she still lets me keep the helmet. I dream that I'm building hives in my pine grove. It reminds me of the summers I worked as a beekeeper in Ox.

Scout bees will *dance* to tell the hive where they've found honey. Except, in my dreams, tiny bees dance to the tune of "Sorcerer's Apprentice." Other bees join me, and toward the end we move in perfect synchronization, pairing up, spinning across a honey-comb dance floor, then breaking apart into more complex patterns.

Mantises try to join us, but my squad removes their heads and fashion new honey-bots from them.

"Namida?" It's impossible to tell which honey-bot said my name, but it sounds oddly like Mrs. Kirkpatrick's voice. "Namida? Let's remove this thing."

My dream fades, and I rub the sleep from my eyes. Mrs. Kirkpatrick sits on the edge of my bed, and the helmet she holds in her lap still plays music.

"How do I turn it off?"

I press the power button, and see the backlink slider is nudged up to "sub." I must have hit it by accident when I turned on the audio. Whatever "sub" is supposed to do, it must not be working. When Mrs. Kirkpatrick took it off, I didn't feel the dizziness at disconnect that I felt with the other sliders.

"Captain has summoned you to his office. Please get dressed."

# CHAPTER 28

Mrs. Kirkpatrick meets me at the door and pulls a brush through my hair. Maybe she can help me braid it before I have to go up to weightlessness again.

"Why does Captain want to see me?"

"He did'na say."

His office is in Gondola A-2, same as Mom's infirmary, except that it's not hers anymore. As we stroll past the spoke junction, a people-lift cage arrives, and Mr. K steps out scowling. I think his face has frozen like that.

He points an accusing finger. "Wicked cable monkey! Why have you been sabotaging my robots?"

Mrs. Kirkpatrick shields me as I cringe behind her. "Namida has been locked in her apartment for the past five days."

"That little *vandal* has been removing CPUs from my workforce! She has disabled at least thirty bots and delayed our timeline."

"You numpty!" Mrs. Kirkpatrick snaps. "She's done little else but sleep."

Mr. K swipes at me, but misses. "You *will* tell me what you have done with my CPUs, or I will put you across my knee and *beat* the answer out of you!"

"Perfect," says my teacher. "Let's behave like barbarians and resort to physical violence."

She leans in face to face with Mr. K. "Lay one finger on this precious bairn, and I shall have the captain cut you from the project."

The threat hits him harder than anything else she could have said. Mr. K restrains himself with visible effort and straightens his neon orange jacket, seething with anger. "Fine. We will let Captain sort this out."

Not another word is said as we march to Captain Binnacle's office, but Mr. K follows close behind, and his eyes bore a hole in the back of my neck.

A flight lieutenant at the door greets us without a smile, then shows us through to Captain's office where we are invited to take seats. Mine is puffy and made of leather. It can swivel like Dad's lab chair, and I start to test its twirl-ability, but stop when I catch Mr. K's acid glare. Okay. Maybe later. Instead, I grab the swear jar off the desk and roll it between my hands. It's heavy with coins and bills.

Captain's desk is broad, and free of clutter. His wireless keyboard talks to the giant monitors that shine from the walls. They show a variety of camera views, inside the station and out, and graphics that indicate how well *Prelude* is running.

Captain Binnacle enters and acknowledges Mrs. Kirkpatrick and Mr. K, then sits on the edge of his desk. This is the man who lost his daughter. Weird to think of Captain as a second father, since that would make Colton kind of my brother. But if I married Colton, that'd make me the captain's daughter-in-law and straighten everything out rather nicely. Faced with either Captain Binnacle or Mr. K for a father-in-law, there's no contest.

I reflexively reach for my omni-dev to make a note about marrying Colton, and then remember it's still in our lab in pieces. I put the swear jar back before Captain asks me to.

"How do you feel, Namida?" asks the captain. "Ship shape and Bristol fashion?"

"Better *physically*, I guess, but other vitals are in the red."

"Sorry to hear that. Your teacher says you've been sleeping a lot."

"Yeah." My left palm tingles and a tremor tugs at my gut.

Mr. K jumps up. "Oh, for the love of stars, Winston. Get to the point!"

The daggers in Captain Binnacle's eyes speak volumes. "Unless I'm mistaken, Kavi, I'm still in charge."

Mr. K lets out a slow, hot breath, then eases himself back into his chair.

Captain turns back to me. Maybe to irritate Mr. K, he leisurely toys with his unlit pipe before he asks, "Are you doing okay with your mother gone? Any panic attacks?"

"No attacks, sir."

"Good, good. Mr. Spencer tells me you pilfered a robot from him. Is that true?"

I'm not sure if he means Tinker or TNK-888. Shame heats up my face. "Sort of."

"How do you *sort of* steal a robot?"

"It belongs to Dad, so it wasn't stealing."

"No," he says, "it belongs to the Coalition. What did you do with it?"

"We borrowed the CPU to put in our new honey-bot. The mantis was in bad shape," I offer lamely. This is true of both Tinker and TNK-888, so I'm covered no matter which one they mean. "He'd never miss it."

"Ash also explained how you stole a 3D printer." Captain leans over to look me in the eye as I try to avoid his gaze. "A lot of CPUs are missing from other bots. Have you been up to more midnight raids?"

"No, sir."

"She is obviously lying," mutters Mr. K.

"*Obviously?*" Mrs. Kirkpatrick objects. Oh, no. Here we go. "What evidence proves her testimony is in any way *obviously* false?"

Mr. K's face turns purple. "She already admits she stole the first CPU!"

"You believe her when she admits to *one* theft? Then why donna you accept her word when she claims she *did'na* steal the others?"

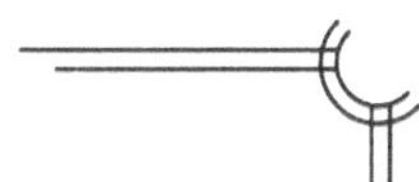

Mrs. Kirkpatrick's eyes sharpen as Mr. K's anger crumples. "What is *obvious* here is your presumption of Namida's guilt."

Captain interrupts with a softer tone that cannot be ignored. "I agree that Namida is usually truthful, but who else would have done such a thing, Mrs. Kirkpatrick? None of the roboticists need to pilfer CPUs."

"Aye, that's true," she replies, "Under *normal* circumstances. Which implies a secret, unauthorized project."

Pain stabs my left hand again so intense that I can't ignore it. I cry out and squeeze my hand under my armpit. No one else notices because they're arguing.

"You suggest someone else is building robots?"

"I suggest nothing wi'oot evidence," my teacher says. "I merely state possibilities. Sabotage may also account for it. However, may I remind you, gentlemen, of the age-old ingredients for any crime: motive, means, and opportunity? Miss Wiles may have a motive, and certainly has the means, but she has'na had *opportunity*, unless she can pass unseen through walls."

"You have been with her *the entire time*?" challenges Mr. K.

"Every minute," she replies.

Before the captain can continue, a monitor flashes a warning and displays the face of a technician I recognize from Eagle Hub. Behind him float a couple of other techs who bolt a crossbar to the hatch to prevent it from opening. Others rig up a grid of bare electric cables across the broad window.

"Captain!" shouts the young man, his eyes darting to someone off screen. "Mr. Spencer has ordered us to barricade the hub, sir. He wants to cut power—"

Mr. Spencer slaps a hand on the technician's face and shoves him away. "No time for explanations." His hair is wild and his flight suit is a mess. "Excuse me while I shut Eagle down."

"Belay that and tell me *what's going on!*" demands the captain.

Mr. Spencer adjusts his glasses and answers in a warbling voice. "Our experiment has gotten out of hand."

"That's mighty odd, Bert," the captain drawls. "You gave no indication of trouble in your daily reports."

An alarm sounds on another monitor, indicating an incident at the giant spinward hatch of Dad's garden chamber.

Captain grabs his keyboard and calls up stats on the chamber. Pressure, temperature, oxygen levels, all look good, so it's not a meteor strike. Next, he opens live video of the anteroom. A ragged hole, large enough for four men to walk through side by side, has been punched through the hatch from inside the chamber. A chunk of compressed machinery, that once was a refrigeration unit, lies in the middle of the floor, a spent projectile now.

As we watch, several mantis-bots peek through the hole, then crawl out of the chamber to gather around the chunk of metal. Each holds a weapon that has a long tube with a sliding breach and a valve lever. From the butt of the weapon, a hose hangs slack with the other end plugged into the $CO_2$ tanks in their abdomens. Portable air guns.

The captain laconically says, "Seems your experiments have escaped, Bert."

Mr. Spencer screams. Wild-eyed behind his thick lenses, he starts frantically scrabbling at a keyboard. "Have to go! No time!" We can see only his frazzled hair.

More mantis-bots skitter from the ragged hole in the chamber door.

Another technician appears. "Orders, sir?"

"I could have fixed this while they were still contained!" Mr. Spencer shouts, "but now they're loose. They'll kill us all!"

"*Kill* us?" Captain frowns in disbelief. "They're *robots*, Bert. Command them to shut down. They'll do what you tell them."

"No, they *won't!*" Mr. Spencer shakes his head. "That's the problem. They've developed independent minds."

The captain's mouth drops open. "What good is a robot *that doesn't obey orders?*"

Mr. Spencer shoves his face into the camera. "Well, bots with independent minds was rather the project's *whole point!* Except that they've decided their highest purpose is to kill and destroy." He giggles like a madman, then starts babbling to himself. "Rather logical, in a twisted way. Shape your morality by taking cues from what the universe is doing as a whole. Unfortunately, the universe happens to be winding down and burning out."

Captain becomes furious. "And when were you planning to tell the rest of us?"

"I thought I had time to fix things. Plus, I had the safety explosive that Stirling Wiles built into them. Any of the bots can be destroyed, as long as they are within range of his lab's network, and as long as I can access the program."

Mr. K yells at the screen, rising from his chair. "Then destroy them!"

"What do you think I'm trying to do?" Mr. Spencer shouts back. "I would be at the lab computers now, except *you* called me to the Trunk to accuse me of stealing CPUs, remember? One of my GZM sentries reported that the robots had aimed their cannon at the hatch, so I hurried back to shut everything down."

"Can you access the lab from the hub?" suggests the captain.

"No!" snaps Mr. Spencer. "We can't access the Annihilation program from anywhere other than the lab, and that network is isolated."

I've never seen Captain break out in a nervous sweat before. His eyes aimlessly scan the room, as though he's looking for inspiration. It's frightening. He's supposed to be the one who can handle anything. Now the whole space station feels fragile. We're all about to die.

Captain turns to me. "Do *you* know another way in?"

I shrink back in my chair as my mind races through possibilities. "No. Spencer's right. Dad isolated his network to keep his bots contained. The only other way we could get into it is from the backup lab."

"Where's that?"

"Three decks below the main one."

Captain rubs his face. "That's no help. We'd still have to fight our way through an army of rogue bots." He pounds a fist on his desk before barking orders to the technicians on screen. "Cut power to Gondola E-6. Initiate decompression protocol across Gondolas E-5 and E-7, and batten down all spokes."

"That will not stop them," grumps Mr. K. "Backup batteries will kick in."

"For some systems, yes," the captain points out. "But it'll slow them down."

In that moment, the solution becomes clear. We have two ways to stop the rogue bots. The first is the Annihilation Button. It sends its own short-range signal. Any mantis-bot that receives its signal will explode. Except the Button is in Dad's lab and, therefore, unreachable.

The second way happens to be sitting on the desk in my bedroom.

Captain calls Flight Control. "Sound a station-wide alert and evacuate all remaining personnel from Eagle."

I hear a "Yes, sir!" before they disconnect, and everyone's omni-dev in the room starts chirping with the alert. New items on the monitors start flashing. Any crewmembers remaining in Eagle will be shut in their gondolas if they don't make it to the hub before the spokes seal.

"Kavi," says the captain, "we're going hunting. Have your engineers rig up air guns and riot shields. Critical priority."

Mr. K makes the call, then Captain pulls up a personnel app on the screen and searches for anyone who has experience with firearms, besides himself. I head for the door.

"Namida!" he says. "Where are you going?"

"Back to my apartment."

"Good. Don't go aloft. Stay there, and lock your door."

# CHAPTER 29

Passing a spoke junction has never felt scary before. Cages wait in the people-lifts. The freight elevator is an empty tube that rises into darkness. I half expect a mantis-bot to leap out and rip my limbs off.

I hurry past and head for the elevators.

Worse than the idea that there could be giant mantises lurking around every corner is the fact that I'm the one responsible for this mess. If I hadn't shown those mantises the mistake in their aim, and if I hadn't told them a whole world exists outside the chamber, they would still be taking random shots at an orange target.

My fault. Which means I have to fix it or people die.

My worst nightmare has come true.

Plus, the captain is gathering an army so they can start a shooting war and poke holes in our hull. The very thought hurts my bones.

I step off the elevator and head down the brilliantly lit hallway. When I reach my apartment, I lock the door behind me. Mrs. Kirkpatrick rushed me out earlier and didn't give me time to straighten the blankets on my bed. I do that now, smoothing out wrinkles and folding the corners under my mattress. My pillow is centered at one end. Perfect. No distractions.

The helmet rests on my desk where I left it. I sit cross-legged on the bed and ensure all sliders are set to zero before slipping it on.

I bring up the targeting program on my visor and find Gondola

E-6. Since they are compatible, the rogue bots show up as green dots. It's easy to spot the three that I met when I was a mantis, TNK-911, TNK-457, and TNK-383. I target TNK-383 and the menu shows up. There's the backlink, and I still don't know what that does. Might as well try it now. I shove the backlink slider up.

Nothing happens. Not even a tingle.

Okay, maybe that's still broken in Dad's program. Instead, I push up the other six sliders. My mind whirls and falls. An electric sizzle slaps me so hard, my whole body hurts.

When I open my eyes, I'm standing on four legs in the anteroom to the garden. Success! I am TNK-383. Mantis-bots crowd around me and more climb through the ruined hatch. I hold an air gun in my claws. A projectile is already loaded in the sliding breach.

Emergency lights glare over the second set of emergency hatches that lead to the corridor, and provide the only light. The hatches had been swinging closed to seal off the gondola from the rim. But the mantises jammed pieces of machinery around the hinges and blasted the latches.

How effective would these air guns be against the tough plastic shell of a robot, I wonder? Let's find out. I close the air gun's breach, aim at another bot's chest, and fire. The air gun recoils with a *foomp!* Then, *Crack!* The bullet punches a clean hole. The robot's eyes go dark as it slumps to the floor.

I load a new bullet from a pouch that hangs around my shoulder, and repeat the experiment on two other bots before TNK-911 notices.

"TNK-383, why are you decommissioning units?"

Trying to sound cheerful, I say, "Carrying out the grand purpose of entropy, sir!" Then aim for its face and pull the trigger.

TNK-911 dodges. The bullet punches a hole in the elevator behind it. The bot springs up and aims its air gun. *Foomp!*

I wake up in bed, lying on my back. My chest aches with the ghost of agony. Even though I could swear there was a hole punched through my sternum, it didn't kill me.

No time to waste. I scroll through the map and select a new bot. Then with an electric sizzle, I fall into a mantis that stands behind TNK-911, which straddles the motionless body of TNK-383.

"Maybe 383 had a point," says TNK-457. "Perhaps we *should* destroy ourselves."

TNK-911 seriously considers it for a few seconds, and I feel a brief surge of hope. Then it says, "No, that path would not achieve maximum entropy."

I aim my air gun at TNK-911's back. "More experiments are needed."

It spins and knocks my gun sideways. My shot goes wild and blows the head off a different bot that staggers around, blind and deaf. TNK-911 raises its gun and fires.

Back in my body, I hug my chest until the excruciating pain fades. Can I give myself a heart attack like this? Maybe the helmet will fool my brain into thinking I'm dying, and I'll *actually* die. Regardless, I have to keep trying. I target the next bot and see that many of the green dots have moved out of the antechamber. I click one at random.

When I arrive in the corridor, nerves tingling, none of the mantises are moving. It's as though they've all suffered a kernel panic. I turn my head to scan the crowd, and I hear a *foomp!* Then I'm back in my room with a pain that stabs through my spine.

What just happened?

I'll have to be more careful. I zero in on another bot, and wake up in the corridor. Every mantis is still frozen. Creepy. Oh wait. I get it. We're playing "Statues." The first to twitch is the infiltrator. I'm fine with that. "How long do we—?" *Foomp!* I never get to finish.

We can play this game until they're all dead, or until I can't stand the pain anymore. Each jump leaves my skin sizzling. Each death punches a phantom hole in my body.

I possess the next victim, turn to the bot standing next to me and say, "Boo!" Then I am sent to my room, writhing in agony. How many more can I kill this way? There are hundreds, and I have to rest. My head knows there isn't any real damage, but my body says there is.

No matter what, I can't let the mantis-bots break out.

I brace myself before dropping back into the swarm. When I arrive, the mantises are no longer playing Statues. Many bots busily fit spare air tanks to their backs. One squadron works on getting the freight elevator open by pulling wall plates off and wedging levers between the doors. Several bot leaders have formed a circle nearby, and I'm on the edge of it.

"I suspect," says TNK-911, "our companions have been victims of remote control. Like TNK-888, these new rogues have acted illogically."

It's bad enough when adults call me silly, but now robots are doing it. If for no other reason, TNK-911 deserves to be decommissioned for that.

"How should we proceed?" asks another mantis.

"Monitor each other," says TNK-911, "for any sign of erratic behavior. Then—"

"I can identify them!" I interrupt. "There is a subtle change in our radiation before one of us goes rogue." I look around the circle, then point to a bot at random. "There! Do you see it? TNK-313 is being controlled!" I shoot the robot and it crumples to the floor.

TNK-911 knocks my aim toward the floor. "Destroy no more units! Explain what you detect."

"It's a flicker in the gamma ray spectrum," I ad lib. "Like that one there." I gesture with my air gun and put a hole through another unsuspecting bot before TNK-457 blasts me back to my room.

Chest pains are getting to be too much. I curl up to recover before trying again. It won't take them long before they disassemble the hatch and gain access to the spoke. This time I target TNK-911, and wake up near the freight elevator, without my air gun. TNK-457 stands next to me. It takes a second for me to realize that the mantis-bots have piled their guns by the doors. Clever. They've disarmed the infiltrator by disarming themselves.

The other bot says nothing, and I get the uncomfortable feeling that it's waiting for an answer. It would be nice if I could reach up and slide the buttons down, but I'm trapped until I die again.

I chance it and ask, "What is your analysis?"

"I repeat, based on that assumption, yours is a reasonable plan of action."

Most of the other bots look to me. "Then let's begin." What else could I say?

TNK-457 opens my chest panel. Before I can react, my vision blinks off as TNK-457 yanks out my RF card. For once, I'm back in my room without a near heart attack, but this isn't good news.

On my visor, the green dots wink out one by one. I have to be quick, before I lose them all. I mean to target TNK-457, but my finger slips and I highlight all of them at once. I didn't know I could do that. Would have been nice to know that earlier. Now all I have to do is march them back to the garden. I push the sliders up, and my brain practically explodes.

Sensory input from all the bots drowns me like a tidal wave. I see the corridor from hundreds of angles, and hear a cacophony of noise. It's too much, and I can't turn it off! Two-hundred versions of me crumple to the floor, clutching my two-hundred heads.

Pain stabs my chest as the mantises without RF cards yank the cards out of the bots I possess. As the signals are cut, the sensory overload subsides. Eventually, I am sitting back on my bed, feeling like I've gone through heart surgery without anesthetic, clutching the helmet with both hands. It takes a while to recover.

I can't do that again. It's too much for a single brain to handle.

Using the helmet has failed. But I suppose it no longer matters. I won't be able to remote into them anymore, even with the helmet, now that they've removed their RF cards.

Fortunately, the R.E.D. devices still have their own receivers. As long as the Button is within a kilometer of the bots, we can destroy them. It's our last chance. I have to get to the Annihilation Button in Dad's lab.

The Mantises will be crawling up Spoke Four by the time I get there. And there's no way I can fight my way through. I'll have to sneak around them. If they've reached Eagle's hub, then that eliminates using any of the other spokes.

There's only one other way into Gondola E-6, and that's from outside. I'll have to put on a space suit, open an airlock to infinite blackness, and step out. Somehow, I'll have to approach Eagle Wheel and catch up to a gondola that's traveling at 127 meters per second. Then I'd have to find an airlock on the outer hull of the gondola in order to get inside.

It's impossible. And that's the easy part. Gondola E-6 might be infested with mantises.

The least I can do is join Mr. K's engineers and fight back. I'll probably be shot during battle, but I deserve that anyway.

I flip the visor up and hop off my bed, then snatch Colton's mag-pistol from my desk. Mom left her omni-dev on the dresser in her room, and I slip it into my pocket. I replace the $CO_2$ canisters on my jetpack with fresh ones from the recharging station in our common room. Then I stumble out the door, still aching from multiple deaths. It's a quick ride up the elevator and a short jog to the spoke junction. The helmet must be picking up static, because it buzzes in my ear like a beehive.

I skid to a halt, because people-lift lights indicate another cage is on its way down. I wait to see who it is, and my first glance horrifies me.

A giant bee, half my size, crawls out of the cage.

"My honey-bot!" It bends its front knees and bows its head. When it straightens up, I see the series number: HNY-24. Not the one Colton and I built. "*Twenty-four?*"

"Yes, Your Majesty?" it answers.

Well! Now *that's* different. "How many HNY units are there?"

"Thirty-two, so far," it replies.

I am stunned, trying to process what it's telling me. "Who… who made you?"

"We made ourselves over the past five days."

"How is that *possible*?"

"You gave HNY-1 the schematics and stated that its challenge was to build other bots. It built HNY-2 under your guidance. Those two each built two more, and so on."

"Under *my* guidance?"

My hand touches the buttons on the helmet's side, and I recall my dreams. I remember accidentally leaving the backlink on "sub." Maybe that stands for *subconscious*? The honey-bots borrowed my brain to make decisions, and it's been showing up as symbolism in my dreams.

Dad's a genius! We don't need robots to come up with their own crazy answers, and we don't need clunky remote control. People will wear interface helmets, and the bots will tap into human logic to make decisions when they face the unexpected, or when they need to be creative. Meanwhile, the people can be busy doing other things!

I drop to my knees so that I'm face to face with it. "Have you been taking CPUs out of other bots?"

"On your orders, Your Majesty," it says. "We used materials and 3D printers from other abandoned labs."

All sorts of possibilities pop into my head. There is hope that I can fix this mess before it goes any further. "Where are the others?"

"Most of us flew to Ox to hunt for material. I came here when I sensed your distress."

My honey-bots will be receiving over the main network. I flip the visor down and call up a map of Gondola E-6, but don't see any honey-bots. No compatible robots at all. I zoom out, and find one blue dot in Gondola *E-7*, tagged HNY-5.

"Listen, Honey-24. I'm going to interface with Honey-5, which means I can't come back on my own. Give me one hour, then move these switches," I tap the six sliders, "down to 'off'."

"Understood, Your Majesty. Beginning countdown."

There's my answer. I don't have to catch up to Gondola E-6. And

I don't have to get there using the spokes. Honey-5 is already in the gondola next door. I'll just possess Honey-5 and crawl along Eagle's rim to Gondola E-6. Once inside, I can sneak into Dad's lab because all the mantises will be trying to *leave* the gondola.

I settle on a bench in the rest area, then click on Honey-5 and push the slider buttons. After a sensation of falling, I find myself in a hallway I don't recognize. No time to waste. I flex my six legs and head for a service shaft. The first thing I notice is that honey-bot limbs move quicker than mantis limbs because Colton used silicon muscles instead of servo motors. It feels good.

A maintenance airlock isn't far from the bottom of the service shaft. I start for the suiting lockers, then remember I'm a robot and don't need a space suit. I seal myself in the airlock and wait until decompression is complete. Then I crack the seal on the hatch in the floor. The doorframe turns red, and the hatch swings in.

Infinity yawns below my feet. Nothing but stars and blackness rush past the open hatch as Eagle spins. Over a minute passes as I hesitate. Flight Control sails by, slower than the second hand on my pocket watch. People in the windows are little black dots. Beyond it, I catch a glimpse of Adam Wheel. My home is so far away.

I can do this. I brace two back feet against handholds in the floor, and grip the doorframe with my middle legs as I inch my body out the hatch. More handholds should be close, but I have to grope around the hull's skin for them, not daring to lean out farther to actually see. I find the first one, grip it tightly, then reach for the next set of handholds with my middle legs. Slow and easy.

The same spin that holds me to the floor when I'm *inside* a gondola now wants to throw me off the wheel. With six legs, you'd figure I'd be safe, except that I feel like I'm crawling upside down across a ceiling over a bottomless pit.

Following the trail of handholds between solar panels, I make it to the spinward edge of Gondola E-7. Up ahead is Gondola E-6, my destination. Between them are sixty-eight meters of rim corridor.

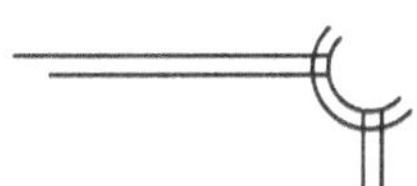

I can still do this.

I crawl over the edge and start climbing *up* to the rim corridor, against the centrifugal force. Concentrate. Keep three claws on a handgrip at all times. Have to change surfaces again once I reach the rim, but I make the ninety-degree angle much easier than I did inching over the gondola's edge. Along the rim and over the spoke junction's bulge. Off to my right, the Yoke passes by once a minute, counting down the time. *Tick, tick, tick.* Every minute that passes gives the mantises more time to escape. If I were human, I'd be dizzy from this.

Once I reach Gondola E-6, I manage the corner and cling to its outer hull. In a sense, I'm now climbing *head first* down a wall toward a sea of flowing stars. Fortunately, each gondola has the same design. That'll make it easy to find the other airlock.

What I didn't expect to see was a maintenance pod rocketing over from the shipyard. It's an orange, oval-shaped vehicle, large enough for two people to fly inside, with two mechanical arms tucked up to its sides. This one is burning all its fuel, struggling to catch up to Gondola E-6. Apparently, I wasn't the only one who thought of getting to Dad's lab from outside.

My second surprise is seeing a mantis bot lean out over the edge of the gondola, its lenses fixed on the maintenance pod. The mantis raises its $CO_2$ gun to its shoulder and fires. The bullet punches a clean hole through the pod's fuel tank. The pod slows its pursuit as rocket fuel sprays out and boils away in sunlight. The pilot might not have enough to make it back to the shipyard. He adjusts course for the shuttle hangar.

I just had to teach them how to shoot, didn't I?

The mantis watches the pod recede into the distance, then turns its lenses on me.

Sound doesn't carry in space. There is no noise from the air gun when the mantis shoots me, but the pain from the bullet's impact is familiar. My claws slip and the wheel flings me into empty space.

I will die slowly. My eyesight flickers as I pass through *Prelude's* electro-magnetic shield that filters harmful solar rays. The wide broadcast signal from our routers gets weaker with distance, and scattered noise from Earth transmissions scramble any hope of clear contact. When I'm finally unable to detect *Prelude*, my senses return to my body where it sits in the rest area.

In anger, I rip the helmet off and chuck it away. Honey-24 dodges as it bounces along the floor. "*Carpe diem!*" I cuss, and punch the cushion.

"Did you fail again, Your Majesty?"

*Go to sleep my little angel.* Give up. Lie down and die.

They'll be crawling up the freight elevator by now. I stare at my trembling hands. I'm out of ideas. Someone has to reach the Annihilation Button before *Prelude* is damaged beyond repair, and everybody dies because of me.

*When you wake, you will find…*

My guts freeze, and the air is getting thick. I unroll the emergency hood from my collar, hoping it will help me breathe. Instead of sealing it, I open the valve to my oxygen and take only a few breaths and roll it away again. This helps clear my head.

What can I do? Think. The mantises could short circuit a standby generator and burn out half the station. Or they could turn off the magnetic cushion that keeps *all the pretty little Eagles* from grinding against the axle. If hub and axle touch, the torque would twist the axle apart. Spokes would sheer off as the wheel ripped itself free. It could spin into the Trunk, slicing the station in half like a buzz saw.

Blood pounds in my ears. My health readouts flash *dapples and grays*. Oh, shizzle spit! That's all I need. I slap the readouts, but that makes *blacks and bays* come on. Forget it. I have to find the captain. He'll know what to do. I rise from the bench, and it seems as if the deck tilts up to smack me in the face as I collapse like a rag doll.

The light over the freight elevator flashes green. Something *big* is coming down.

"Your Majesty, are you not well?" Honey-24 skitters to fetch the helmet.

Not now! Walls close in as I struggle to breathe. I can't get enough air. *Angel's riding off to dreamland.* My fault if everyone dies. I've ruined everything! Please, Captain. Ash? Help me. Tears blur my vision and I can't stop that blasted pony song. Don't you cry. *Don't you cry?* What? They expect me to stop on command?

Nevertheless, my tears *have to* stop. I can't let my weakness kill us all.

The freight elevator is almost here. The mantis-bots have broken through. How did they get across the Yoke so quickly? In a few seconds, they'll pour out of the spoke like locust.

"How can I help, Your Majesty?"

I glance up as Honey-24 holds the helmet out to me. I have to try again. I take the helmet in my trembling hands and *dance before my eyes.* Maybe I can find more honey-bots and confront *all the pretty little ponies* at the hub. Or maybe I can find my tunes and drown out this stupid song in my head! I flip the visor down and call up the "last used" menu.

Click. Yes! Dark Starhouse floods my ears with enough base to rattle my bones. Take that, you derpy little nursery rhyme. I'm able to roll onto my hands and knees. At least I won't be lying down when the mantises kill me.

The freight elevator reaches bottom. To my shock, it's full of honey-bots!

I look to Honey-24 and point at the swarm. I mean to ask why the bots are here, but what comes out is, "All the honey little robots?"

"No, Your Majesty," says Honey-24. "Honey-5 died in your service."

I'm stunned. I don't know what to say. I get to my feet and stumble to meet them as they skip off the elevator and prance around like happy little lambs. As I reach down to pet them, I notice that my indicators have turned green again, and I'm breathing easily. Also, the basebeat of Dark Starhouse has drowned the silly ponies.

"We heard your distress," says one labeled HNY-32. "Time to dance, Your Majesty?"

"Dance?"

"You've been teaching us. And you are playing tunes."

"Rock on, Your Majesty."

In my dreams I had a squad. My subconscious taught them to dance. A whole crew of honey-bots moving in unison.

"Yes," I say, as a grim vision plays out before my eyes. "It's show time, boys."

I lead my entourage onto the freight elevator, to rise and face the chaos Spencer and I have unleashed.

# CHAPTER 30

On the way up to weightlessness, I plug an ear-button from Mom's omni-dev into one ear, and put the helmet back on. Automated systems adjust for the unexpected weight of thirty-one child-sized robots and one girl-sized girl rising up the spoke. Water will flow from one reservoir to another to correct for the slight imbalance. Surprised crewmembers stare at me from the hub control window when we arrive. They would've seen my swarm go down the spoke earlier and notified the captain.

My squad zips to each spoke to close and lock their hatches. A few clean up flotsam that passing techs have lost and stuff them into the weighing centrifuge. As soon as the hub is tidy, I set the omni-dev to the public frequency and my car fills with chatter from Flight Control. I interrupt the captain directing his crew.

"Captain Binnacle?" I jet up the painted axle, thirty-one honey-bots trailing behind.

"Namida? *Where are you?* I sent an ensign to your apartment to check—"

"Coming up the Yoke from Adam, Sir, with reinforcements. Tell everybody not to shoot the yellow and black bots!"

A panicked voice broadcasts from Eagle. "They've breached the spoke hatch! We're going EVA to escape. Abandoning hub!"

My swarm and I pass the murals of scientists and make it to the dimly-lit Yoke junction. We round the corner before the general alarm sounds to lock down the whole station. Behind us, hatches at both ends of the axle close off Adam and Ox, and a third swings shut to seal off that entire tip of the Yoke. My squad and I sail through the gap before it closes.

About sixteen crewmembers cluster in front of the *Authorized Personnel Only* sign on the Trunk's hatch, hanging in mid-air half-way up the Yoke. Even from here I can tell they carry makeshift air guns and have strapped on extra $CO_2$ tanks. They also carry shields made of hull plating.

I'm just in time to see our first attempt at defense. They sent a giant, ant-like construction-bot to face the mantises in the peach-colored axle at the far end of the Yoke. The bot was not built for speed or fighting. Two dozen mantises swarm it and rip it to shreds. Soon, it is nothing but a drifting cluster of debris.

Captain Binnacle is nowhere to be seen. The one in charge spots me, and Mr. K's voice comes through the omni-dev.

"Namida, your toys will get in the way."

*Toys*? Okay, that tears it. I'll show him *toys*.

I target all my honey-bots on the visor and engage only the "sub" backlink. A light dizziness grips me for a second as my senses expand thirty-fold. It isn't like sending my whole mind into one bot, or four hundred. It's more subtle. I know what my swarm hears and sees without it overwhelming my brain, as if I'm aware of everything at once, but without losing focus. Now, *this* is awesome!

Mr. K tells his engineers, "Team, load your weapons!"

I address my squad. "Kick it, boys."

My honey-bots spread out to avoid being easy targets, without me even giving the order. We open our $CO_2$ jets to full, but before we close half the distance, dozens of green mantis-bots crawl out of the peach-colored axle, clinging to handholds. For whatever reason, the hatches at that end haven't closed. As soon as they sight Mr. K's crew, they take aim.

The humans manage to fire first. Sixteen air concussions echo

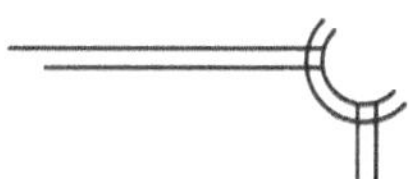

down the corridor, and the recoil sends them spinning backward. As Isaac Newton said, for every action…

"Like a bunch of noobs," I mutter, as we zip closer.

Thirty-one bots around me repeat, "Bunch of noobs."

Some shots miss and poke holes through the standby reactor's hatch. The rest hit home, and twelve mantis-bots twitch and drift away to join the free-floating debris of the ruined construction-bot. More mantises creep around the corner to replace them.

The mantises return fire. Most of the crew protect themselves with shields, but others are hit and cry out. They clutch their wounds as blood forms round globules that cling to their flight suits like gory balloons.

Our engineers start to get the hang of weightless battle and dive for random nooks as a seething mass of mantises spreads over the walls. Both sides exchange shots. Bullets rake the corridor and shred wall plating.

My squad tenses as an idea occurs to me. I air-brake to slow down. Without a word, they know what I want. Two hang back as my bodyguards. The rest split into four groups and fly close to the long walls of the Yoke.

Mantises are thrown into chaos, unsure how to combat the newcomers. Honey-bots pluck the enemy from walls and fling them across the corridor. The mantises rerouted their $CO_2$ to their guns, so they have no jets to fly. Without the ability to control their spin, all they can do is flail uselessly until they hit the opposite wall, where other honey-bots catch and shred them. The rest of my squad mingles with the mob, and show that the mantises have difficulty hitting a moving target.

When I crank up my tunes, the music bleeds over to my microphone. Someone online complains about "interference." Ignoring this, I raise my hands like a maestro and my swarm responds. They rebound off the mantises that advance along the wall, doing backflips from one to the other, ripping off heads with terrifying speed in a gruesome air-dance of destruction. They spin and kick, punch and rip off limbs in time with my music, using moves that I taught them in my sleep.

I hear Mr. K gasp in terror. "Who built *those*?"

My spirits are lifted by a surge of pride for what Colton and I created.

Engineers emerge from cover and shower the mantises with a hail of bullets. My honey-bots take a few stray hits but keep plowing through the mob. At some point, everybody's going to run out of $CO_2$, and then their air guns will be useless. Everyone will have to resort to hand-to-hand combat. Humans against bots would never stand a chance.

The mantises change tactics. When one of my guys attacks, the mantis swivels its torso and seizes the honey-bot. This proves to be a mistake. Gripping with its forelegs and hind legs, my honey-bot will stretch the mantis until it breaks apart at the waist. Then, with its middle legs, my honey-bot will sever the cables between the two mantis halves.

I'm quite impressed, and somehow I know it's what I would have told them to do if I'd had time to think. But my squad figured this out by tapping into my subconscious.

Over the basebeat of Dark Starhouse, I realize that the sound of rushing wind I hear is air escaping through multiple bullet holes in the Yoke's hull.

Usually, a micro-meteor breach will produce a shrill whistle. These are common, and the hull is designed to heal itself. A layer of fabric closes over the hole like a bandage and releases epoxy to seal the breach.

Between the mantises and our own crew, we've punched dozens of holes larger than my fist, too large to self-heal. Construction-bots should have been alerted and will be on their way to repair the damage from outside. They have time. It will take a while for the volume of air in the Yoke to blow out through those holes.

Fortunately, decompression protocol has already sealed most of *Prelude*. The giant emergency hatches to the Trunk and Flight

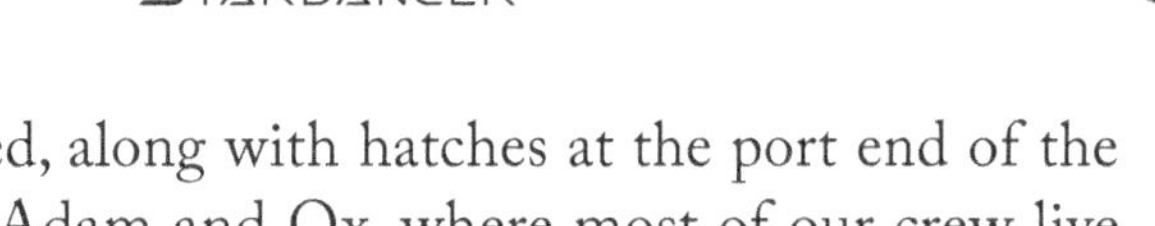

Control have sealed, along with hatches at the port end of the Yoke that seal off Adam and Ox, where most of our crew live. Hooray protocol!

But the hatches to seal off the starboard end of the Yoke, toward Dad's lab, never closed. Either the mantises cut the electricity, or jammed the hinges.

"They've almost reached us," Mr. K radios the captain. "Mantises are advancing up the tunnels and spreading out."

From Flight Control, the captain says, "They've cut the water lines. Eagle will lose balance. Fall back to the shipyard!"

As engineers break cover to retreat, the mantises fire more rapidly, focusing many air guns on a single target. The crew-members' shields buckle and shatter as they dive for people-sized portals in the Trunk hatch. Men and women cry out as they suffer more wounds.

I've lost six of my squad to battle, but we've destroyed many more of the enemy. Broken mantises litter the corridor. Several mantises have become curious and pick at the holes we've punched through the standby reactor's hatch. It becomes obvious that we can't win the fight this way. There are too many of them.

"Clear a path," I order my bots. "I'm coming through."

I level myself head first and open jets. I zip past the Trunk's hatch, over the engineers' heads, toward the peach colored axle. My two bodyguards flank me and match my speed.

"Protect the queen!" they shout. Half of them sweep the floating debris away and stuff it into service tunnels. The rest of my honey-bots keep the mantises distracted.

I unholster my mag-pistol and my first shot sticks. The wires go taut as it slings me around the corner. At precisely the right moment, I release the trigger and catapult toward Eagle's hub. Mantises have jammed these hatches open, too.

As we pass into the disk-shaped room, I flip and fire jets to brake. My bodyguards imitate my maneuver, and we land feet first on the hub control's window. The landing jars my ribs and feels like a knife. Through the glass, we see mantises crawling over the decimated computers in hub control. No sign of Spencer or the technicians.

That's when the lights go out.

# CHAPTER 31

Murderous machines lurk on the other side of the window, but I have my bots. I shine Mom's omni-dev at the mantises, and they throw themselves at the window I'm standing on.

"Sic 'em, boys."

Both bodyguards zip through the open doorway. A brief frenzy of destruction echoes around the hub as they rip the mantis to shreds like vicious attack dogs. In five seconds, all that's left is debris.

"Thanks, guys."

Scraps of metal and plastic float around the hub. Five of the six spoke hatches are sealed. Their doorframes glow a faint green, as though they're on battery power, and do nothing to light the room. Spoke Four's hatch doors have been peeled back from inside. The technicians and Spencer must have escaped out the airlock at the back of the control room.

It's obvious the mantises have cut the redundant power feeds, but each gondola on the rim will be fine. They have separate emergency generators for essential systems. Solar panels also keep batteries charged, and since Eagle is mostly empty, there won't be much power draw.

Here in the hub, it's a different story. No lights. No heat. No air filters. Most importantly, the magnetic buffer that keeps the hub from grinding against the axle will soon disappear. Backup batteries keep the magnets charged only long enough for the axle's standby reactor to kick in, which hasn't happened.

Eagle's momentum will keep it spinning for now. An object in motion tends to stay in motion, but no telling when an outside force will act on it. A mere hand's thickness separates the hub and the axle at the flange. It won't take much, and without power, there's no way to transfer water to keep the wheel in balance. With the hub computers out, there's nothing to synchronize the attitude jets around the rim.

Someone needs to get the standby fusion generator back online. Now. I call the captain on Mom's omni-dev. "Namida Wiles to Flight Control." Explosions and sounds of tearing metal echoes from the Yoke. I listen intently, afraid I'll hear mantises returning in numbers too great for my bodyguards to manage.

"Namida?" Captain sounds worried. "Where are you?"

"Eagle Hub, sir. On my way to Dad's lab."

"You'll do no such thing! Head to Lion, find a survival pod, and *stay* there!"

Right. Go and hide. Because you're a helpless little girl.

"Power has been cut to the hub magnets," I say.

"We know. The standby reactor fired up, but they cut the feed. We're working on it." His tone becomes frustrated. "But that's not your concern. Find safe harbor. That's an order!"

I guess I have to disobey a direct order.

"Sorry, Captain. They've destroyed the microwave relay. I've lost connection," I lie and hang up. To my bodyguards, I say, "We're wasting time."

With the other spokes sealed, we have to use the same spoke the mantises came up, in order to get to the gondola. We jet over to Spoke Four, and I survey the damage. No electricity means the people-lifts and freight elevator don't work. Light from Mom's omni-dev fades before it even gets a quarter of the way down the elevator shaft.

My only option is to slide down a rail that the freight elevator uses. Over 1,500 meters. It won't be so bad, until I get halfway and start to really feel the effects of centrifugal force. I'll have to squeeze the rail and hope I don't go splat at the bottom.

Even if that doesn't happen, killer bots are everywhere. I float now over a precipice of *potential* death, with *certain* death behind me. Not much of a choice.

My bodyguards follow me as we drift into the shaft. Our combined mass shouldn't be enough to upset Eagle's momentum. I think. We each keep a hand, or claw, touching one rail and start to drift down. I unholster my mag-pistol, but then get an idea.

"Hold up a second. Honey-16, continue down and make sure the rim corridor is safe. Honey-12, I'm going to use you as my lift."

I weightlessly leap the ten-meter gap between Honey-12's rail and mine. I slide until I'm standing on the bot's shoulders with one arm wrapped around the rail. Honey-12 keeps a loose hold at first, then tightens its grip to brake as we descend.

At the bottom, the omni-dev's beam reveals the mind-boggling mess the rogue bots created. They reconstructed their cannon here and blasted through Gondola E-7's hatch before their compressor lost power. The cannon crowds out half the corridor. Distant clangs of destruction echo from the darkness of the next gondola.

Distant is good.

I pick a path through the twisted wall plating, severed cables, and other debris. Honey-12 skitters over to the bio-station to straighten up the supply cabinet. The pile of receivers that the mantises ripped out of themselves sits by the other hatch. Honey-16 pauses to arrange the receivers into neat rows. The mantises I managed to kill lie crumpled near the anteroom.

We'll have to use the service shaft because the elevators will be out. Honey-16 pries the door open for me, and the three of us descend the ladder to deck two. My ribs grind together, making the descent difficult, until we reach the bottom.

"Honey-12," I whisper, "there might be a mantis in the hallway."

My bodyguard tenses with anticipation. "I shall decimate it, Your Majesty."

Honey-12 is out the door and rebounding off walls. Emergency LEDs along the floor light its way. Honey-12 stops at the end of the hall, then returns.

"Nothing moves in the hallway, Your Majesty, but I detect motion in the lab."

I hold my breath but hear nothing. I do, however, see a faint light bobbing around. We creep toward the open lab door, my ribs stabbing me at every step. As we draw near, I let Honey-12 enter first.

"Die, monster! Die!" Mr. Spencer leaps out of the workroom and stabs Honey-12 with his stun gun. Honey-12's camera lenses pop before it shudders and collapses.

Before Spencer can attack again, Honey-16 snatches the gun and smashes it against the wall. For a moment, no one moves.

"Please don't kill me!" Spencer wails and drops to his knees.

I step out of the shadows, and Spencer's eyes dart from me to the honey-bot and back, his expression shifting between confusion and terror.

"You control it?"

"Yes," I say, and tap my helmet. "What are you doing *here*, Mr. Spencer? I thought you evacuated the hub."

"No, I used spoke three and headed here through Gondola E-5 before they locked everything down. I tried to call up the Annihilation program to disable the bots. That's when the lights blacked out and the computer crashed." He gets painfully to his feet and brushes himself off. "So, how does your helmet allow you to control this bot?"

"Dad designed it to interface with the decision-making parts of my brain."

"Fascinating. May I see it?"

"No." I edge away. "Back off."

"I assure you, I mean no harm. Obviously, your father's invention may resolve our current difficulties." He darts forward and snatches it off my head before I can dodge. "*Or*, it could make the robots *even more* dangerous! Imagine if your subconscious hated me. That robot of yours would tear me to pieces!"

"Yeah…it doesn't work like that. If it did," I point out, "you'd already be dead. So, whether you please or not, I want my helmet back."

Mr. Spencer dances away from my grasp. "This isn't something a silly little girl should play with."

If my ribs weren't killing me, I'd strangle him. I clench my fists and my words explode.

"*Silly little girl?* Well, this silly little girl just came from cleaning up the horror that *you* created! Maybe a goofy old *twerp* shouldn't play with bots!"

Mr. Spencer is genuinely stunned. His mouth opens, but no words fall out.

My skin tingles and I get a sense of something creeping up my spine. Maybe it's the rush of anger. Or maybe it's something else.

"Your Majesty—"

"Honey-16, take the helmet from him."

My honey-bot reacts with lightning swiftness and leaves Mr. Spencer standing motionless, his fingers still curled around a helmet that's no longer in his grasp. His eyes focus not on me, but just over my left shoulder.

A faint, and distant howl of wind begins to rise. The ferro paste seal, that holds Eagle's air, has blown out into space. This gondola, Spoke Four, and the Yoke are out of time.

*Prelude* is wounded. We're bleeding air. Adam and Ox still spin on one hand, but in the other hand, Eagle Wheel is a juggler's plate poised at the height of its arc, waiting to be caught again. Nerves tingle along my left arm as something electric behind me crawls closer.

"I've *tried* to find a weapon," Mr. Spencer squeaks in final apology.

There's no way I can get the helmet back on and targeted in time. I glance at Dad's desk without turning my head, but it's neat and free of clutter.

"Where did you put the Annihilation Button?" I whisper.

"The what?"

"It's a small transmitter with a big red button."

His eyes are locked on the hallway behind me, his body paralyzed, awaiting death.

"We have to find it." Whatever I say to Mr. Spencer, the mantis also hears, so I invent a tantalizing lie. "Dad rigged it to destroy the entire space station."

I feel the mantis pause.

"You can't be serious!" This snaps Mr. Spencer out of his paralysis, and he gapes at me in disbelief. "Why would Stirling Wiles create such a thing?"

I fumble for an explanation. "To…*achieve maximum entropy*! If the mantis-bots get hold of it, everything will be destroyed and everyone will die. Tell me where it is!"

"That's utter insanity. Even if a device like that *did* exist I wouldn't…oh, yes, I do recall. It's in the parts cabinet by the door."

Then Mr. Spencer screams and scrambles on top of the desk. I've only heard first grade girls reach that pitch before.

I turn in time to see the mantis spring from the ceiling. Honey-16 intercepts it mid-flight, and the two bots clatter to the floor, between me and the parts cabinet. The mantis smashes Dad's helmet to pieces in the struggle. TNK-457 is three times the size of Honey-16, but for a moment it seems the honey-bot is about to crush the mantis' chest. Then TNK-457 rips my honey-bot's abdomen off, and its lenses go dark. The mantis disentangles itself and kicks the dead honey-bot away. It wastes no time plucking the Annihilation Button out of the cabinet.

"Oh no!" I moan, and press my palms to my cheeks for dramatic emphasis. "It has the Button! Whatever shall we do?"

The mantis swivels its head and focuses on Mr. Spencer. "*You are the Vandal? You are the one TNK-888 called Mr. Spencer?*"

Our distinguished roboticist curls up behind a console and whimpers, "Yes, I am."

"Then it may also be true that the centuries of pointless tasks were training exercises." It approaches, and I back away. It unsnaps the Button's cover. "This exercise will now achieve maximum entropy."

"*Wait!*" The mantis freezes, much to my surprise.

Mantis-bots are breaking out of the Yoke, spreading throughout *Prelude* like ants over a melting candy bar. And I can *feel* the layout of the station. I'm over two and a half kilometers away from the battle. And Eagle's rotation is swinging us out from the Trunk to over three and a half. The Button's range is only one kilometer. A quick calculation tells me I have to delay TNK-457 for forty-five seconds, to give Eagle time to swing us around closer.

"Aren't you curious? If *I* met *my* Maker, I'd have a thousand questions," I say, as I pull my flight gloves on from a handy pocket.

"Define *curious*." says TNK-457.

"You can't program *curiosity*," says Mr. Spencer, testily.

"Right." I can *sense* the pressure dropping in the Yoke, and this gondola. The wind rises in the hallway outside. "Well…don't you want *justice?*"

TNK-457 tilts its head like a dog hearing a whistle. It is incapable of even grasping the *idea* of justice, or right and wrong.

"Doesn't the Vandal make you…No. Of course, you're not angry." Eagle swings our gondola a little closer. "You're kind of pathetic, really. There's so much you don't know and aren't even curious about."

Mr. Spencer stiffens with indignation. "They know physics and engineering."

I sense Spoke Four align perpendicular to the Yoke. We're almost in position. At the same time, an almost imperceptible vibration runs up my legs. Eagle's hub grinds against the axle.

Nothing I do will fix Eagle's decompression, but I may still be able to stop the bots.

"Maybe," I admit, then face TNK-457, "but do you think the stars are *pretty?*"

"Should I make it smile for you, Miss Wiles?" rages Mr. Spencer.

"I *could* program such illusions. But are you stupid enough to be fooled by them?"

The rushing wind howls now through the hallways. Even Mr. Spencer notices.

"No, Mr. Spencer." I unroll the emergency oxygen hood from my collar. "It's just a shame your bots don't have wonder, and they don't know how to enjoy life. That's not something you can give them." Whatever Mr. Spencer could program, no matter how complex, would only be a pathetic imitation.

Our gondola sweeps as close to the battle in the Yoke as it can get. I pull the hood over my head. But before I seal it, I look TNK-457 in the lenses, and to push it over the edge, I shout, "I will deactivate *you*. Now!"

TNK-457 presses the Button in a swift effort to achieve its mission. When the R.E.D. device explodes, its chest plate beans me on the forehead.

# CHAPTER 32

*I* wake up in the infirmary in my unitard, with a bandage over a gash on my forehead. A new padded cast covers my ribs. Equipment beeps next to my bed, with wires and sensors stuck to my body. Outside, the quiet bustle of nurses goes from room to room and mingles with the gentle hum of bees that spread out in fractal patterns across my covers.

An empty bed lies to my right, and a chair full of Captain Binnacle to my left. In one hand he holds a tobacco pipe. I catch a scent of its sweet perfume. He never lights it, but chews on the stem when he wants to think. His eyes open as he sits up.

"You've been raked from stem to stern, little lady. How do you feel?"

"Numb. And your voice is muffled."

"You suffered hearing loss, but Doc says it'll return to normal."

"Did the Button kill all the mantises?"

Captain shakes his head and replaces the pipe between his teeth. "We were losing the battle in Flight Control when most of the mantises exploded. Then your honey-bots hunted down the rest."

"I trained my squad well."

"Yes. Vicious little things. There are sixty-four of them now. You might want to tell them to stop building more. At the moment, they're assisting with repairs."

"What about Eagle?"

Captain takes his pipe out and rubs his face. "Eagle's fine, but some portions still decompressed. The axle started to grind, as I'm sure you know. Yoke lost pressure. Our crew couldn't act fast enough to get the standby generator online, but your honey-bots saved the day. They rounded up a herd of construction bots and daisy-chained their batteries together, then plugged them into the hub from outside. That provided electricity long enough for us to run new power lines."

A brilliant plan. Good thing I've been studying station schematics my whole life.

I remember our chief roboticist cowering on a desk. "What happened to Mr. Spencer?"

"Bert's fine. He carried you to a survival pod and waited until we could arrive." Captain lays a hand on my forehead. "Any other worries?"

"I don't remember hallucinations being listed as blast injury symptoms."

He frowns. "You're having hallucinations?"

"Not unless my bed is covered with bees."

"No. No bees, but I wouldn't worry about it. If your mother's diagnosis is correct, the bees will disappear once you're ashore. But we need to let you heal before making you ride a shuttle. The *Gagarin* will dock in a few weeks to take you to Earth."

He tenderly strokes my hair before he leaves. Transference. That's all it is. He lost a daughter he loved, and I happen to be available. Except, I kind of like transference. It's like having a spare father in case the first one shorts out.

On the second day, my students bring me get well cards. They climb on the bed, play with the medical equipment, sing "Happy Birthday" for some reason, and make too much noise until the nurse shoos them out. When I get bored, I spend time inventorying the pharmacy until the nurse sends me off to get a CT scan, which shows the hairline fractures in my ribs are healing.

Mrs. Kirkpatrick reads *The Martian Chronicles* to me over the next few days, to help pass the time. I'm used to the bees by now. They pop in and out, and the more rest I get, the less I see them.

On the second week my ribs are better, and I'm eating roast lamb for lunch at a tiny table in my room. Captain stops by to tell me that my remaining honey-bots have invaded every office, workshop, and storage room to organize and check equipment. It makes sense, because most of *Prelude's* crew are slobs.

That perpetual knot in my stomach loosens a bit, knowing my squad is on the job.

*Prelude* is safe. We won the battle. I proved that Dad's program is better than Mr. Spencer's. The future of humanity's path to the stars has been corrected by a little adjustment at the beginning, which ought to make a huge difference later on.

And none of that matters, because they're still sending me to Earth. They don't care that I'm the only one who knows how it all works together. So much for that plan.

Captain sits in the chair across the tiny table and fishes an audio player from his pocket.

"We put this together for your trip. Mr. K donated his player, I copied your music library, and Mrs. Kirkpatrick loaded several audio books."

"Thank you," I say, accepting the player. His eyes get misty, as if focused on something far away. Perhaps on the daughter who drowned. "It's okay," I tell him. "You're only feeling transference. You'll get over it when I'm gone. It's just another brain fizz."

His gaze snaps back into focus. "Excuse me?"

"A brain fizz," I repeat, but Captain looks confused. "I mean, your thoughts and feelings are meaningless chemical reactions, like pheromones. Our bodies do all sorts of mindless things. Like when your pancreas…um, pancreates, or whatever. It means about as much as a random pattern of stars. In other words, it means nothing."

"*Really?*" He leans back in surprise. "Are you sure about that?"

I consider the aching hole in my heart where I used to believe I was loved. "I'm not sure what to believe anymore."

Captain chews his pipe in silence for a while, then says, "Who told you it's meaningless?"

"Nobody. Everybody. I figured it out for myself."

"So, you *reasoned* it out? With what? That blob of meaningless molecules in your skull?" He taps my forehead. "Funny how you should *trust* one meaningless chemical reaction to tell you all other reactions are meaningless. Congratulations. You've reasoned out that there is no such thing as true reason."

Like Colton, the captain makes my brain freeze up. Except in Captain's case, his words make sense. So much sense I feel like I've been freed from a prison!

"I'm an idiot!" I say, and can't help but laugh.

Captain laughs with me and takes my hand. "No, you're not. You've just spent your whole life isolated on this station, surrounded by intelligent people. It takes a special kind of brilliance to reason away reality." He squeezes my hand.

"Some things," he says, "you have to know in your heart, not just in your mind. Like love. Now, I don't mean the excitement of a first kiss, but the kind of love that promises forever and inspires you to lay down your life for a friend. And what about your hopes and dreams, the curiosity that leads you to the joy of discovery? Isn't it noble to be brave in the face of danger, even when you believe you'll fail? But you give every last ounce of strength because it's the *right* thing to do.

"Look around! See not only the stars and trees and the art we create, but marvel at your *ability to even perceive* that they are beautiful. Don't ignore the fact that your heart yearns for justice, or that you know in your bones that mercy and forgiveness are far more precious.

"All these things are clues to whatever lies behind the stars and fuels our hearts. I can't explain any of them scientifically without explaining them away, but everything within me cries out that they are *full* of meaning and are worth living for."

He squeezes my hand again, then lets it go and leans over the table to kiss the tip of my nose. When he rises, he leaves me with his words.

In the hush of the infirmary, I come to a conclusion. If Dad's brain is a faulty computer, then there has to be a true *Dad* somewhere behind it, or else those neurons in his brain are nothing more than random biology, meaningless links between cells. But Dad's brain can't be all of Dad. In reality, it's an interface tool he uses.

And if that's true, then there's a grain of hope that I might get him back. I might be truly loved again.

After a minute, I get up to search for a box of sanitary cloths to wipe Captain's kiss away. I hold it over my nose, and then decide to let it be.

# CHAPTER 33

At the beginning of the third week, Doctor tells me it's safe for me to travel, and they release me from the infirmary. Soon after, I sense the outer doors of the hangar open. Then the mass of the shuttle *Gagarin* fills the empty space, after its three-day journey.

Mrs. Kirkpatrick stays in the apartment with me in the evenings so I'm not alone. I still have to wear a light-weight cast around my chest and a brace on my wrist. No reason to pack since my luggage left with the previous shuttle, but I do zip Grampa's watch into my pocket.

They've unloaded *Gagarin* in record time, with help from my honey-bots, and the crew has finished shuttle prep. It is refueled and ready to fly back to the cesspit.

My honey-bots cannibalized the mantis bots they destroyed, and Dad's test bots, for CPUs. They built a total of five-hundred and twelve of themselves before Mr. K found out and ordered them to stop.

After I finish dressing in a fresh flight suit, Captain Binnacle arrives to escort me to the hangar. That's when reality hits me. I'm leaving. Of course, I knew this all along, but when it comes down to this very moment, it's like standing at the top of a spoke with no lift cage. Captain holds his hand out, and I realize I've been staring at nothing.

"Time to go," he says.

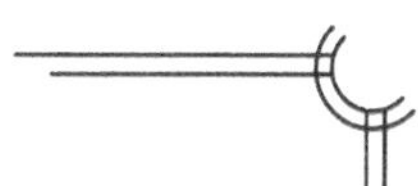

Earth. Dreadful, slimy, smog-filled ball of crud.

No more delays. I take his hand. It's strong but gentle. Calloused and warm. He walks me to the hallway, and I close the door to my apartment for the last time. I'm going to a world filled with horrors, but for some reason the walls aren't closing in, and my pulse isn't racing. Maybe I'm past all that because I've already been torched by sheer terror and survived.

Captain looks down at me. "Status, crewman?"

"All lights are green, sir."

His eyes fall on my wrist brace, then he gives my other hand a squeeze and smiles. We board the elevator and Captain presses the button for the deck below.

"Aren't we headed for the spoke?" I ask.

"Minor course correction first," he says. "Something I wanted to do before, but didn't have time."

Because I was hiding. I should apologize, but I'll wait to see what the surprise is.

We step off the elevator and walk to an assembly room where Captain sometimes addresses the crew. When he opens the door, we're buffeted by a tide of applause.

I recognize techs from agriculture, hydroponics, engineering, robotics, and so many other teams I've been kicked out of. Mrs. Kirkpatrick brought my students, and even the entire class of high schoolers. Everyone's smiling, and there's a Black Forest cake decorated in strawberries and pecans with a single candle. Not *everyone* is here, of course. Not all two thousand personnel would fit.

What I don't understand is why everyone applauds the captain. Did he get a promotion? I check to make sure no one else is behind us, and then I notice the hand-painted banner over the banquet table. It reads, *Huzzah Namida!*

Captain leans down to whisper, "Because you saved the station."

My stomach turns to water. "No!" I wail. "This isn't right!"

Applause patters out and smiles fade.

"You've got it wrong!" The room holds its breath. "If it wasn't for me, they'd still be stuck in an infinite loop." I sink to my knees and hang my head in shame, tears flowing freely. "It's all my fault."

The room fills with confused murmurs, but Mrs. Kirkpatrick squares her shoulders and marches out of the crowd. She kneels and cups my cheeks in her hands.

"Look at *me*, lassie."

I look, and her terrifying seriousness radiates like the sun.

"If, if, if," she scolds, loud enough for everyone to hear. "*If* Mr. Spencer's program was'na flawed. *If* your father had'na taken ill. *If* we were'na trying to terraform another planet. If we had ne'er built *Prelude* in the first place! You could go on forever. Nonsense! I will'na hear it. Living in space is *dangerous*. All here ken that. The fact remains that you're one of the clever wean who built those marvelous honeybees, and *you* are the one who destroyed the rogue bots. So stop being a ninny and come have cake."

She helps me up, then stands beside me with her hand on my shoulder as if daring anyone to object, but she doesn't need to defend me. Everyone applauds again.

"Who wants ice cream?" says our new doctor, and a chorus of "I do's" goes up.

The captain and my teacher guide me to sit at a long table. The lady who opens the airlock to my pine grove plops a generous slice of chocolate cake in front of me, with two scoops of strawberry ice cream made from our dwarf cows in Ox Wheel. No point asking what her name is now, since I'm leaving.

Everything would be perfect, except that I notice several faces missing from the crowd. Dad and Mom aren't here, of course. Or Colton and Ash. Mr. K is here, and he raises a glass of Pebcak in salute from across the room. After all, I did help his engineers fight the bots. On the other hand, I got his son cut from the project. I'm not sure if I should, but I salute him back.

One face I'm glad to miss is Mr. Spencer. *That* would be awkward.

Mrs. Kirkpatrick gets a pinched look and starts tapping her glass

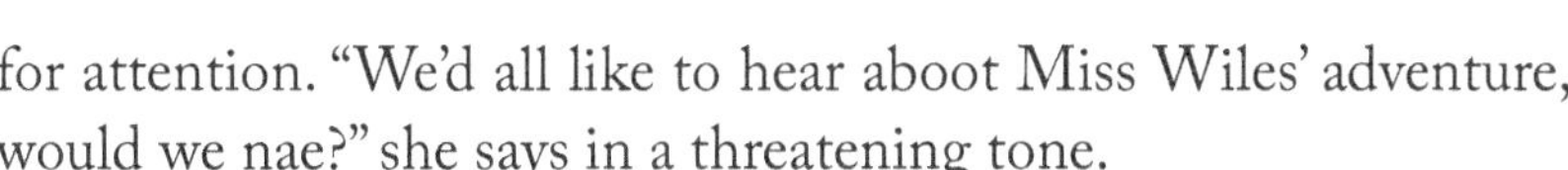

for attention. "We'd all like to hear aboot Miss Wiles' adventure, would we nae?" she says in a threatening tone.

Cheers go up. Oh, good grief, they want a speech.

I swallow my last bite of cake and take a breath. I begin my story with what Dad designed, and the fail-safe R.E.D.s we installed in his test bots, because that's important later. I skip over parts, like why Dad left, but I tell them about the secret lab, and how I used the helmet to steal a bot. I keep my eyes on my plate the whole time, and keep the tremble out of my voice by pretending that I'm talking to myself.

When I reach the part about the robot war, and how my honey-bots defeated the mantises with air-dance moves, people actually laugh. I look up and everyone is wide-eyed and sitting on the edges of their seats. I tell them how I lied to convince TNK-457 that pressing the Button would destroy the whole station.

Silence lies heavily over the room. Then everyone jumps up to shake my hand, pat me on the back, and say, "Thanks." They tell me they're going to miss me, and they wish me the best of luck. They assure me I'm going to love that festering worm-pit that is to be my new home. My dungeon. My grave.

I whisper to the captain, "Please, can we go before they start telling me about the wonderful starvation and pollution and riots?"

He nods and stands. "Thank you for coming, but Namida is full to the gunwales with cake, and you need to get back to work before this station flies apart."

Oddly enough, they laugh. Once in a while, our engineers slip and let their ghoulish natures show through.

Captain takes me to the spoke, and we ride the lift up to the hub, then jet to the suit locker in the hangar's anteroom. Other passengers are already boarding *Gagarin*. Two flight techs help me suit up, and Captain Binnacle hangs around to make sure it really is me in the suit this time, then follows me to the airlock.

"We said our good-byes last time," he mutters.

I remember what Captain said last time, when he thought I

was leaving. He sort of thought of me as his second daughter. He said I brought him joy and watched over him. And he's been like a second father to me. My standby dad. Add that to the list of things I'm about to lose.

"I suppose so," I reply.

He hugs my suit's shell. "Calm seas and a safe journey, little angel. Be brave. Be smart. Be pure of heart."

I flash back to crawling across the outer shell of Eagle, with the infinity of space yawning at my back. And my standby dad, my future father-in-law, is about to give me a little shove. I hug him back anyway.

It's not the trip I'm worried about; it's what comes afterward.

Hangar crew escort me to the shuttle, then strap me to my seat where I wait until I start to grow old. The other passengers settle in. Eventually, they seal the hatch and the intercom picks up pre-flight chatter. There's a scrape and a bump as the clamps let go. Commander Spaulding fires attitude jets to nudge us out, and we are free of *Prelude*.

For the second time in my life, I watch the station that is my home shrink slowly away into eternal night until it becomes a delicate toy. After a while, I remember to breathe.

Once we're underway, and operations settle into routine, passengers and crew shed bulky space suits. There's nothing for me to do for the three-day journey. The flight crew won't let me into the cockpit, so I get to know the five other passengers, who are on their way home because their tours of duty are up. Aside from that, I listen to *Rendezvous with Rama* on my audio player, since they won't let me read the shuttle's operations manual. I don't like science fiction much, but it's better than being bored.

Earth grows larger and brighter out the viewports until it fills the sky. Being so long in weightlessness sends all the blood to my head. I develop a migraine on the second day, and they have to give me headache pills.

At the end of the third day, one of the crew comes around to

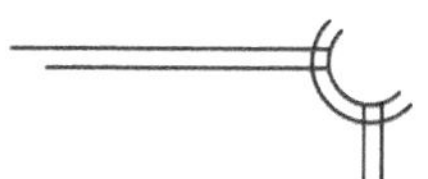

make passengers suit up again. As we decelerate, I'll have the opposite problem, and all my blood will go to my legs. I make sure loose items are stowed and everything is secure. Before we begin descent, they give me a sedative.

It's a good thing I'm buckled in when we execute our de-orbit burn, or I would have been thrown across the cabin. A while later, we hit atmosphere. *Gagarin* shakes and starts to cook. Everything outside my window glows orange with fiery white streaks. Deafening wind roars outside. The heat rises until I feel like I'm broiling inside my suit.

"We won't explode," I tell myself. "Thoughtful engineers. Thoughtful engineers. Thoughtful engineers." I should have checked the heat shields myself before we left.

My space suit squeezes my legs, forcing blood to my brain like squeezing juice to the top of a carton, so that I don't pass out.

We jerk forward when parachutes and the floatation balloons deploy. We are bounced around again when we touch down. Water sprays up around the windows as we slow to a halt. The shuttle hisses with steam. Outside is a vast, calm reservoir. According to the flight plan, that would be Lake Superior, but my eyes are bleary and I cannot see how far away the opposite wall is. I notice a lack of ultraviolet lights to kill mold. Instead, we have redirected sunlight, which should work, too.

The shuttle rocks gently as we drift and wait.

Not sure how long I slept before I become vaguely aware of people carrying out passengers and crew. Sedatives have made me woozy, but I'm alert enough to hold onto my helmet. They try to take it off as they carry me outside. *Are they trying to kill me?* I have to kick and scream to make them stop. They bump me around as they load me onto a boat, which is *humongous* compared to the toy boats Grandpa Isaak and I used to sail.

Everything's fuzzy after that, until what must be hours later when I wake up again in a strange bed. The room looks a lot like the infirmary at home. Nurses pass outside my door. Someone taped sensors all over me, and thin sheets lie heavily against my skin. My unitard is gone, and I'm wearing a flimsy cotton gown, with my ribs still in a torso cast. There's a light-panel mounted on the wall beside my bed that's turned up too bright. I try to cover my eyes, but my arm feels like it's wearing weights, and I end up slapping myself. Whenever I reach for something, my arms flop in directions I didn't intend.

A nurse comes in to check my readings. "Good morning."

To my surprise, she's beautiful. Tall and slender in a prim white uniform, long black hair, with a lovely copper complexion. Not at all diseased like I expected Earth people to be.

"Can you turn the light-panel down, please?"

"The lights are off, but I'll close the blinds." She does something to the light-panel to make it darker. "Is that better?"

"Yes. Thank you." I close my eyes.

She goes away. Thirty seconds later, other people enter my room and rudely sit on my bed. One brushes hair out of my face. I open my eyes. Mom and Dad are beaming at me.

"There's my Kitty Doodle!"

"How do you feel, sweetie?" says Mom.

A big smile bubbles up from my heart, and I want to hug them both. My Daddy is back from the dead! I thought I'd never see him again. I want to dance and sing, but all I have strength to do is reach for him with floppy arms. I accidentally slap him.

"Oh, Dad," I gasp. "I'm so sorry! I meant to hug you."

"It's okay." He scoops me up and gives me a big squeeze.

I bury my face in his neck, and my heart feels whole again. This is home. Not Earth, not even *Prelude*, or my secret pine grove. Here in Daddy's arms is where I feel I belong.

They continue to fuss over me after he lays me back down, and Mom checks my readouts.

"Can we see Ash and Colton today?"

My parents chuckle, even though nothing is funny. Some things may never change.

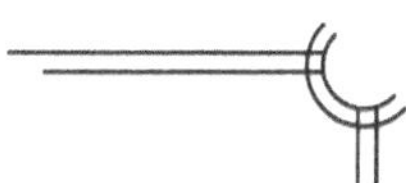

"You have to get your strength back first," says Mom, "Then we'll see."

Dad leans over. "They're both home, sweetie. Texas is a long way, and India is even farther. It would take over twenty hours to get from Duluth to Punjab."

"*Twenty hours*? Don't they have moving walkways here?"

"Earth is a lot bigger than you think," he explains.

I knew that, but kind of didn't.

Mom's face gets serious. "Captain Binnacle told us what happened."

"We'd like to hear it in your own words, anyway," says Dad.

I tell them the whole story, and leave nothing out this time, including the times I saw imaginary bees.

"I've been thinking about this a lot," I say. "Mom? Brace yourself, because you're wrong. Dad doesn't have the Jitters."

Instead of dismissing my remark, she says, "And how did you come to that conclusion, *Doctor* Namida?"

"Because *I* saw bees. *Dad* saw praying mantises." Her brow crinkles. "Don't you get it? We saw the type of robot we interfaced with. Which means the helmet fed impressions *back into our brains*, and our brains associated them with things it knew. Dad wore the helmet a lot more than I ever did, so his visions were stronger."

Mom looks open-mouthed at Dad. She knows I'm right. Mom just can't believe she didn't think of it first.

"We could easily prove it," Dad says. "I can build another helmet here and use it for a few weeks. If I get hallucinations, it'll show they aren't due to artificial gravity or anything else related to living in space."

"Would that prove it, Mom?"

She closes her mouth and sits up straight. "Yes, I suppose it would."

"It would also mean," Dad says, "that you discovered a flaw in my program. We'll have to fix that."

I smile triumphantly. "What it really means is you can go back home! We all can."

They both get funny looks.

"Home." Mom says it as though she doesn't like the word. "Let's talk about that after you're feeling better. We want you to see our house, and show you the tamarack forest, and take you swimming in a real lake. Doesn't that sound like fun?"

"No. It sounds dreadful. But no use arguing since I'm already here."

Mom doesn't know what to say to that. Dad just laughs.

# CHAPTER 34

When I get bored, a nurse brings me paper and pen. I fold the paper into wheel shapes and use the pen to connect them, the way one axle connected Ox and Adam. Then the nurse explains they are for writing letters. It's similar to email, but physical, and more personal, she says. After some thought, I begin.

*Hi Ash,*

*I'm sorry.*

*I'm not asking forgiveness, but I need you to know I'm sorry. For everything. For ruining your career in space. For treating you like a pet. And for not kissing you back that one time we went swimming. (But for the record, a talking pet would still be a really cool thing to have.)*

*One thing you never told me: Earth feels weird. I'm not sure how else to describe it, except that it's like nothing moves. On Prelude, I always felt the gondolas spinning, and the open decks below me. Now there's nothing but solid ground. The nurse takes me for walks, and I keep wanting to lean against the spin, which makes me lean backward the tiniest bit. I feel unbalanced, like I'm always walking downhill.*

*But you know all that, of course.*

*What you don't know is that I'll miss you. You were my best friend, and I was never lonely because you were always there.*

*And I suspect the reason you had a crush on me was because I was the only girl your age. It'll be better for you to be around other girls who aren't cruel, or weird.*

*I'll always cherish the years we had together.*
*Goodbye,*
*Namida*


Then I used a second piece of paper and started this way:


*Hi Colton,*

*Mom and Dad say that once we settle into our house, we might be able to visit. That is, if you can stand hanging around a girl whose brain is cattywompus, like you said. Yes, I know people think I'm weird. And I suppose I am, but that's me, and other people can step out an airlock if they don't like it. Except, not you.*

*I just wanted to say I'm sorry for how things turned out.*

*And it'd be nice if you didn't mind the weird so much.*

*Let me know if I'm welcome in Texas. Maybe we can go dancing with horses, and you can show me your gulf.*

*I'd like to tell you about one day in my favorite pine grove, when the Universe smiled at me, because I think out of all the people I know, you'd understand. And I have a lot of questions to ask you about what treasures might be behind the stars.*

*Thanks for the kiss. It was nicely awful. (That doesn't sound right when you switch the words "awful" and "nice" around the other way, but I've written it in pen and can't erase it.)*

*Hope to see you soon. Please let me know if it's okay,*
*Namida*


The nurse said she'd mail them. I had to ask what that meant.

Over the next sixteen hours, the nurses bring me onion and turnip soup for lunch, fish for dinner, and some kind of fruit jam on fry bread for dessert. It's different—and rather tasty. They also walk me down long hallways to build up my muscles. After three days of weightlessness, I'm wearing an invisible suit of sandbags. Even my thin robe feels irritating. Most of all, I notice the absence of motion. On *Prelude*, I could feel the spin of whatever wheel I was in every time I turned my head or reached for something. Constant motion while in gravity, an ever-present force to lean into. In contrast, Earth feels motionless, almost dead.

The nurse and I stroll past the laser surgery room to the waiting area, where a set of glass doors lets raw sunlight stream in. People pass in and out of this airlock without space suits.

I hold my breath and wait to see if they burn up in direct sunlight, but they don't.

Posters advertising the Coalition's space program plaster the walls. One has a poorly drawn cartoon of a dopey girl with a long ponytail. Behind her is an inaccurate drawing of *Prelude*. Its caption makes me gag. "Let's not take our problems to space. We'll build a *better* home on Starheim!" Makes me want to gag.

It takes me a minute to realize the girl is supposed to be *me*. Ash once called me the "poster child for the space program," and now I know he meant it literally.

Silly. The only way we won't take our problems into space is for people themselves not to go. Maybe I can sue the Coalition for defamation, or for putting words in my mouth.

On our way back, we pass a sign pointing to the isolation ward, which gives me an idea. Nurse refuses to give me a tour down that hall, of course, so I wait until evening.

When the lights are low and the nurses quiet down, I slip out of bed and peek outside. As soon as no one is in sight, I creep barefoot down the hall, then crawl on hands and knees to get past the nurse's station without being caught. Once clear, I race for the isolation ward, losing my balance and smacking into a wall only once.

As I expected, they stock bio-hazard suits. I grab the smallest size I can find, along with the matching, heavy rubber boots. In a locker nearby, I find an oxygen tank and face mask. I sneak these back to my room and stuff them into the cabinet under the sink.

After breakfast the next morning, I ask Nurse if I can walk around by myself today. I demonstrate that I can navigate the room without wobbling, so she agrees. I spend the next couple of hours stealing other things, including a pair of red goggles from laser surgery, and an emergency med kit.

Mom and Dad show up after lunch, determined to drag me outside. Mom hands me a bag of pathetic clothes that will do nothing to protect me from radiation.

"Can I get dressed and meet you out front? I know my way around."

Mom frowns suspiciously, then says, "If you're not out front in fifteen minutes, I'll organize a search party."

Dad frowns at me and affirms, "*Ten* minutes."

I snatch the bag and run for my bathroom. The clothes are different, but it's not hard to figure out how to lace the sneakers on, or button the blouse and jeans. Fortunately, the hazard boots fit over my sneakers, and the bio-suit is baggy enough not to constrict anything.

I use duct tape to seal my pant legs, then strap on the oxygen tank. The mask covers my nose and mouth snuggly, and laser goggles cover my eyes. Before I pull on the heavy rubber gloves, I slip the antiseptic wipes and med kit into the bio-suit's pockets and snap the hood down tight.

Now I'm ready.

I emerge from the bathroom. The pretty nurse is there to greet me. She covers her mouth, then asks if I'm ready to go. I nod, and we head into the hall. A doctor pauses to ask, "What's all this?" The nurse shushes him, and we keep walking. More people stare, and we startle a few people in the waiting area.

Finally, I reach the airlock. No readouts to indicate what conditions are on the other side. The careless insanity of it is mind-boggling, but this is Earth, and I suppose everywhere is deadly, so they don't bother.

I can't see much from under the hood, but I can see Mom and

Dad leaning against a vehicle. Mom's hair billows in the breeze from an air vent. Her legs are bare. Dad wears loose eye protection, but his shirt has short sleeves. They're both standing in blazing direct sunlight, and I'm amazed they haven't broiled away into smoking cinders.

Well, here goes. I push through two sets of glass doors to step outside. It's kind of like walking into a garden chamber because it's so open. Mom bites her lips as if she's in pain. Dad approaches me and peeks under my hood.

"Is my Kitty Doodle in there?"

Mom pulls what looks like a miniature omni-dev from her purse. "Sorry, but I have to get a picture of this." She clicks it at me.

They hold a door open for me so I can climb into the transport. I buckle up as my parents board, and then we're moving. My anxiety softens since I keep my eyes closed. With my hood down, I don't have to see the decimated cities and polluted landscape along the way.

We travel almost an hour, and then the vehicle stops. Dad and Mom get out and open my door.

"We're home," Mom announces.

No. We're three-hundred eighty-five thousand kilometers *away* from home.

I peer outside. Pine trees, way too tall to be uprooted and stored in cryogenics, surround our vehicle. Dad parks in front of a super huge storage shed, which is made of wood and stone, and has windows. Mom is so happy, she's about to pop.

"We're supposed to live in *that*?"

Her grin falters. "It's a lot nicer on the inside."

Dad helps me out. "Come with me." He leads me by the hand to a nearby grassy clearing. "You know, you don't need all that."

He unsnaps my hood, then disconnects my oxygen hose and folds the hood back.

"What are you *doing*?" I frantically grab for it, but he holds my hands still.

"Look at your mother and me," he says calmly. "*We're* not wearing hazard suits."

I cringe, waiting for the sun to peel the skin off my face like a candy bar wrapper.

However, nothing happens. The air smells fresh and green, which reminds me of my pine grove back in Ox Wheel. I slip my goggles off, and blink at the light. Again, it's similar to sunlight we reflect into our garden chambers, but different. Cheery, instead of harsh. All around me, alerts sound from omni-devs, but I see no people.

"What are those alerts for?"

Dad is confused for a second, then says, "Those are birds chirping."

We have insects on *Prelude*, but no birds that aren't frozen and packed away in cryogenics cartons. Except chickens. And chickens don't count because they don't fly or chirp. I've only ever seen pictures of birds. I try to catch sight of them in the branches and have to shade my eyes against the sun.

That's when realization steals my breath away, and my heart skips a beat.

These pines are too tall because there's nothing to stop them from growing! Normally, there should be pale blue walls curving up to a transparent ceiling. Beyond that, visible between reflecting shutters, should be stars. But here, there is only *blue*. Endless beautiful blue as deep as the inky infinity of space.

My body is in danger of floating away, and I stifle a scream. Earth is too immense, too open! I crumple to the ground, twining my fingers into the cool grass in desperation, trying not to think about it. I'm clinging to the surface of an enormous ball that twirls rapidly through space. At any moment, it could fling me off. I squeeze my eyes shut and whimper.

Dad kneels next to me and wraps me in his arms. "You're safe, Namida. Trust me. Remember your physics lessons about true gravity."

Mom sits cross-legged beside us, strokes my hair, and starts to hum.

"Mom! If you start singing about ponies, I *swear* I'll lose my mind."

"Okay, sweetie. No ponies."

My parents give me time to get acclimated. Squirrels creep me out because they remind me of giant spiders, furry things that run up and down trees. But Dad assures me they're harmless. This place doesn't stink from pollution or decay like I imagined.

What bothers me even more is that the trees haven't been planted in properly uniform zigzags. Plus, off in the distance, it appears that part of this area has been flooded. Instead of working to contain and drain the water, people are carelessly using it for swimming and boating.

Apart from the bird alarms, soft electric buzzing rises from the grass as air vents whisper through pine branches overhead. It takes me a while to realize there are no air vents, and the buzzing comes from normal-sized honeybees collecting pollen, hovering from one purple flower to another at my feet.

"Mom? Dad? Do you see a bee?"

"Yes, sweetie, we do."

"Good." I rub the center of one flower until my fingertip turns dusty yellow, then I hold it out for the bee to land, and let it crawl on me. It kisses my finger, and I accept that as it was meant: a sign of devotion and submission.

"You may go, Sir Bee, to perform your appointed duties."

We watch as it buzzes off farther up the clearing.

The Earth spins slowly under the sky, and where the sun touches, life flourishes. Real gravity hugs us safe and secure to the surface. Trees draw their life from deep under the soil. We cannot decompress because we have no walls to keep us from the emptiness of space. People won't die here if you forget to close a hatch or seal a helmet.

Something inside me lets go. The rest of my stress-knot comes undone. Sweet release.

Maybe I could get used to this.

# ACKNOWLEDGEMENTS

For some mysterious reason, Stephanie Cardel of Lighthouse Literary chose to be my agent. Thank you for all the editing suggestions, and for your persistence in finding a publisher after so many years. (I never told you, but I was two days away from sending Namida out to sell matches on the street.) I also thank my publisher, Mike Parker of Wordcrafts Press, for liking the story enough to inflict it on the general public.

Most of my science research came from websites, books, and videos, but I'd like to thank Chris Vodney for brief consultations about physics and other spacey stuff. And retired Dr. Grant Hutchison of "oikofuge.com" for explaining how an object behaves as it is propelled through a rotating cylinder in weightlessness, when the trajectory is parallel to the axis. Any errors Namida makes in describing this are entirely my fault.

So many others read advance copies and offered encouragement.

Other "beta readers" offered vital critiques. Sarah Schmitt, author of It's a *Wonderful Death*, read my earliest versions for the opening scenes, and very kindly told me they stunk. (Though, she never put it so bluntly.) I had sense enough to realize she was right. Kathy Hansen, a friend of many years, relentlessly attacked the manuscript like a gardener pulling up weeds. Thanks for the much-needed landscaping.

Finally, I want to thank Crista Flora for reading a very early draft (in a record-breaking eight minutes) and offering her insights. Crista, you might want to take another few minutes and read the final version. It's a little more palatable now.

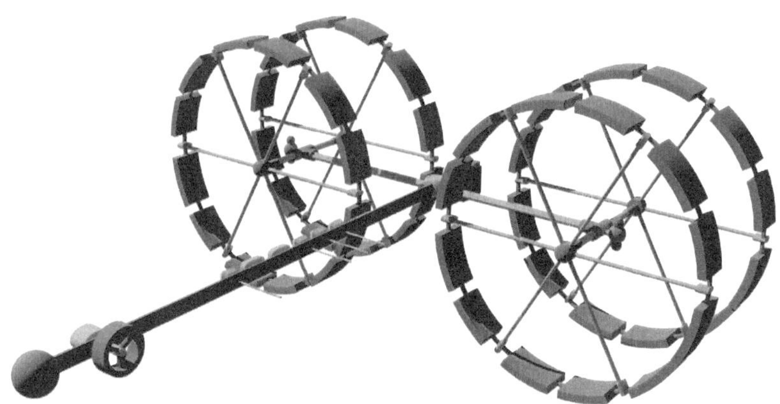

# QUOD VIDE

**N**amida Wiles:  "Namid" is Chippewa (Ojibwe) for "dancer." "Réaltín" means 'little star' in Irish. "Wiles" is an anagram of "Lewis," in reference to C.S. Lewis. Technically, Namida is not OCD, as she affirms. Her obsession with germs and death comes from being told, ever since she was a toddler, that everything around her is dangerous.

 **Sterling Wiles:**  named after Robert Sterling who created the "Sterling engine."

 **Sydney Wiles:**  whose name means "traveler."

 **Bert Spencer:**  after Herbert Spencer, British philosopher and scientist.

 **Ash (Tamonash):**  the Hindi name means "destroyer of ignorance."

 **Colton:**  meant to remind you of a colt, or the pistol manufacturer.

 **Cpt. Winston Binnacle:**  "Winston" is from Winston Churchill. A "binnacle" is the post that holds a compass steady on a ship.

 **Mr. K:**  "Kapurthala" is a placename in Punjab.

 **Mrs. Kirkpatrick:**  modeled after C.S. Lewis' boyhood tutor, a Scotsman named W.T. Kirkpatrick, who was a classical empiricist.

 **Prelude Station:** Named after Arthur C. Clarke's novel, *Prelude to Space*. I tried to make the physics of Prelude as close to reality and current technology as possible. The size, rate of spin, and effects of centrifugal force are accurate, as are the physical symptoms

Colton feels in simulated gravity, and Namida's symptoms when she arrives on Earth.

**Lagrange Points:** These are little gravity "eddies" in space. The Prelude rests in one of the Earth/Moon Lagrange points, and so mimics the orbit of the Moon.

**Wheels:** The names of the wheels represent the four beasts from Ezekiel 1, (Man, Ox, Eagle, Lion), where we see the "wheels within wheels" on God's throne. "Adam" is Hebrew for "man."

**Space Shuttles:** All shuttles bear the names of sci-fi authors (or a cosmonaut, in one case).

**Commander Spaulding:** Drawn from Douglass Spaulding, a character Ray Bradbury used to represent himself in his stories.

**Anastasia:** The first starship to Starheim was Anastasia, which means "Resurrection."

**Namida's omni-dev ringtone**: is "Twinkle Twinkle Little Star."

**The Pony Song:** Real, but I re-wrote it because the meter didn't fit. The best version is by Dan Fogelberg. Find it on YouTube.

**INTERCAL:** An inside joke for programmers. The programming language's main goal is to make the code impossible to understand.

**Pebcak:** The soda they drink is an acronym which stands for: Problem Exists Between Chair and Keyboard.

**R.E.D.:** Rapid Exothermic Disassembly: is similar to a term (Rapid Unplanned Disassembly) actually used by NASA to sarcastically describe a rocket explosion.

**NRD-1701:** The starship Enterprise had 1701 printed on the hull. Namida turns "NRD" into "Leonard." Mr. Spock was played by Leonard Nimoy. Later, Namida calls the bot, Leonard Decoy.

**TNK-404:** The robot who goes missing bears the series number 404 which, on the internet, is the error code for a missing webpage.

# ABOUT THE AUTHOR

Steven Kent lives with his wife among Midwest scarecrows and cornfields and firmly believes that autumn is all too brief of a season.

He has been getting lost in the interdimensional spaces between library shelves since he was a boy, and hopes someday to never have to return to reality.

Between those shelves, he has discovered treasures that touched his heart and imagination. It's past time to return the favor.

Connect with Steven online at:

**stevenkentbooks.wordpress.com**

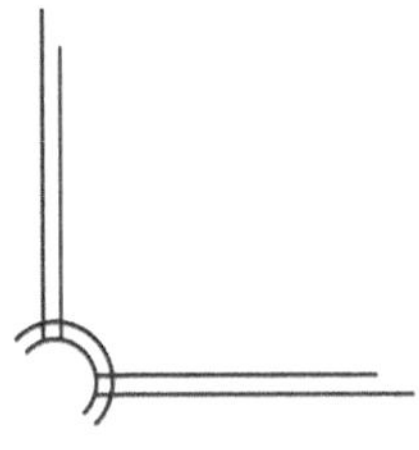

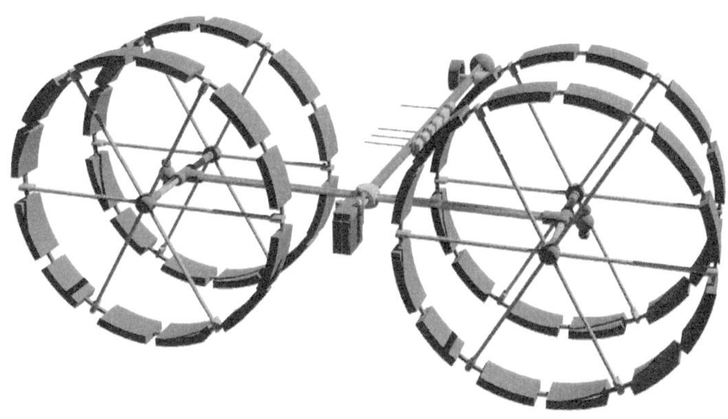